THE GENE

Annette Keen

Published by Sunbird Publishing

A CIP catalogue record for this book is available from the British Library.

ISBN 978-0-9574080-0-5

Cover design by Strumpet Design

Prepared and printed by:

York Publishing Services Ltd
64 Hallfield Road
Layerthorpe
York YO31 7ZQ

Tel: 01904 431213

Website: www.yps-publishing.co.uk

This book is dedicated to my Dad.

With thanks to all my family and friends for their on-going support and enthusiasm for this project, also the team at YPS for their professionalism.
I couldn't have done it without you!

Special thanks to Sue at Strumpet Design, for the cover artwork.

Love,

Annette

x

THE GENERATION CLUB

2 ladies (central Horsfield) with elderly dependent relatives WLTM other people in a similar situation, for mutual support, social events etc. Together we could do the difficult and the downright impossible.

SOH restored if not still intact.

Email to: cathsal@chatbox.co.uk

CHAPTER ONE

ONE BIG STEP FOR WOMANKIND

Jo Taylor has spent ages faffing around and changed her clothes four times, but now she's finally ready to leave. It's not as if she has an extensive and varied wardrobe to choose from, as Jo's social events are few and far between, but in the end she's settled on black trousers and a white top with black spots on it. She hopes she looks smart but casual. Shoes are her next problem. The sandals she would like to wear are no good for driving in so she ends up in a pair of elderly flat casuals, with an option to take the sandals and change when she gets there. Things like this are major decisions for Jo, who is already stressed enough at the thought of meeting a room full of strangers.

It's a mild evening for April, so she decides not to bother with a jacket. She checks the mirror one last time, takes a deep breath and leaves her bedroom and personal comfort zone.

With her sandals dangling by their straps from one hand, Jo goes into her father's study to tell him she'll be off soon and give him last minute instructions.

'Your coffee's all ready to make Dad, and the biscuit tin's on the table so all you have to do is boil the kettle. I don't suppose I'll be late but go to bed if you want to before I'm back.'

Don Taylor turns round from his computer. At eighty-two, retired from the bright lights of city life and London dancehalls to the small-town Sussex backwater of Horsfield, he is making a late run at being a technophile.

'OK dear. Don't worry – I'll be fine. Do you know, I've just picked up an email from an old pal who's now living in Florida! Isn't that something?'

He looks up at her, schoolboy excitement splitting his face into a smile.

'He used to play the clarinet – we worked the Mecca halls together in the Fifties. Amazing. I thought he was dead.' He coughs a bit, wheezes and takes as deep a breath as he's able to.

Jo lingers, she's ready to go, but putting it off. Don, who can read his daughter better than most fathers are able to, takes her hand in his.

'I think it's very good, you meeting these people. You should get out more, I've always said so, and this will give you the chance to do just that.' He pauses for a bit to catch his breath. 'It's no life for you cooped up in this flat with me all the time, you need to be with people of your own age. And you'll have something in common with them straight away. It's a great idea, Jo.'

Jo squeezes his hand and smiles. They both know this is a big step for her, and possibly an important one. At times like this Don is aware that he's venturing into territory a mother would be better equipped to cope with, but he's been standing in for her since Jo was four and he's had to learn. There have been mistakes, situations not talked through adequately and advice handed out clumsily, but with this one he feels he's got it just about right.

'Anyway,' he continues, not wanting to overcook the point he's making, 'This Ray, he's still in touch with some of the others from the Mecca circuit and he's given me their email addresses. One of them might remember something I can use in the book…'

He can't bear to watch the panic rising in his daughter's face any longer so he turns back to the screen.

'Mind how you drive, love.'

It's like seeing her off to school on her first day, and in his eyes she doesn't look that much different – long brown hair tied back, little wispy fringe getting in her eyes. Don can't see the silvery streaks in Jo's hair, or the lines left by the intervening fifty-two years of coping with situations she doesn't feel equipped for. Jo had faced her first day at school with trepidation, and all the things she feared about it had been pretty much how the day had turned out for her. Now she's got that look again and he's just hoping it'll be better this time.

Don can no longer focus on the screen clearly because his eyes have welled up and there's a tightness in his chest that's only partly to do with the emphysema and his breathing difficulties, but he doesn't let on or she might change her mind and not go. And it's important that she does.

Jo kisses the top of his head.

'Bye Dad. See you later.'

In the hallway she hesitates again. But because there's nothing else to stall her, she picks up her car keys, looks back for a second, then leaves the flat.

* * * *

'Scrabble?'

Mavis Henderson sighs. Her sister Dorothy looks at her accusingly, from the several pillows that are propping her up in her bed. Sadie, her black cat, is on the bedspread as usual, leaving hairs that Mavis will have to clean off tomorrow with her sticky roller brush.

'No it isn't, but I told you I was meeting up with some friends tonight, didn't I?'

'Friends? My friends?' asks Dorothy, immediately confused by a concept she can no longer relate to.

Fat chance, thinks Mavis, who has had enough for one day, but then immediately feels awful for thinking it.

'Janet from next door will sit with you till I get back. And I'll see you in the morning Dorothy.'

Dorothy strokes Sadie and looks back to the television on the chest of drawers opposite the bed, which is blaring out a re-run of *Celebrity Big Brother*. Dorothy hasn't any idea what's going on, but it quickly gets her attention.

Mavis goes back into the lounge.

'Won't be too long, Jan. She'll just nod off to sleep soon so you can slip in and turn that TV off if it's annoying you, or it'll wait till I get back. Either way it won't disturb her. If you need me just ring my mobile and I'll come straight back. Thanks for helping out, you're a saviour.'

'You know I'm happy to do it – just have a good evening and don't give us a second thought,' says Janet.

Mavis heaves a sigh of relief as she gets outside into the spring evening. The sky is clear and still light, and she pauses for a moment on the doorstep, just enjoying the small window of freedom that has chanced her way. She wonders if there'll be other nights like this but she supposes it'll only happen if Janet agrees to sit with Dorothy and in spite of what she's just said there's a limit to how much Mavis can impose on her. It's a big responsibility, she knows this. But Mavis also knows that she's near the edge and this might just save her from going over.

She walks quickly to the address she's been given. It's only a couple of streets away and Mavis wonders if this Cathy Lawson will turn out to be someone she recognises. Only if we shop in the same supermarket, she thinks grimly, since she never goes anywhere else to recognise her from. Except the Scrabble club, and there are no Cathys there.

She turns into the street, pauses and looks at the numbers to orientate herself. The house she's looking for is a good size, and the garden is neat and well cared for with shrubs and little bedding plants that haven't quite got going yet. Mavis doesn't have time to do anything to her garden and has had the whole of the front concreted over. Slabs, or those nice decorative bricks would have looked better, but concrete was the only option she could afford, so concrete it was.

She hears the bell ring through the house while all this is going on in her head, and then there's the sound of approaching footsteps and Mavis straightens up and plants a smile on her face.

* * * *

They've been sitting in Cathy Lawson's living room, nervously waiting for the doorbell to ring, for what seems like hours. Cathy and Sally had put postcards in many of Horsfield's newsagents, and to their surprise about a dozen people emailed in reply. Once they'd weeded out the simply curious and the frankly pervy, they were left with three ladies and these are the people they expect to ring on Cathy's doorbell any time now.

'What if we don't like them?' says Sally. 'Just because you and I hit it off right away doesn't mean to say we'll all jell. I hate strained atmospheres.'

Sally always fears the worst, but as she explains to Cathy that way she's never disappointed.

'I don't think we have to become bosum pals to be mutually supportive – but we already know we have at least one thing in common, so that's a good start.'

Cathy is the optimist. Nothing is out of reach to her, nobody without hope, until proven otherwise. Cathy wants the group to flourish, for herself and Aunt Stella, for her new friend Sally Bennett and her mum, and for the others who are, at this very moment, making their way along her street and up her drive.

The doorbell rings, and Cathy goes out into the hallway. Sally stands up and re-arranges the things on the tea tray, then puts them all back where they were. She could do with a glass of wine but knows she'll have to wait till she gets home. The living room door opens – Cathy ushers in a lady of a similar age to herself, and suddenly they're up and running.

Once the opening hellos are over, Jo perches on the edge of Cathy's sofa, looking ill at ease in spite of their best efforts. They can see it's taken a lot for her to come here tonight, and it's obvious she's apprehensive about the whole thing. Sally sits next to Jo and strikes up a conversation and at just that moment the bell rings again.

Mavis bustles in with the words 'I can't be too long', but she looks pleasant enough and after Cathy has introduced them all and Mavis has settled herself in one of the armchairs she seems to relax a bit. The conversation, slightly edgy at first but gradually settling down, has moved on to take in the county library scandal, and seems to be going along quite well. They all read the local paper and all but Jo have expressed an opinion on the alleged goings-on, when the clang of the front gate heralds another arrival. Cathy goes to let her in and the others fall silent as they each ponder the group dynamics changing again so soon, just when they were getting to grips with things as they were.

Cathy re-appears with Karen, looking glamorous and much younger than she really is, and she settles in the armchair opposite Mavis.

'This is Karen Kennedy,' says Cathy, and proceeds to introduce everyone else while they all weigh the newcomer up.

From behind her own Varifocals Sally ponders on the fact that Karen's not wearing glasses – probably got contacts, she decides. Cathy spots the designer jacket (label on outside of sleeve gives it away), which Karen is wearing with jeans and spiky-heeled shoes of the sort she remembers having years ago but wouldn't wear now for fear of spraining an ankle. Mavis wonders if Karen's trim figure and tanned skin have been achieved by natural means or with interference, and Jo just thinks how lovely her hair looks and wishes she had the courage to have blonde highlights put in hers.

Cathy makes tea and brings it into the living room, and Sally passes the chocolate biscuits round. Everyone seems to settle a little further down in their seats as they start to tell each other which part of Horsfield they live in. Cathy, who has been used to conducting business meetings, lets this go on for a bit, then glances at Sally over the top of her specs, and makes a start.

'Well, it's traditional at times like this for everyone to take a few minutes to talk about themselves.'

Jo's heart sinks. She hates this.

'But I think we should break with convention, because the reason we're all here is because of the people we care for, our dependants. So maybe we should start with them.' Cathy waves a hand in Sally's direction, and this is what they'd agreed on so naturally she's ready for it.

'Sally, tell us about your mum.'

'It would have been my parents' diamond wedding anniversary in a few months time,' Sally begins, 'But my Dad spent five years in a nursing home suffering from Alzheimers, and although we visited him every week, most of the time he had no idea who we were. This was very tough on Mum. All the time he was alive she soldiered on as always. It gave her something to tell him about, although he didn't really understand much, and in a way I think it kept her going, as if she wanted things to be just right for when he came home again. But we both knew he wouldn't come home. When he went, it was as if her purpose in life went with him. She's had poor health for a few years – a couple of minor strokes and an on-going problem with angina.'

Mavis ventures a question. 'Is she in a wheelchair? My sister Dorothy is, and that's one of the things I find really hard, coping with getting her in and out because she's a real weight, and all the performance of getting places – not that we go anywhere much now.'

'No she isn't, not all the time, but we get one for things like the supermarket...' Here Sally grins across at Cathy, who throws in a quick explanation.

'It's how Sally and I met, she was pushing Queenie round Sainsbury's and I sort of eavesdropped on their conversation,' she says.

'Hardly eavesdropped – not only is she deaf but the entire store could hear me some days when I reach the end of the line. I expect we all know what that's like.'

Everyone but Jo murmurs agreement.

'Anyway, she can't walk far and actually can't manage much at all now on her own – so last year I sold my house and moved in with her.' Sally pauses. This is the bit they hadn't rehearsed but she thinks it needs saying anyway.

'This idea, the Generation Club, was Cathy's – and I think it's a brilliant one. Everyone in our situation needs a support network, and obviously none of us has got one or we wouldn't be here tonight. Together, we lose our isolation, and if the club works, so do our dependants.'

Jo thinks of Don and her throat tightens up. He still has his group of pals, not all of them in the virtual world of emails either. But every few months it seems he loses another one and she hates to think of him being the last one left with nobody to talk to who knew him in his glory days. Jo hopes she won't cry but she's nervy and feeling fragile and this is a danger zone for her.

Cathy takes the reins back and goes next.

'I look after my Aunt Stella. She's independent and bloody-minded, but reluctantly – and I have to say quite elegantly – accepts my help because she knows she needs it. Like Queenie, she can't walk far now although she's OK getting around at home from room to room. She suffers from diabetes, which brings its own problems, and her eyesight is failing, which saddens her because she loves to read.'

Jo pipes up for the first time in ages.

'Does she get those audio books? Because I think they'd be good…' Her voice tails off as she realises this is something Cathy would certainly have thought of herself by now.

'Good point Jo. I could look in the library, couldn't I? She was never much of a one for fiction – but they might have biographies, or something else that would interest her.'

Jo beams. 'It's worth a try,' she says, suddenly feeling surer of herself.

'She can still manage the TV news though,' continues Cathy, 'so that's bridging the gap at the moment, and she reads the local paper very laboriously with a strong magnifying glass. She doesn't live here by the way, in case you were thinking she might put in an appearance at any moment. We live separately, although her flat's only just around the corner, so I do still have my own life. But she's only got me to rely on, and I can't just go away and leave her to her own devices for any length of time. And it's only going to get worse.'

Straight away Mavis feels deeply envious of Cathy and the life she has that's her own, then hates herself for it. And she's right, of course. One day Cathy's Aunt Stella may be as dependent on Cathy as Dorothy is now on her. It makes sense to Mavis, banding together like this.

Things move along, Jo stumbles through a description of her dad and they all marvel at his late incursion into the computer world and the memoirs he's writing. When she mentions some of the bands he worked with on the London Mecca circuit Mavis surprises them all by knowing the names.

'I used to love dancing,' she says, looking animated and smiling broadly at the memory. 'I probably danced to him and his saxophone sometimes! Oh, weren't those Mecca ballrooms glamorous?'

'Not backstage, they weren't,' pops out of Jo before she knows it's coming, for without a mother at home she spent much of her childhood and adolescence hanging around Mecca dressing rooms at Don's gigs, and knows that behind the façade the reality was more grubby than glitzy.

Karen can't remember ever going to a Mecca ballroom.

'I think our nearest became one of the first discos. I went to that, not that it was what you'd call glamorous – trendy, though, at the time.'

Sally knows she never went inside one as her evenings out were taken up mostly with the cinema and Cathy lived in a village in mid-Sussex so she never even saw a Mecca ballroom.

'I spent much of my youth performing amateur dramatics in village halls,' she says. 'It was the basis of my social life – still is in fact. And going into town in the evenings just wasn't an option then – none of us had cars.'

'Well you don't know what you missed! I met my first husband at the Streatham Locarno...' says Mavis, leaving the rest of the story hanging in the air.

Cathy glances at Karen who has a question ready on her lips, and it's one she'd like to ask too, but this is not a road they need to go down this evening so she moves on to ask Mavis about Dorothy.

Now that Jo's got her piece out of the way she's loosened up a bit more and while Mavis is talking she starts to take in the details of Cathy's living room, and then the rest of the group. Don will be asking for a blow-by-blow account in the morning and she doesn't want to disappoint him or leave anything out.

Although it looks as if it's due for re-decoration, Cathy's living room is tasteful and tidy. There's a darker square of blue on the wall facing Jo where a picture has obviously been removed and not replaced and the curtains are definitely well past their best. But it's comfy and inviting – a good place to have started off this enterprise. A tabby and white cat is curled up on a footstool by the window, seemingly asleep although every so often it opens an eye, stretches a leg and re-curls itself.

Cathy and Sally have dressed pretty much the same as Jo herself – at least I got that right, she thinks. They seem like old friends – Jo can hardly believe they've only known each other a few weeks – and they seem to be living proof of that old adage about opposites, at least in terms of looks. Neat little Sally, petite and pretty with her glossy dark bob has to look up about ten inches to make eye contact with Cathy, who's model-girl tall and slender with a platinum-white layered cut.

Side by side they make quite a comical pair. Jo reckons they're both about the same age as her, whilst Karen is obviously younger, although it's hard to put an age on her. Mavis, probably the oldest of the group, is short and dumpy, wearing a navy dress that does nothing for her and a V-neck cardigan with a button missing.

'...and the twenty years between us is still a huge gap, especially so now that her dementia is getting worse. We're no company for each other.'

Jo realises she hasn't been listening and makes more of an effort to concentrate although the tabby cat has climbed down from its footstool now and is distracting her by cleaning itself with one leg delicately pointing towards the ceiling.

Mavis is coming to a halt.

'I just never have any life of my own any more. I can't get out of Horsfield, let alone Sussex. Heavens, I've got grandchildren I'd like the chance to see, but the way things are there's no possibility of me actually making the trip to see them. '

Nobody asks at this stage where these phantom children are, or why their parents aren't doing something useful about the situation. Mavis bucks up again after she's got all that off her chest, accepting another chocolate biscuit and the offer of more tea, and while Cathy goes to the kitchen to brew a second pot the rest of the group take the opportunity to look out at her back garden.

It's a bit chaotic but pretty in a country sort of way, with a lilac tree just getting ready to flower, honeysuckle scrambling untidily up one wall and great unkempt clumps of grape hyacinth and aubretia in the borders. When Cathy returns to the living room with fresh tea it's at the point where Karen is in the middle of a gardening story about her dad.

'...so in the end I had to stop him from going. He still does the garden at home but that's only just outside the patio doors so he can find it without too much trouble. But getting to and from the allotment was just too much of a memory test. It got to be a regular thing, the police bringing him back in a squad car when he got lost.'

Sally hands an empty cup to Cathy for a refill, and winks. It's going well, better than they'd hoped. Even Jo seems less tense now, more receptive.

The conversation turns to the question of finances. Everyone agrees that the Carer's Allowance they receive is pathetic, and somehow they all have to subsidise it in whatever way they can. Cathy's Aunt doesn't need her all the time, so at the moment she can still hold down her part-time job in a travel agency. Karen works from home, and luckily her expertise is in graphic design, which is something she can do from her own computer. But it's Jo who's been most enterprising in turning her dressmaking hobby into a way of making extra money.

'Bridesmaid and Prom dresses mostly,' she says, which impresses everyone and immediately has Jo playing the whole thing down.

'Nothing too fancy though,' she adds, modestly.

'I run a home shopping catalogue,' says Sally. 'It's good at Christmas time but not great the rest of the year. It helps out a bit with the bills.'

Mavis just struggles on with hers and Dorothy's pensions and Social Security. As she's telling them this she glances at her watch and realises she's already been out longer than she'd planned.

'I'll have to go soon,' she says, and Sally notices the 'soon'. Considering Mavis's opening shot when she arrived she's certainly relaxed into it.

Then it's Karen's turn to tell them about her father, which she does accompanied by a lot of gesticulating and combing her fingers through the front of her shoulder-length hair. Sally can't help wondering what Karen's own story is, but they have agreed that this is not their brief for tonight.

'We'll find out about each other as time goes on,' Cathy had said, 'Let's put the spotlight on the dependants to start with,' and as an ice-breaker it seems to be working. They are beginning to open up to each other as they recognise similarities in their own situations.

'This dementia is a terrible thing,' says Karen. 'It robs them of their present and future and hasn't even got the decency to leave them with their past intact. It takes away their precious memories and turns them into different people. But every so often you see a little glimmer of what they used to be through a crack in that outer shell. And then they come back to you, just for a moment. After a bad day it's what you need to keep going.'

For a short while they're all silent, and the loudest sound in the room is the cat licking itself.

'Anyway,' says Karen after a pause which nobody else feels they should be the one to break, 'that's the way it is with me and Dad. I've never left home and now I never will because I'm all he's got.'

She combs her hands through her hair again, climbs back out of the hole she's fallen into and smiles across the room. Cathy admires this quality in Karen, her ability to turn things around in a few seconds.

'So, how do you see this club progressing?' Karen asks.

Cathy puts her cup down.

'Well, if you all want to be a part of it then it's not for me to decide – we make the ground-rules up according to what everybody thinks. But I suppose the way I saw it originally was a means by which we could come together on our own every so often as a social group, like this – but also that we could have some days out with our dependants, all of us together.'

'Wheelchairs are easier to handle on trips out if you can hire an adapted mini-bus, for example,' cuts in Sally, pushing the idea forward. 'Together, we could do that.'

'And things you wouldn't dream of doing on your own can be achieved if there's a group. Possibly even holidays away.'

Jo's nodding in agreement, but she's wondering what her dad would make of all these seemingly dotty old folk. He doesn't fit into the normal dependent category, not in the sense in which the others seem to, but now that she's getting keen on the idea she wants him to be enthusiastic as well. She ventures the point.

'It wouldn't just be them and us though, when we're out?'

Cathy has already spotted Don as being potentially an odd one out and is anxious to promote Aunt Stella's similar cause.

'I don't think my aunt would have much truk with that, Jo. I can't get her to any of the old people's clubs that currently exist because she just wouldn't have anything to say to most of the other people there – or to put it more accurately, they wouldn't have enough to say to her. She's still very alert, loves a good conversation, studies the news avidly and knows more about what's going on in the world than I do most of the time. So it would suit her to have all of us around to talk to – I imagine from what you've said your dad is pretty much the same?'

Jo nods.

'Also, we could be a dependent-sitting service for each other from time to time, I suppose,' says Karen, hopefully. 'Couldn't we?' She looks around at the others. 'Everyone taking a turn?' she adds.

They all seem to think this is a fair point, and Karen is quietly jubilant as she thinks of her occasional illicit afternoons and it being easier to organise them if this thing takes off.

The plate of chocolate biscuits goes round again and Mavis takes another one.

'I don't think my sister would have very much to contribute to the group,' she says.

'But that's not a problem, Mavis,' says Sally. 'She would get something out of it – any excursion or outside contact would do her good, and the whole thing would be good for you. And *you'd* be making a contribution.'

Mavis seems happy with this – seems happy with most things at the moment actually. They chat on for a few minutes then she catches sight of her watch.

'Heavens! Look at the time! Janet will think I've run off.' She pulls herself out of the armchair she's sunk into and brushes biscuit crumbs off her dress and onto Cathy's carpet.

'I'm sorry to break up the party, but I really must get back now.'

'Don't go without leaving us your contact details', says Sally, pushing a pad and pen at Mavis, who sits back down to write, passes it on to Karen, then hauls herself upright again.

'Listen girls,' she says, 'it's really been good to meet you all. I'd certainly like us to get together again, if the rest of you are still interested in the idea.'

Without exception, they all agree. Karen gathers her bag and jacket and follows Mavis to the door, offering her a lift as they go off down the path together.

Jo lingers over writing her address and phone number on the pad until Cathy and Sally come back from the front door. She's been brought up to say thank you to the host before going home, and old habits die hard with her.

'I had a really nice evening, Cathy. Thank you both for being so welcoming.'

Sally feels a sudden fondness for Jo, and gives her a hug.

They see Jo to the door, and watch her drive off down the road.

'Well, that went better than I thought it would,' says Sally, as they close the front door and start gathering up the cups in the living room.

Cathy laughs at her. 'God, you are such a pessimist!' she says, then adds, 'But you know what, I really think we're on to something here. Those girls were certainly enthusiastic, and it's great to know we're not the only ones who think it's a good idea. Now we just have to push it forward.'

CHAPTER TWO

ANXIETY AND E-SEX

The minute Karen turns onto the driveway she knows her dad is agitated.

He's standing at the front room window, arms wrapped around his chest, staring out onto the street and rocking from side to side. As she walks up to the front door and he realises it's her, relief floods his face.

She turns her key in the lock and reminds herself that she mustn't get tetchy with him since it's her fault for leaving him on his own in the first place. It's something she wouldn't normally do but her 'sitter' cancelled at the last moment and rather left her with no option. She's also much later than she expected to be, thinking it would just be a dry old meeting that she could leave after an hour.

'Hello Dad!' she calls out as she closes the door behind her. Bill Kennedy rushes into the hall to greet his daughter, anxiety and relief in equal measures stirring him into an unusually high level of animation.

'I didn't know where you were – you didn't say you were going out – I've been worried all evening...'

'I told you Dad, I said I was only just around the corner with some friends. Don't you remember? Before I went out I told you where I'd be. '

Bill looks confused, puts his hand to his forehead as if the effort of remembering is giving him a headache.

'You didn't say...I thought you'd gone...' he says, getting himself worked up again as the horror of Karen's disappearance hits him once more.

Karen takes off her jacket and slips it over the end of the stair rail.

'I wouldn't go and leave you Dad.' She puts an arm round his shoulder. 'Now, let's get a cup of tea and see what's on the TV, shall we?'

'You might have had a car crash...or been hit by another driver when you were just walking... just walking along the road... you might have been killed... you might have had a car crash...'

'But I didn't, did I? See, I'm just as good as when I went out.'

'What if someone had phoned for you?'

'And did they? Did someone call?'

'No, but they might have done...'

Karen guides Bill into the living room and switches on the TV. Luckily, there's a gardening programme on which immediately gets his attention. She brings in some tea for him and a strong black coffee for herself. She's got work to finish before she can go to bed and needs a caffeine fix to help her through it.

They sit together in the lounge, not talking because Bill's wrapped up in a piece about growing unusual vegetables without the need for a greenhouse.

'That's something different I could try up at the allotment,' he says all of a sudden, forgetting that he no longer has an allotment. 'That'd surprise them all,' he chuckles. And Karen agrees because there's no point in going into it all again and she doesn't want to upset him any more for one evening.

She drains her coffee, then goes out to the kitchen and pours another one. She's drinking too much of the stuff, but the work's got to be done and the best time is when Bill's in bed and she can really concentrate.

Back at the studio garden they've moved on to trailing begonias and Bill's telling her he needs several trays more than he's first calculated. She knows he hasn't calculated at all, in fact the idea of begonias in hanging baskets has never occurred to him before.

'We'll go to the garden centre tomorrow morning, if you'd like to do that,' says Karen.

'Good idea. See what sort of selection they've got there. You can choose the colours, you're better at that than me – I just grow the things.' Bill smiles at her, he's getting enthusiastic and in that moment it's hard to believe he's not just the same old Dad he always was. This is one of the glimmers she talked about at the meeting, and her heart sings to see him back again, if only briefly.

There's a photo of Karen's parents on the mantelpiece, in the same spot it's been standing for years. It's a Garden Club dinner and dance, Bill's all dressed up in a tuxedo, and Karen's mum is next to him in a fresh perm and borrowed fur stole. Bill's proudly holding up the silver cup he won that year, for growing something he's long since forgotten about. The smile's the same, but something in his eyes has vanished.

The flashlight bounced straight off the trophy so it's never been possible to read the inscription on it but Karen has always assumed it was the late fifties. She would have been starting school, whilst across London Mavis was falling in love at the Streatham Locarno and Jo's dad was playing tenor sax at the Hammersmith Palais with the Joe Loss Orchestra. How strange, to think that they should all come together now, at this time.

Karen feels terribly sorry for Mavis, who seems to have the worst deal of all.

'Between you and me,' Mavis had said in the car on the way home, 'I can't go on much longer like this. This club could literally be a life-saver for me.'

Karen has taken Mavis' phone number and intends to ring her the following day. She wonders if it would be too intrusive to just turn up on her doorstep instead with some iced buns and the offer of a chat over coffee. But there's the question of what to do with Bill while this is going on – she hasn't been able to get him to the day centre recently for some reason he can't articulate but obviously feels strongly about, and she doesn't want to force him to go. It's been a bit like getting a school-phobic child off in the mornings. Also Karen's watching her carbs and never actually eats anything like iced buns, not even in a good cause, which is what Mavis undoubtedly is. All round, the phone might be best, she decides.

By the time the programme has finished Bill has wound down enough to get ready for bed, although Karen knows he'll have a disturbed night after the anxiety of the evening – which means she will too.

'Come on, Dad. Let's get you settled down for the night. Big day tomorrow – we're going shopping, remember?'

Bill looks confused.

'We're going to the garden centre first to look for trailing begonias, then off into town to find you another cardigan.'

'Yes, that's right,' he says, although he has no recollection of needing a new cardigan, nor of the incident which resulted in the sleeve of his old one getting burnt.

Karen knows that when they get to the garden centre Bill will have no idea what he wanted to buy, but she'll see it through anyway, helping him choose the best plants and reminding him of the TV presenter's tips.

'Yes,' he repeats. 'Garden centre first, then cardigans. Jolly good.'

Once his light is out Karen goes into her study and looks again at the programme she was working on earlier. It's a theatre brochure – the first one she's designed for them – and although it's not a complicated layout there's a lot of information to get in and it requires a degree of juggling to fit everything coherently into the space available. The theatre administrators have asked for the first draft by the end of the week but Karen would like to get it to them before their deadline.

She glances at her watch. Almost 10.30, time to get an email off to Graham first – and wonder of wonders! For once he's on-line at the same time as her, which gives them the chance to chat.

Is this a good time? she starts, because she can never tell who else might be in the room looking over his shoulder and you can't be too careful.

Hello you. Yes, all alone at the moment, the message comes back from Graham. **Working late?**

Just about to start. I was out at a meeting, just got back. How are you?

Missing you, says Graham. **What meeting? Work?**

No. Other people with elderly dependants. Good chance for sitters next time you're in town. Could get a room for whole afternoon! Karen cannot contain her excitement at this unexpected turn of events and wants to share it with Graham. She hasn't seen him for a couple of months and the longing is growing.

There's a pause before Graham comes back to her.

What are you wearing?

Karen smiles. It's one of their games.

Jeans, red tee-shirt, red heels.

Underwear?

Of course! What sort of woman do you take me for?

What colour?

What do you think?

Umm. Black?

No. Try again.

Red?

Correct!

The lacy set?

No, satin. Tee-shirt Graham — try to concentrate!!

Oh believe me, I am concentrating. Picturing you in it. Bet you look great. Do you miss me?

Karen hears Bill blowing his nose. Not asleep yet, she thinks.

You know I do. It's been ages. There's a pause while Karen listens out for Bill. She types in another line to her message. **I wish you were here.**

Me too. What would you like to be doing if I were?

All of a sudden Karen hears Bill out in the hallway.

'Karen? Karen — where are you?' Bill stumbles into Karen's study, knocking over a pile of folders as he comes through the door.

'Dad, it's OK, I'm here.' Karen says, leaving her desk and guiding him along the hall to his bedroom and back into bed.

By the time she gets back to her computer the wretched 3D Pipes are growing all over her screen, Graham has gone and she has to send him an email to explain her sudden departure.

Bloody typical, she thinks. We have enough trouble getting it in real life, now we can't even manage e-sex.

CHAPTER THREE

LADIES WHO LUNCH

It's a week since the first Generation Club meeting, and although they've been in phone contact Sally hasn't seen any of the others since. She has arranged to meet Cathy in town today for lunch, and she's taking Queenie along with her, as she can't find a sitter. Cathy is not bothered by this, and Queenie has quite taken to her on their previous couple of meetings and is looking forward to having lunch out. It's a real treat for me, she keeps telling Sally, as if ordinarily she never goes anywhere. This is a good sign in a way, as Queenie will obviously be up for all the Generation Club has to offer. But Sally is miffed, for reasons she can't quite fathom, or doesn't want to admit to herself.

Queenie has been getting on her nerves all morning. She's been in one of her more belligerent moods, and nothing Sally does quite passes muster. The cake she made this morning (cherry and almond) failed to rise and it looks as if the cherries have sunk to the bottom. Queenie tuts a bit, then makes her pronouncement.

'You should have washed those cherries off first and tossed them in flour,' she says.

Sally grits her teeth and pushes back the retort that springs to mind. She can't recall her mother being much of a cake-maker, her birthday cakes were always shop bought.

'Still, we can put it under custard I suppose, rather than waste it,' Queenie goes on, oblivious to Sally's silent rage. The tip about the cherries is something she heard only yesterday on daytime TV, and she's delighted to have the chance to show it off before she forgets it completely. Cakes didn't feature much in Queenie's culinary repertoire, but she made amazing pastry, light and crumbly. She likes to think she still could, but she's got out of the habit now. Sally does everything these days, and Queenie lets her.

They go along to the local shops later, at a snail's pace, Queenie refusing to take her walking stick and leaning heavily on Sally's arm instead. Ordinarily it's a walk of only a few minutes, but it actually takes them fifteen to reach the Post Office. Once inside, Sally sits her mother down, and joins the queue. Queenie has a birthday card to send off to a friend in Canada and when the deed is done and she hears the cost of the postage is horrified.

'It's not worth that – why didn't you ask me first? Isn't there a cheaper way?'

'Yes, it could go by sea but it'll take weeks and we don't have time now for that. If you didn't want me to send it why bother getting the card in the first place?'

Sally has to bellow this to her mother above the background noise in the Post Office, so naturally the rest of the queue are in on the conversation and some of them turn round to see what sort of dreadful daughter would speak to her mother like this. Just as they are leaving, an old friend from their road comes in and starts chatting to Queenie, who appears to have no trouble hearing her and is now in no rush to get to the other shops and then back home.

Leaving the two of them together to have a gossip, Sally takes the opportunity to nip along to the newsagents for her mother's *People's Friend* and when she gets back to the Post Office finds them still at it. Eventually, she prises them apart and they begin the slow crawl in and out of a couple of other local shops before setting off for home.

This is a trip Sally can do without. But her mother has used these local shops for all of the sixty years since she first came to the house as a newlywed, and it's part of her routine. They have, by negotiation, got it down to twice a week and now it's more of a social event than a shopping necessity as the weekly supermarket trip could cover all their needs. But to Queenie Wednesdays and Fridays are a lifeline and a non-variable part of her week, and Sally can see the difference in her afterwards.

Now, on the way home, Queenie can just about find enough puff to tell Sally what she's just learned of everyone else's business. Sally's wondering if the cherry cake disaster has been Queenie's contribution to the gossip pool today, because there's precious little else for her to bring to the table. She doubts that the Generation Club has featured yet.

'...ungrateful little boys, both of them. No time for their great-grandma...'

There's a bit of a slope from the end of the road up to their house, and Queenie has to rest more heavily on Sally's arm, and stop talking, in order to manage it. This gives Sally a chance to get in.

'Eleanor's coming back from university next weekend. It'll be lovely to have her home again, won't it?'

Queenie stops and turns to Sally, panting a bit to get enough breath to speak.

'Just the weekend?' she manages to get out.

'Going back Monday,' confirms Sally, with a nod and a weak smile. She doesn't want her mother to see that she's disappointed by such a brief visit after a long absence, but Queenie isn't easily fooled.

'She'll be here when you need her,' she says. 'Daughters are. I thank God I had a girl.' Queenie pats Sally's hand and turns her face forward, towards home.

As they set off again Sally thinks, but I need Eleanor now. I need her here right this minute to help get you back home, then spruced up and ready to go out again into town to meet Cathy. And I no longer give a stuff about her university course and the degree she'll eventually get but never make any use of because she takes a job in a shoe shop or goes off with a man who wants to raise sheep in the Falklands.

Queenie pauses at the gate and turns to her daughter.

'Will she be seeing her father, or do we get her all to ourselves this time?'

'I don't know Mum, she didn't say. It was only a quick call this morning.'

'It always is,' says Queenie, as she strides off unaided, up the path towards her front door.

There are a few bits of shopping to unpack once they get in, and Queenie needs a sit-down with a cup of tea and a biscuit before she can face going out again. Sally leaves her with the *People's Friend* while she empties the washing machine and then hangs the sheets and towels outside.

'I think I'll wear my green jacket to go into town,' says Queenie, as Sally comes through the back door.

'It's in the cleaners, Mum.'

'What?' says Queenie, fiddling with her hearing aids.

'The cleaners,' says Sally, a few decibels higher. 'It's in the cleaners.'

'Is it? I thought you picked it up the other day – you said you would.'

'I ran out of time,' lies Sally, who had completely forgotten it. 'Didn't have enough left on the parking ticket and you know how hot they are in town these days.'

'What do you think about my tweed one then? It doesn't really go with this skirt – maybe I should change into a different one. What do you think?'

Sally's thinking that if so many decisions are required for this trip it's maybe not such a good idea to go.

'Mum, you look perfectly fine as you are. We're only going to the coffee shop in Barkers.'

Queenie can remember when Barkers was a posh department store where the staff called you Madam and the prices were beyond her means. In those days you got bone china and linen serviettes in what was then called the Luncheon Room, and she can't get to grips with the way it is now.

'Well you know I like to make an effort when we go into town. At the very least I'll need to put on fresh lipstick and do my hair.' Queenie pulls herself up from the table, and heads towards her bedroom.

Sally is pleased really that she still cares about how she looks and takes a pride in her appearance. So now she starts to feel guilty about snapping at her.

'Let's take a look at that jacket, then,' she says, following her mother into her room.

* * *

Cathy has already got a table and a coffee by the time Sally and Queenie arrive. She gets up to greet them and can see straight away that Sally has had a bit of a morning.

'Are we late?' asks Sally, guiding her mother into a chair. 'Had terrible trouble parking, the world and his wife must be in town today.'

'No, I was early, so don't worry.' Cathy turns to Queenie with a smile.

'What a smart jacket,' she says, loudly enough for Queenie, and the rest of Barkers coffee room, to hear. 'Lovely colours in that tweed, and it looks very nice on you.'

Queenie beams, then realises that Sally has put her in a chair facing away from the room and into a wall.

'I can't see anything here, dear,' she says. 'I'll sit round there instead.'

She hauls herself up, holding on to the edge of the table and tipping it so that all the menu cards fall over, and Cathy and Sally manoeuvre her in and out of the chairs till she's re-located opposite.

'Just move that wall a bit to the right while you're on your feet,' Sally mutters to Cathy, who winks back at her over Queenie's head.

Finally, they are all settled and the menu is consulted. Queenie looks around for a black and white clad waitress to take their order but of course there aren't any. She starts to tell Cathy about the way Barkers used to be, when she was a young wife and Sally was a baby.

'Mum, just decide what you want and I'll go up to the counter and get it,' says Sally, impatiently, because she hasn't eaten since a bowl of cereal at 8am, and is in need of nourishment. Queenie snatches the menu back from her.

'I don't know what all the rush is, anyone would think you had a train to catch.'

'Aren't you hungry then?'

'Hungry?' Queenie puts on a world-weary look. 'I haven't been hungry for years, dear.'

'Well you won't be very pleased if I get up there and then find they've run out of whatever you decide to have. Now, what do you fancy...'

Queenie takes her time over choosing, stuck between the Welsh Rarebit and the ham omelette. Finally, the order is complete, Sally reaches down to pick up her handbag and, with a little shriek, finds to her horror that she's wearing her slippers.

'Oh, my God, I've been walking about in these all morning,' she says. Cathy and Queenie look down at the fur-trimmed black velvet mules, then back at Sally. She looks as if she might burst into tears.

'I'll order the lunch,' says Cathy, immediately getting to her feet. 'What size?'

'What?'

'Shoes – what size?'

'Four. Don't tell me you've got a spare pair with you.'

'This is a department store – my guess is they'll have something wearable downstairs. Give me five minutes,' says Cathy, and then disappears to the counter.

She re-appears at about the same time as the sandwiches and Welsh Rarebit come onto the scene, and hands Sally a Barkers carrier.

'You're in luck – they've got some quite nice reductions. I might take a look myself after lunch.'

Queenie, who has been silent up to that point, suddenly starts laughing. Cathy looks at her, in trepidation. Sally looks at her in astonishment. Then she sees the funny side, and starts to laugh herself. Cathy sees the two of them laughing, and it's infectious so the girl who has brought over their food ends up just leaving everything in the middle of the table because now none of them can tell her who wanted what.

After lunch they go to the shoe department, and in the end they all leave with Barkers carriers. When they part company Queenie tells Cathy she hasn't had such a good time in years and although initially Sally is a little put out by this, she has to admit that today's outing has done them both good.

Later that evening Cathy rings Sally. She's had an idea.

'What we need is a code-word,' she says. 'For those times when it all gets to be a bit much – we need someone else to de-fuse the situation by saying something that's only known to us, the carers. It would just help to pull us up short at moments of extreme irritation.'

Sally can see how it would work – how it would have worked a couple of times today for her, let alone each of the others in their own situation.

'What sort of word?'

'Anything, it doesn't matter as long as we all know what it is. There's a Gilbert and Sullivan operetta where they do something like this, I think they used the word Basingstoke. We could use – oh, I don't know – what was the name of that ballroom where Mavis met her future husband?'

'The Locarno', says Sally.

'There you are – that would do. Locarno. Must remember to mention that to the others next time we meet up...'

QUEENIE

One of my girlfriends from work warned me off him, but I was young and silly and thought I knew better.

'That Arthur Jones is a bully,' she said. 'If you take up with him you'll never have a moment's peace.'

I should have listened to her. But he was handsome, and I was flattered by his attention. I wasn't the first woman to fall for that, and I won't be the last either. I just hope my Eleanor doesn't make a similar mistake, I might have to tell her the truth about her Grandad if it came to it and I wouldn't really want to do that. In some ways he was a good husband, he wasn't afraid of hard work and we always had food on the table, even though there were times when it was a struggle. And he was a good father to Sally. He never laid a finger on her and like most little girls she knew just how to wind him round her little finger.

But that girl – I wonder what her name was? She had red hair, I remember that much. Anyway, she was right about Arthur, he *was* a bully and once we were married he wanted things all his own way. He liked to control everything – except the kitchen and the housework, that is – he had nothing to complain about there, I made sure of that, and so he didn't interfere in those departments. I never said anything to any of the other girls around here – we were all young married couples in these houses – but they could see how it was. Their husbands gave them enough freedom so they could do things outside the house – many of them worked, or joined Young Wives and some went to cookery or needlework classes. I'd have liked to go along with them but Arthur wouldn't hear of it. 'You're needed here at home,' he said, 'not out there gallivanting around with that lot.' Anyway, he couldn't stop me meeting up with them down at the shops or in the park with the kiddies.

But you make the best of things, don't you?

We had Sally, and she was a good child. It's a pity we didn't have any more children, I'd have liked a boy and it might have softened Arthur a bit if he'd had a son. But I had a terrible time with Sally and after that they told me I wouldn't be able to have any more children. Anyway, it's a girl you need as you get older to step in and do the things you can't manage any more, boys aren't much good then. And if you're lucky she'll have a husband who can turn his hand to bits and pieces around the house too.

I liked Ian, not that he was ever any good at DIY. He was brought up too posh for that, his parents were a bit hoity-toity so we didn't have much to do with them over the years. But I was sorry when he and Sally got divorced because he was very good to me, and he's always been a wonderful dad to Eleanor. She's turned out such a lovely girl, she loves her old Grandma.

Arthur went into a home more than five years ago, which was a blessing because I couldn't cope with him at home any more. It was shocking really, seeing such a powerful man as him in a state like that, just like a child all over again. If it hadn't been because Sally wanted to, I wouldn't have kept going in to see him. He couldn't even remember me. But I went along with it for her sake.

When things started to get a bit tricky for me here it was Sally's idea to sell her house and move in with me. I'm glad it turned out that way – I wouldn't have been too keen on moving into her house, nice though it was. I could have had my own bathroom there. But I don't know anyone in that part of town, this is where I belong. I can walk down to that parade of shops and

I guarantee I'll meet lots of people I can stop and have a chat to.

I sometimes think Sally's got more of her father than me in her. I'm not allowed to do anything. She won't let me anywhere near my own kitchen now in case I have an accident with the cooker or some such daft idea. Not that it looks much like my kitchen any more, now there are new cupboards in there. Of course all my old pots and pans had to go when Sally brought her own stuff in, or bought new. I'd been using some of them for years, nothing wrong with them that I could see.

It's all very well her taking over the cooking, but she's not got what I'd call a flair for it. I reckon my pastry could have won competitions, even Arthur praised me for that. I watch those cookery programmes on telly, and I think, they can do all that fancy stuff and make it look pretty on the plate with blobs of this and sprigs of that, but I bet they can't make a decent bit of shortcrust pastry to save their lives. Neither can Sally if it comes to that. But I'm not allowed to cook now, though I bet I could still give her a surprise or two, given the chance.

CHAPTER FOUR

GETTING TO KNOW – WHO?

'What you have to remember is to deadhead all summer long.'

It's a Saturday afternoon and the first time all the Generation Club members, with their dependants, have been together. The venue is Karen's house and luckily, since she'd planned a garden event, it's the kind of early June day that should be predictable but is actually all too rare – brilliant, warm and splashed with sunshine.

Bill's trailing begonias are not in full bloom yet, but in general his garden is a showpiece and he's enthusiastically pointing out its best features to Jo, Don and Cathy's Aunt Stella. A lifetime non-gardener, Don is struggling with this but Stella is showing a lively interest in Bill's rambling descriptions of the herbaceous border even though she's unable to see any of it clearly. Jo would like to slip away and join Sally on a seat by the pond, but doesn't know how to do it without seeming rude. There's also the added problem of having Stella hanging on to her arm, because at the moment they're standing about on the garden path. In one of life's strange quirks, Bill, the keen gardener, has unwittingly found himself in a sub-group with the only people present who live in flats.

Karen has been having a chat with Mavis, and trying to include Dorothy at the same time, but she suddenly spots the predicament and comes across to rescue them.

'Dad, get chairs for Stella and Don will you? Bring a couple over from there,' she adds as Bill looks about him in some desperation.

'Sorry, you got a bit stuck there, didn't you?' she whispers to Jo, who passes it off with a smile and a wave of the hand.

'It's nice to see them all getting on,' says Jo, noticing her dad and Stella settling into a chat now they've left the unfamiliar gardening territory behind. She has come armed with Don's portable oxygen system in the car but so far he hasn't needed it. Stella is making allowances for his wheezy speech patterns and giving him plenty of time to say what he wants before she comes back with her own contribution, and it seems to be working.

Meanwhile, having accomplished the chair task, Bill has moved across to where Cathy and Queenie are talking about clothes. He has a couple of pink roses in his hand, which he gives to them, one each.

'Mind the thorns, I haven't taken them off, see?'

Queenie is charmed by this gift.

'My next door neighbour grows roses,' she tells them. 'Sometimes he brings some over for Sally and me, but they're always full of greenfly. Isn't that right?' she adds as Sally joins them with a tray of glasses and a jug of fruit juice.

'Oh, pervy Tom,' says Sally. 'I don't accept anything from him. He's a lecherous old sod, always has been.'

Bill laughs hugely and inappropriately at this, not really taking it in but feeling part of the social group by contributing in this way. Mavis, pushing Dorothy along the path to join the group, interprets his laughter in the usual, but as it happens quite incorrect, way.

'Well, you lot are having a jolly time. What's the joke?'

She gets one wheel stuck in a dip in the flagstones at this point and Cathy helps her to get free.

'Hardly a joke,' says Sally. 'We were talking about our next door neighbour. He gives me the creeps. Even as a little girl I thought there was something funny about him. Dad couldn't stand him, could he Mum?''

'I remember he used to give you sweets and you always threw them straight in the bin.'

'And he's still doing it – box of chocolates last week.'

'What?'

'Mum, turn those hearing aids up,' says Sally, irritated, then repeats the bit about the chocolates.

'Really?' says Queenie, and her hearing aids whistle a bit as she adjusts them. 'I didn't see them.'

'That's because they went in the bin too.'

Bill laughs again, this time slapping his knee for added effect.

'It'll all come out in the wash,' he observes.

Sally, confused by this, looks across to Karen, who shrugs and pulls a face.

'I've got no idea,' she says.

'Chocolates,' says Dorothy, her only contribution since arriving.

'Dorothy loves chocolates, don't you?' says Mavis, although everyone present could have guessed that. Years of over-indulging and lack of activity have made Dorothy huge. No wonder it's a job for Mavis to handle her, thinks Cathy, even given that Social Services send people in to help with personal care.

'Next time I get chocs from pervy old Tom I'll save them for you Dorothy,' smiles Sally.

'And marzipan,' says Dorothy.

Karen passes fruit juice around to everyone. She has made a couple of cakes for the afternoon and is getting started on who wants what, when they hear the phone ring in the house.

'They'll ring back,' she says, determined to ignore it. But Bill, wanting to do his best to help out, is already on his feet.

'I can answer it,' he says as he heads for the French doors.

'Oh dear,' says Karen, quietly to Mavis and Jo, who are taking plates from her and passing them round, 'I don't like him answering the phone, he'll just get confused and get it all wrong. Then one or both of us will get upset.'

It takes only a little time for Bill to re-join them in the garden but he hangs back on the edge of the circle for a few minutes fingering Karen's silk cardigan where she's abandoned it around the shoulders of a shepherdess statue.

'It's somebody Conrad,' he says finally, then adds, 'Joe, I think. He's still on the phone.'

Karen slams the cake knife down.

'Joe Conrad? I don't know anyone of that name. Are you sure?'

Bill shrugs. 'I think so,' he says, less confidently. 'Each to his own,' he adds.

'Dad, I wish you wouldn't...' Karen starts, then goes up the steps into the house.

From the open door they hear her at the phone.

'Yes? Oh, Simon, it's you. Look, I've got people here, I'll ring you back.'

As Karen re-appears on the patio Don comes in right on cue with a wheeze, a cough and an anecdote.

'I used to know a Joe Conrad,' he starts. 'Played second trumpet in the Ken Mackintosh Band. Can't be him though, he fell under a tram on the seafront at Blackpool back in 1957. He was chasing one of the show dancers at the time. She was more nimble obviously and better at dodging the traffic than him.'

Mavis is the first one to laugh, then Stella joins in and soon they're all laughing quite out of proportion to what was said but just enjoying the release of tension that Don has engineered. It all comes to an end in a few more seconds.

'Shut up! Shudupshudupshudupshudup...'

They turn to see Dorothy with her hands over her ears, shouting into her lap, saliva dripping onto her knees as she does so. Mavis goes across to her, reaching out to take her hands away from her head.

'Come on now Dorothy, it was only a little bit of fun...'

Dorothy reaches out and whacks Mavis across the arm, not hard enough to hurt but the spiteful, truculent action of a child who's not getting her way. Mavis scolds her and gets another slap for her trouble.

There's a brief silence, which Karen steps into.

'Chocolate cake, Dorothy? I bet you'll like this,' and she hands her a plate with a wedge of cake on it.

Dorothy takes the plate and eyes up the cake, and for a moment it looks as if it'll be all right. But then she hurls it down on the patio, and broken china and chocolate cake bounce all over the slabs and onto the grass.

Mavis is mortified and apologises to Karen in as many ways as she can think of. 'We'd better go home,' she says.

'You don't have to, Mavis. Please stay a bit longer,' says Karen, but it's clear that Mavis won't feel comfortable after Dorothy's tantrum so Cathy helps her push the wheelchair back up to the side gate and Karen comes with her to say goodbye. They each give Mavis a hug, and watch as she sets off to walk the couple of streets back to her house.

'Poor Mavis,' says Cathy. 'Out of all of us she's probably the one who most needs these occasions to work.'

'I'll ring her later,' says Karen.

By the time they get back to the others Jo and Sally have picked up the pieces of broken china, and thrown the cake into the shrubs for the birds to find. Meanwhile, Bill has discovered a few wayward stems on one of his plants and has the secateurs out, and Stella, Queenie and Don are having a natter about something on the television, so in general it looks as if the afternoon is going well.

'That whole thing kicked off because Dad answered my phone,' says Karen, taking her dustpan and brush from Sally.

'You can't blame him, he was only trying to help. He couldn't have known what it would lead to.'

Bill wanders across just at the moment the phone rings again.

'Stay right here Dad,' says Karen, wagging a finger at him. 'I don't want you going anywhere near that phone.'

Sally and Jo, both nearby Karen at this moment, lean in towards her and stage-whisper in unison.

'Locarno.'

Karen stops in her tracks, looks at them, and her shoulders drop.

'OK, maybe you're right. What does it matter anyway? I'll pick up the message later. Now, more cake anyone? More juice?'

Later, as they're starting the washing up, Jo and Karen look back on the afternoon with a feeling of achievement. It's gone well, apart from the incident with Dorothy, and everyone seems to have enjoyed the time spent in each other's company.

Sally and Cathy come into the kitchen with the remainder of the tea things from the garden, leaving the oldies chatting in the late afternoon sun. Every so often they hear laughter, and a wheezy cough from Don.

'Anyway,' says Cathy, 'Where do you think your dad got that name from? Joe Conrad?'

'No idea. I've never known anyone called that and as far as I know, neither has he. It was a friend called Simon Cross on the phone, so nothing like it. But by the time he got back to me he'd have forgotten Simon's name.'

Sally has brought Karen's silk cardigan in, and as she puts it over the back of a chair she starts to laugh.

'I can see where he got it from.'

She holds the cardigan up for them to see. The label inside the neck reads Jasper Conran.

Out in the lengthening shadows of the garden the oldies turn in the direction of the kitchen, from where the sounds of laughter are drifting out towards them.

'Well, just listen to that,' says Queenie, who has now taken the trouble to get her hearing aids just right so that she doesn't miss anything. 'They're having a good time,'

'Good, they deserve it,' says Stella, and Bill slaps Don on the back, making him cough, then throws his head back and roars with laughter.

CHAPTER 5

AS LONG AS SHE NEEDS ME

Cathy lets herself in to Stella's flat and calls out as she does so.

'Only me, Stella. Where are you?'

Stella's voice drifts back from the living room and Cathy drops her two bags of grocery shopping in the kitchen and goes through to join her aunt. This has become their routine – once a week, on a Friday, Cathy goes to Stella's on her way home from work and they have lunch together. Unlike the weekly supermarket trip, this is an opportunity for them to catch up on each other's news, and surprisingly, in view of the fact that she seldom leaves the flat on her own, Stella usually has more to tell than Cathy. It also gives Cathy the chance for a surreptitious clean around the kitchen while she's getting lunch ready. Later on she'll go to the bathroom and have a go in there as well. She doesn't blame Stella, whose eyesight is now so bad that she just can't see when things need a clean.

This Friday the living room appears to be under siege from the national press. Stella has the local newspaper delivered each week, and reads it avidly, but today there's more than the usual quantity of newsprint spread across the dining table and Stella is bent close to the pages with a large magnifying glass, her glasses abandoned alongside her.

'Big story breaking that I don't know about?' Cathy asks.

'More upheaval at the BBC,' says Stella, 'Boardroom revolution etcetera, etcetera. My neighbours only ever read the gossip and sports pages, so I thought I'd get the whole spectrum of opinion on what's happening from their papers. The Guardian to The Sun – it's an interesting comparison,' she adds shuffling the pages back together, folding and moving them off the table.

'Anybody you know involved?' asks Cathy.

'One or two who were just office boys when I knew them. Things are so different now to how they were in my day – they need a Charles Hill or Trethowan at the top again to keep the lid on things.'

Cathy moves to the oak sideboard for cutlery and dinner mats.

'And you, I daresay, to slap wrists when necessary!'

'Sadly I was never in a position to do that – not much in the research department affected what went on at the top. But the whole atmosphere was different then.' Stella clears the last of the papers and her magnifying glass onto the coffee table, puts her glasses back on and spreads a tablecloth out.

'I still miss it, you know,' she adds, 'but none of us can go on forever. The body lets you down even when the brain still thinks it's got plenty left. Don was saying much the same the other day at Karen's house.'

'You got on very well together, didn't you?' asks Cathy, as she fetches glasses and plates from the kitchen. 'With Don in particular, I mean.'

'He's an interesting man,' says Stella, 'I admire him for starting on computers at his time of life. That shows a huge willingness to embrace new thinking and quite some determination to get to grips with the nuts and bolts of it. He's going to let me read some of his memoirs.'

'Great – I bet that'll make fascinating reading.'

Cathy moves into the kitchen and rummages in the shopping bags for the things she has bought for lunch while Stella carries on chatting from her chair in the lounge.

'He was telling me about his ex-wife, Jo's mother. She simply walked out on them one day and for months he didn't know what had happened to her. The police treated it as a missing person case, but didn't turn anything up, then I suppose they lost interest and the file was put to one side. Eventually she got in touch, but Jo wouldn't have anything to do with her from that day on. She's coming over soon.'

'Over? Over from where?' asks Cathy, who knows nothing about Jo's mother because Jo has never mentioned her.

'New Zealand. She and Don email apparently. Her name's Jean.'

'Well you seem to have found out a lot in a short time. I wonder what Jo thinks about this trip.'

'Oh, this conversation wasn't at Karen's – Don phoned me in the week.'

In the kitchen Cathy stops squirting cleaner onto the worktops and pauses, J Cloth in hand.

'Oh?'

'Yes,' Stella continues, 'I might be able to help him with some research for his writing. He wanted to give me some information.'

Cathy smiles to herself and leaves it at that.

Over lunch neither of them mention the Generation Club again. Stella wants to hear about Cathy's job at the travel agency, about which places are popular at the moment and where the Government has advised people to keep away from.

Cathy has been to most of the popular destinations herself, back in the days when she worked full time as an agent and had money to spend on holidays – and when she didn't have Aunt Stella to look after. So in many cases she can speak about resorts from personal experience, and Stella – who has never travelled outside the UK and knows she never will now – likes this window on the world. A lifelong fear of flying may have condemned her to being an armchair traveller but her curiosity about the wider world has never diminished.

'Would you go there again?' Stella asks when they discuss one of the Greek islands.

'Couldn't afford it now,' says Cathy. 'I had the benefit of cheap flights, and sometimes if it was a work trip I'd go at the agency's expense. But no concessions come the way of a part-timer, no free lunches or excursions, nor salaries that can stand the expense of foreign travel. It's the price you pay if you want more time for yourself.' And for you, she adds to herself, but would never say aloud.

Stella is adept at reading between the lines, and tactfully changes the subject.

'How are the rehearsals going?'

'Early days. Nobody knows their lines yet, but I think it'll be OK. Andrew Simmonds is taking the male lead again – which has irritated one or two people no end. I keep out of the politics as far as possible.'

In spite of her failing eyesight, Stella always attends Cathy's plays and is a staunch supporter of the Horsfield amateur dramatic group. Through Cathy she knows most of the members by reputation if not personally.

'Well, he's always very good. Maybe that's what irritates them more than anything else.'

'You're probably right, and like most groups there isn't too much competition from other men. It's a different story with the women though – auditions can go on for days.'

It's true that in Horsfield's terms Andrew Simmonds delivers an Academy Award winning performance each time, but Stella also knows that her niece is more than a match for him. They are the only two with a real on-stage presence, and each of them steals every scene they're in. When cast opposite each other Stella has often said that they light up the stage as well as any professionals she's seen.

The afternoon passes quickly, as it always does, and after Cathy has washed up she makes a sandwich for Stella to have later. Neither of them mentions the fresh smell of cleanser that's coming from the kitchen. Cathy assumes Stella doesn't notice and Stella chooses to say nothing about it.

It's a small deception that suits them both.

* * *

Across town, Mavis is knocking on Karen's door. It's an unscheduled visit, Mavis taking advantage of the short break afforded by the daily visit of Social Services to attend to Dorothy's personal care routine.

Mavis likes going to see Karen. Everything about her is the opposite to Mavis herself, and the same can be said for her house. Karen has an eye for colour and design, which is reflected in the way both she and her house look. Where Mavis is old-fashioned and mumsy, Karen is chic and elegant. Largely due to financial considerations, Mavis's house is tatty and faded, but Karen's is smart and shiny – and it's not because she can lavish money on herself or her house. Karen can come up with the ideas and she has the knack of doing things on a shoe-string that end up looking a million dollars. Mavis is of the opinion that Karen could show the TV make-over people a thing or two.

So it's never a hardship for Mavis to pop round to Karen's place, it actually brightens her day. Today, she just needed to get out of the house for a while and hasn't really got time to stay for a cup of tea, but Karen presses her to do so and she lets herself be talked into it. They head for the kitchen and Bill wanders into the hallway at this point and stops by Karen's elbow.

'Dad, you remember Mavis, don't you? At our garden party? With her sister Dorothy?'

Bill looks completely blank, having no recollection of Mavis at all.

'Yes, yes,' he finally manages. 'Yes, Margaret. Of course.'

At the first opportunity he scuttles off to the garden, and Karen and Mavis settle down at the kitchen table.

'You should have said, "Dorothy who had the hissy fit and flung her cake on the ground." He might have remembered then,' says Mavis.

There has been a general feeling among the GenClub girls that Mavis's family is worse than useless. Up to now nobody has felt they could ask her what their problem is, but today Karen's in the mood for it, though she is uncharacteristically hesitant.

'Mavis – your family, your children – I was just wondering – why is it they don't occasionally help you out with Dorothy? A little respite, you know?'

'Well, it's a bit of a journey for them,' says Mavis, in a classic piece of understatement. 'I have three boys – Stephen lives in Italy, Robert in the USA and Martin in Australia. They don't know how bad Dorothy is now because there's no point in telling them – they'd only worry about me and what can they do from that distance?'

'Oh, well that explains that one,' says Karen. 'And your ex-husbands? Ever hear from them?'

'I'd be surprised if I did. Both dead,' says Mavis cheerfully as she heaps sugar into her tea. 'And my four brothers, too. I'm good at seeing them off – plenty of practice. So you see there's really nobody else to share the burden of Dorothy. Shouldn't say 'burden', though in truth that's what she's become.'

Karen pushes the biscuit tin across to Mavis.

'When did you last see your boys?'

'Stephen came over with his partner at the end of last year – I met them in London, so he didn't get to see Dorothy, thank goodness.' Mavis dunks a biscuit in her tea. 'I haven't seen Robert or Andrew for longer – three years or so. They both have young families and their own businesses so it's difficult for them to get away. I've never seen some of my grandchildren.'

Mavis is very matter-of-fact about it but Karen can see through the cracks and there's a lot there that makes her want to weep.

'Well,' she says, struggling to find something positive and encouraging to come back with, 'One of these days you might win the Lottery then you'll be able to go off and see them all.'

'I doubt it,' says Mavis, 'I don't buy a ticket.'

* * *

Don is watching an old black and white film on DVD when Jo gets back from the shops. It's something he's been sent by one of his old musician pals and in some of the nightclub scenes are people he once played with. He's not really interested in the rest of the film, so he keeps fast-winding it forward, missing the bit he wants then fast-winding it back again. It's a frustrating business and after a while he gives up and comes out into the kitchen to help Jo put the shopping away.

'There's something I wanted to tell you,' he says, passing tins of soup and baked beans up to Jo, who is standing on a chair and stacking them at the top of the cupboard.

'Your mother's coming over on holiday soon.'

Jo stops what she's doing and turns to look down onto Don's upturned face.

'Oh? How do you know that?'

'I had an email from her last week. She'll be here in September – and naturally she wants to see us.'

Don has kept in touch, sporadically, with his wife Jean since she set up home in New Zealand. He no longer tells Jo when she's been in touch because it causes friction between them, but this time he can't avoid it – not if Jean's going to turn up on their doorstep one day soon.

'Why "naturally"? She doesn't have much of a track record at doing the most natural things – take for instance walking out on her husband and child. Well sorry Dad, but I don't want to see her. You can do what you like, but don't count on me to be here when she comes calling. Honestly, she's got some nerve.'

Jo gets off the chair and walks round Don to get to the fridge.

'Just give it some thought,' says Don, 'This may be the last chance you get to see her.'

'Why? Is she dying?'

'No, no. But New Zealand's a long way away, how many more holidays do you think she's going to have over here?'

Jo starts slamming cheese and yogurts into the fridge.

'None, hopefully.'

Don catches hold of Jo's arm as she spins back from the shopping bag with a lettuce and pack of tomatoes.

'No matter what happened she is still your mother and it would be nice if you could find some common ground, Jo. Take some time to think it through…'

'Dad, I was four when she left. I've already had fifty-three years to think it through – how much more time do you think I need? If she's expecting a reply you can tell her I'll be too busy when she's here. Or away from home. In fact, tell her anything you like as long as it prevents me from coming face to face with her.'

Don sighs. He knows this is an argument he can't win and he understands exactly how Karen feels because he used to feel the same. But over the years he's come to the conclusion there's nothing to be gained from bearing a grudge against Jean. She went, and he and Jo stayed, carrying on as best they could without her. It wasn't easy being both parents to a little girl, or to a teenager whose hormones were out of control, but somehow Don muddled through and he reckons Jo turned out just fine. Where Jo is concerned, he knows Jean was the loser. So now he has no animosity left towards her, only a measure of curiosity about what she's like these days and how her life experiences have changed her. And in a funny sort of way, he's looking forward to seeing Jean again.

Jo takes the packs of bacon and sausages that Don hands across to her, and as she puts them in the fridge a kind of dread creeps over her. When it comes to it, when her mother actually does come, she'll have to screw up all her courage to deal with the inevitable confrontation, and do it in such a way to avoid the one thing she can never bear to do – upset her Dad.

Jo takes refuge in her tiny sewing room, surrounded by the mauve silk and artificial flowers of the bridesmaid's dress she's working on at the moment. She hears Don wheeze his way back up the hall towards his computer and wonders if he's going to report back to her mother, or just leave it to chance that things will work out once she's actually on their doorstep.

She unpins the tissue pattern from a piece of mauve silk, marking on some seam points as she goes. This isn't the right time to get the machine on it, not while she's tense – a mistake will be costly, and Jo can't afford either that or the extra stress it will cause her. Instead, she picks up a froth of mauve tulle and smoothes it over the silk, then threads up a needle and starts tacking the two fabric layers together. The repetitive sewing action slowly calms her down and gradually the knots in Jo's shoulders start to ease out.

Maybe she won't come after all, she thinks. There'll be some reason why she can't get here and we'll be able to carry on just the way we are without having to see her.

The mauve fabric is beautiful and it's going to make a gorgeous dress for some lucky girl, who'll look a million dollars in it.

It'll work out fine.

STELLA

I always say, it's no good moaning about health problems as you get older. It's something you just have to put up with. I was lucky; I had the best of health for most of my life, so now I have to accept what's in store for me and keep going regardless.

I don't like having to bother Cathy all the time. She's a good girl – like a daughter to me – and she never lets me feel I'm a nuisance to her, though I'm sure there are times when that's exactly what I am. You never think, when you're younger and hale and hearty, that there'll come a day when you have to rely on others. Then all of a sudden that day arrives, and it's hard, very hard sometimes to take.

Throughout the years I worked at the BBC I was so active that now I can't imagine how I fitted everything into a 24-hour day. After work we used to go and play badminton, or tennis in the summer, and there were always weekend parties and gatherings at one of the pubs or somebody's house. I worked long hours, too. There was no place in those days for anyone who just wanted to coast along – and as a woman I had to work extra hard to prove myself amongst all those men. It was hard enough in radio, but once I moved across to television it was even harder. Women talk now about the glass ceiling, well we had glass walls to scale as well. Television was the new media, success was all there for the taking and people were scrambling over each other to get to the top. My side of things, research, wasn't as bad as some other departments but it was still tough for a woman to do well.

But I loved my job. It was endlessly fascinating and I used to look forward to going in to work each morning. Every day brought me a new challenge and when there was a big story breaking you never knew where your research would take you.

My father used to say I'd not only got my own quota of brains but my sisters' as well. That wasn't fair of course, but they never wanted careers; their priorities were different to mine, that's all. They wanted husbands, children and a nice home – and there's nothing wrong with that, it's just that these weren't the things that were most important to me.

It wasn't that I didn't want men in my life – goodness knows there were plenty of those to choose from. Working for the Corporation meant that we mixed with some very interesting people, some of them quite important in their own spheres, some rather famous too. The only one I might have given it all up for simply wasn't available. For a while we shared a love that was intense but ultimately fated, since he was much too high up in politics to want a scandal on his doorstep. From my relatively lowly position I watched as he soared way above me, finally achieving a Cabinet post and his place in history. And I found comfort in the arms of other, less important young men. It's funny when you think that since time immemorial young people have been under the impression that they were the first to invent sex – we thought it and so do today's youngsters. The only difference today is that it's all made so public, and I don't approve of that at all. We were discreet.

Cathy's my only relative down here. My other sister moved up to the Midlands after she got married, and I haven't seen any of her four children since her funeral three years ago. They don't seem to be able to find the time to trek down to Sussex, and to be fair they have all got their own families now to think about. Cathy was an only child, and both her parents died young.

She always had the same attitude to work and life as I had – work hard and play hard. I don't know why she never married, she had plenty of boyfriends when she was younger and she's still a good-looking woman. There must be lots of men who'd want to share their time with her.

I don't want for much in my life – I have everything material that I need and you can always find someone to talk to. My neighbours are very good, they're mostly about my age and like me they're happy to have a chat about the latest stories in the news. It's so important to keep your mind busy, keep alert and switched on to what's happening in the world. 'Use it or lose it' they say.

Well, I have no intention of losing it.

CHAPTER 6

WITH A LITTLE HELP FROM MY FRIENDS

There are plenty of times later, when Karen remembers the phone call, that she wishes she'd never answered the phone. Or been out. Or, unlikely though this is after the garden party incident, let Bill answer it and get everything confused so that she'd be unable to return the call because he couldn't remember who it was.

But none of this happens, because Karen is in and she does answer the phone.

'Mavis, you sound exhausted. You really have to see about getting some respite, you know.'

'I'd be fine if I could just get some sleep, but all I seem to do is thrash about in that bed trying to get comfy so I can get off. In the mornings the state of my bedclothes makes it look as if I've been having wild, rampant sex all night,' says Mavis. 'In my dreams,' she adds, 'if I had any, which of course I can't since I'm awake all the time.'

She's trying to make light of it, but beyond the flippant remarks Karen knows Mavis is close to breaking point.

'Look, I'll pop round later with some sleeping tablets...'

'Oh, I don't want to get started on those. Thanks all the same Karen, but I know what these tablets do to you.'

'What they'll do is give you a sound night's sleep, which is exactly what you need. I'm not suggesting you take them on a regular basis. I'll just bring you two, for tonight.'

It's a remedy Karen has had to resort to herself sometimes. She's got to bed and then can't get her brain to shut down for the night as the whole ghastly panorama of her current and future life comes up on a big screen somewhere just behind her eyes. It's like being made to sit through a particularly boring film, in wide screen, technicolor, multi-track digitally re-mastered stereo sound, with no option to get a choc ice. The ending is both predictable and unappealing so the film never actually gets there, just keeps grinding on a loop through the endless minutiae and frustrations of Karen's life. She combats the occasional days of exhaustion which follow such episodes by swigging down a couple of small white pills the next night, and they never fail her.

'Well', says Mavis, as Dorothy bellows to her again from her wheelchair in the kitchen, 'maybe you're right. Pick up a couple of Danish pastries from the baker's on the way round and I'll make us some coffee.'

Karen laughs. 'It's a deal,' she says, although she has no intention of buying a Danish for herself, much as she fancies one – way too many calories. But she'll get one for Mavis, and maybe some chocolate for Dorothy as well.

There's a rather expensive lingerie shop in the High Street, almost next door to the baker's, and a little window-shopping in passing would just suit Karen's mood at present. After checking her emails a couple of nights previously, she's on a high. Graham has engineered another business trip to Sussex soon and the anticipation of seeing him again has put a big smile on her face. Even Bill's memory lapses and occasional bizarre behaviour can do nothing to dampen her spirits, as she counts off the days till their next meeting. So with the prospect of the man she loves unwrapping her body like an exquisite birthday gift, high calorie snacks are naturally out of the question at the moment.

The lingerie shop, 'Secrets', has a window display of black lace and cream satin. It's the most expensive shop in this part of town and Karen has never bought anything there, but she's thinking that on the way back from Mavis she might stop and see if there's anything that is both affordable and sexy. Her everyday lingerie is more functional than exciting, although she has one or two sets that she keeps for those occasions when she sees Graham. He must be sick of seeing me in the same things, she thinks, as she looks closely at an exquisite set with the price tag deliberately turned face down. Someone she knows slightly comes out of the shop with a 'Secrets' carrier, and as she peers in through the open door Karen spots one of her neighbours in there. My goodness, she wonders, are we all at it?

Karen would like to confide in Mavis about Graham. For the three years of their affair she hasn't mentioned him to anyone, and there are times when keeping him to herself is a struggle. It's been difficult for him continually finding reasons for a trip to Sussex, there not being much in the way of work commitments for him along the south coast. But he's somehow managed to get there every couple of months, and each time Karen has managed to contrive some time away from Bill. It may not seem like much to an outsider, but it's all Karen has these days, and she hangs on to it desperately. She would like to be able to say his name aloud but is afraid that doing so will break the spell, rather like a magician taking the mystery out of his best trick by showing how it's done. And Karen is under no illusions herself – she knows part of the attraction, for both of them, is the secretive nature of their meetings.

There's also the risk that Mavis may disapprove, though somehow Karen doubts this. However, she doesn't want to take a chance on spoiling the friendship they have, so by the time she turns up on Mavis's doorstep she's already dismissed any fanciful ideas about unburdening her soul.

Mavis takes the white paper bag Karen holds out to her, leads the way into the kitchen and puts the kettle on.

'You're so strong willed,' she says as she takes a single Danish out of the bag. 'Me, I've got the self-control of a cockroach where food's concerned. Ooh, Cadbury's as well?'

'That's for Dorothy actually. Where is she?'

'In the conservatory, staring at the garden – well, the jungle where the garden used to be once upon a time. Go on through, she'll be pleased to see the chocolate so you'll get a good reception.'

Karen gives Dorothy her chocolate and watches her happily peeling the purple foil off the bar. Mavis is right about the garden, she thinks as she looks out at the brambles and weeds that are creeping closer to the house and threatening to engulf the conservatory. The garden is too big for anyone without Bill's enthusiasm to cope with – much less a carer with practically no spare time. Karen wonders if it might be a project for her dad. She could bring him round a couple of days a week and she knows he's got the energy to tackle it. It would be nice for both Mavis and Dorothy to see it come back to life, little by little, and good for Bill to have something to think about other than his own patch where all he really needs to do is titivate. He might even want to grow a few vegetables again and unlike the allotment it's close to home and she'd be with him, which would also be a bit of light relief for

Mavis. Karen makes a mental note to pursue the idea as she wanders back to the kitchen.

Mavis gives her a large mug of strong, black coffee – just the way she knows Karen likes it – and they settle down at the kitchen table.

'What have you left Bill doing?'

'Watching a DVD. It's a war film and he's seen it loads of times but it's one of his favourites. Sometimes when he's watching these old films and I come in halfway through he can go over everything that's already happened, no problems remembering the plot or who's who. I think it's because he first saw them years ago and for some reason the stories have stuck in his mind. But other times he gets films all confused with each other – so we have Fred Astaire dancing with Joan Crawford and they've met in a bar in Casablanca...'

Mavis licks icing from her fingers.

'He's a sweet man though. He must have been a lovely dad to you.'

'He was. I wish I still had him the way he used to be, that's all.'

'You do very well with him Karen. He's lucky to have you.'

'We all do very well. You, Cathy, Sally, Jo – we're all doing our best in spite of everything.'

Karen fishes around in her bag and brings out a folded tissue.

'Here you are, two sleeping tablets. Just take one if it makes you feel happier, but I always go for two then I know I'll get a good night.'

Mavis tucks them into her pocket.

'You're a life-saver,' she says.

***

It's about 8.30 the following morning when Cathy's phone rings, and her first thought is that Stella must need her for something. So she is quite unprepared for Karen on the other end of the phone, and totally wrong-footed by the edge of hysteria in her voice.

'What on earth is wrong Karen? Is it Bill?'

'No...it's...oh poor Mavis...the paramedics couldn't do anything by the time they got there...she must have been dead for hours...I feel wretched...I only wanted to help her but...'

'Karen, just slow down. What exactly has happened?' Cathy brings the tone of her voice down a couple of notches and struggles to fit together the disjointed bits of the story Karen is pouring down the phone line.

'She just called me...'

'Who called you?'

'Mavis.'

There's a pause while Cathy re-arranges the pieces into a different scenario.

'Mavis called you? Then she's OK?'

'Not really – how could she be? Finding Dorothy like that...'

At this point Karen gives up completely and her end of the line goes quiet. Cathy presses her fingertips to her forehead.

'Karen, I'm coming round to you first, then we'll see if we can do anything for Mavis. OK? I need to call them at the office, then I'll be with you – so just keep calm and wait there for me.'

Bill answers the door to Cathy, still in his dressing gown. He recognises her although for the life of him can't remember who she is.

'Someone's died,' he announces in a low voice. 'But it's nobody I knew. Anyway, it's good that you've come because Karen's a bit upset about it. Keep the home fires burning,' he adds, confusingly.

'Bill, do you think you could make me and Karen a cup of tea?' asks Cathy, hoping this will be something he can do unsupervised. He's delighted to have the opportunity to be useful and rushes off to the kitchen whistling.

Karen has pulled herself together sufficiently to tell Cathy quite calmly and coherently what happened.

'Dorothy had a heart attack. It looks as if she tried to get herself out of bed at some time in the night. She seems to have reached out to her wheelchair, pulled it across to the bedside and then she must have fallen over as she struggled out of bed, overturned the chair and got wedged face down across the seat. The paramedics didn't even try to resuscitate her – she must have been dead for hours.'

Karen reaches over to pull a tissue out of a box on the coffee table.

'Mavis didn't hear her call out,' she takes a deep breath here, 'and that's because I gave her a couple of sleeping tablets so she could get a decent night's sleep. If I hadn't done that...'

'It might still have happened. How do we know Dorothy did call out? And even if she did, Mavis might not have heard her if she'd just nodded off without any tablets.' Cathy leans forward and takes Karen's hand in hers. 'It wasn't your fault. It wasn't anybody's fault. It just happened, the way things do sometimes, so don't go blaming yourself.'

Karen blows her nose just as Bill bustles into the living room with a tea tray.

'Here we are girls,' he says cheerily. 'A nice cup of tea and some of those chocolate biscuits you like.'

Bill has tried very hard, although it's a bit early in the morning for the biscuits, but he's found a matching teapot, milk jug and sugar bowl and he's remembered to put spoons out as well.

'Now, who's going to be mother?' he asks.

'I'll do it, Bill. Thank you very much for going to all this trouble,' says Cathy, and Bill beams at her.

'Well, I'll go and get dressed then,' he says, 'and leave you two girls for a good old gossip.' He whistles his way along the hall and Cathy reaches across to the teapot.

'You've made his day,' says Karen. 'I should give him more of a chance to do things but it's usually easier to do it myself. You must bring out the best in him.'

'Not so sure about that,' says Cathy, peering into the teapot. 'He hasn't put any teabags in here.'

* * *

Mavis is quite tranquil and composed when Cathy and Karen see her later in the morning.

'In many ways, it was a blessed release,' she says. 'What quality of life did the poor soul have? Trapped in that room most of the time, with no peace or dignity, and a procession of strangers coming in every day for her personal care. Her only bit of pleasure was the cat.'

As if on cue, Sadie wanders in and rubs up against Karen's leg, leaving black hairs all over her jeans.

'I feel so responsible,' says Karen, reaching across to take Mavis's hand.

'Whatever for?'

'Those sleeping pills – if I hadn't suggested you take them you'd probably have heard her call out.'

Mavis pats Karen's hand.

'Well, you needn't worry on that score – I didn't take them,' she says. 'I must have been so exhausted I just zonked out naturally.'

Karen frowns at her, wanting but not willing to believe it.

'Dear girl, if you don't believe me I'll show you,' says Mavis, getting up and leaving the room. She keeps up a running commentary all the time as she goes upstairs.

'They're still on my bedside table. Never liked the idea of pills – to be honest I was a bit scared of taking them, though I'll admit there were times I was desperate to get some sleep. But in the end the body just gives in and off you go. Anyway, as I said to the doctor at the hospital, who's to say she did call for me? Now, here they are, right where I put them after you left.'

Mavis re-appears in the doorway a few moments later.

'You see?' she says, and in her outstretched hand is the folded tissue with two white pills sitting in the middle of it. 'Just as you gave them to me. So let's have no more talk about blame. Nobody was to blame.'

Karen looks at the pills for what seems like a very long time.

'Mavis...' she starts, but Cathy cuts in on her.

'I think we should go now, Mavis, if you're sure there's nothing we can do. I expect you'd like some time on your own. If you think of anything you need, just call. I'll let the others know and we'll see you again very soon – whenever you want to.'

Karen is still staring at the pills, and above her head Cathy gives a little smile to Mavis, who nods back at her. She squashes the tissue up in her hand and there's a small crunch as the pills crack and break against each other.

'Well, there'll be things I have to see to. There'll have to be a coroner's inquest because of the nature of her going, so the funeral won't be immediate. Perhaps

63

we can all get together in a few days? I'll be needing some company by then I expect.'

Then she sees them to the door and off down the garden path.

In the car, Karen's voice is barely audible.

'They weren't the pills I gave her. I don't know what they were, but they weren't my sleeping tablets. '

Cathy turns in her seat to face Karen.

'I think you're imagining this, because you're upset. You weren't in any way responsible for what happened to Dorothy, and you have to believe that. If Mavis says those were your pills, then they were your pills, and that's an end to it.'

Then very gently, because this fragile side of Karen is one she hasn't seen before and it's both surprising and unnerving, she adds, 'We stick together through these traumas, because we care about each other. That's what this circle of ours is all about.'

Karen nods, and wipes a finger under each eye.

'Now put your seatbelt on,' says Cathy, 'and I'll get you back home.'

* * *

It's a different Mavis who opens the door to the GenClub girls a few days later. Surprisingly, this Mavis is more agitated than the one Cathy and Karen saw on the morning Dorothy died, and it puzzles them because it's not what they were expecting.

'Girls, come in. You won't believe what I've got to show you,' she says, leading them through to the back room. There's a bottle of sherry and a set of glasses on the sideboard and although they've always been there it's the first time Karen has ever noticed them. Mavis uncorks the bottle and starts pouring.

'I need a glass, and so might you lot when you see what I've just found,' she says, handing a generous measure to each of them. She takes a gulp from her own glass and leaves the room for a moment.

'Look,' says Mavis as she bustles back into the room. In her hand is a large wad of old bank notes. She spreads them out on the top of the sideboard – ten-shilling, one pound and five pound notes, all neatly turned around the same way and sorted into denominations.

'Wrapped up in newspaper and hidden at the back of her wardrobe,' she says as they gawp at the strangely familiar old notes. Jo picks up a brown ten-shilling note, crisp and new.

'I had to save my pocket money up to get one of these,' she says. 'It used to take me months.'

'These must have been there for at least forty years,' says Sally. 'Maybe longer – when did we go decimal?'

'And that's not all,' says Mavis. 'Come with me.'

They follow her along the hallway and into Dorothy's room. With the exception of Mavis, who has already downed her sherry, they're all still clutching their glasses. From the depths of an old wardrobe Mavis pulls out a shoebox. It seems at first to hold only photos, but she turns it out onto the bed and at the bottom there are more notes. These are mainly tens and twenties.

'Mavis – how much is here? Have you any idea?'

Mavis fans the banknotes in her hands.

'Several hundred, at least. I haven't counted it yet.' She crams it all back into the shoebox. 'There's more,' she adds.

Sally takes a large slug of sherry.

'How much more?' she asks.

'Look.'

From under the chest of drawers Mavis draws out a small attache case and snaps the locks open. The top layers consist of papers – a certificate of achievement for something, some newspaper cuttings and old insurance documents. But at the bottom there are three tight rolls of banknotes, held with elastic bands, which have perished over the years and lie flaccidly stuck to the paper.

'And I've only just started sorting her things out,' says Mavis.

'Are they still worth anything?' says Cathy. 'Collectors, I suppose, but would the bank change them after all these years?'

'I heard something recently on the radio,' says Jo. 'Banknotes keep their face value for all time. I suppose you might have to take them to the Bank of England though.'

'In a taxi,' says Mavis, 'there and back, and take the scenic route. I had no idea she had all this. What a difference it could have made to her in the last few years – never mind about me.'

'Did Dorothy have a good job, Mavis? I mean, this must have taken a bit of saving over the years.' Sally is remembering the way her parents struggled to take her on holidays when she was little, and the presents under the Christmas tree each year that Queenie had to buy from her catalogue on the never-never. For them there was no chance to save.

'Well,' says Mavis. 'That's the queer thing. I suppose she didn't earn bad money and of course she never had a family to support. But she was just an ordinary working girl all her life, nothing more. No high-flyer or anything.'

'What did she do?' asks Karen.

Mavis bundles everything back into the attache case and clicks the locks closed.

'She worked for a bank,' she says, and Jo chokes on her sherry and has to be slapped vigorously on the back.

'You don't think…' says Cathy.

'I've no idea,' says Mavis, 'and she's not going to tell us now is she?'

'An old lady's savings,' says Karen. 'That's what you say if anyone questions it.'

'More sherry?' asks Mavis, and as everyone seems to need a refill now they file back to the living room. Karen looks out to the conservatory, where only the other day Dorothy was tucking into her chocolate bar while she hatched a plan to get Bill over to sort out the jungle-garden for them.

'I shall sell this house,' says Mavis as she pours the sherry, 'and buy a small flat, something brand new that doesn't need much looking after. And I'll go and see my boys and those grandchildren I don't even know. That's what I'll do, thanks to Dorothy. Cheers, girls.'

There's not a woman in the house who would begrudge any of this to Mavis, but it's a complicated mix of emotions that settles over the circle. Mavis has found her freedom but the emotional cost has been high, as it will be for each of them.

And there's something else; the realisation has suddenly hit them that the GenClub in its current form has a shelf life, and uppermost in each of their minds is, 'Which one of us will be next to leave?'

CHAPTER 7

NEW HORIZONS

'Cathy – just move a little further centre stage as you start that speech, would you?'

The Horsfield Players hold their early rehearsals in each other's homes, and so this is the first time they've actually been on stage with their latest play, *Bring Me That Horizon*. Suddenly, the community hall stage seems more like an obstacle course and they're all having trouble getting used to working around the furniture and set without bumping into anything.

Barry, the writer and director, is a large, middle-aged man in corduroy trousers and braces. He's walking about in front of the stage, with his glasses perched on the end of his bulbous nose so that he can look from script to stage and back again without the need to remove them. Cathy has worked with him lots of times before and considers him to be one of the better directors the Horsfield Players can offer. For his part, Barry knows without doubt that Cathy is the best actor in the group – better than the feted Andrew Simmonds, who gets all the male leads by default since there's not much competition. Cathy takes her turn, accepting both minor roles and leads, and then acts the rest of them off the stage.

Cathy doesn't have the lead in *Bring Me That Horizon*, but her part is challenging and she appears on stage alone much of the time. She has just one scene with Andrew, and they haven't rehearsed that since the early readings. Barry feels, quite rightly, that precious rehearsal time is better spent on some of the less able actors in the group, but tonight there are two key players absent and since Cathy's solo scenes are quite demanding he's giving her a bit of stage time.

She's just coming to the point where she should be interrupted by a ringing telephone, when they are all interrupted by the door banging back on its hinges, and Andrew Simmonds steps in.

'Sorry to be late,' he booms across the hall. 'Train cancellation at Victoria. Forgive the interruption Cathy, Barry.'

'Any chance you could just slip in quietly next time you arrive late?' asks Barry, glaring over his glasses, as the door slams closed again.

'Yes, yes, of course...a thousand apologies. Carry on,' says Andrew, who is not in the least sorry but has achieved his twin aims of making a grand entrance and niggling Barry.

Cathy is not at all wrong-footed by this and carries on where she left off, but Barry has now lost both his place on the script and his patience.

'Bugger it,' he yells. 'Take a bloody break. Five mins maximum.'

Andrew smiles behind his hand. Barry stomps off to sit on his own at the back of the hall, mumbling over his script, and the rest of the group congregate together over at the side of the hall. Cathy comes down from the stage and joins Andrew, now sitting in a wonky chair in the front row.

'You stars are all the same,' she says, leaning down to peck him on the cheek, 'always after the limelight. What kept you?'

'The train – just as I said.' Andrew kisses her hand and pulls her into the seat next to him.

'Don't believe a word of it. I bet you stood outside just waiting for your moment,' laughs Cathy. 'Why do you like winding him up so much?'

'Because it's so easy and he falls for it every time. Anyway, how's it going with the great direc-tor?' he says, pulling out the last syllable for added effect.

'Fine, till you arrived. He won't put you on stage tonight you know, not after that.'

'Good – I can just sit here and watch you, then.'

'And don't start trying to corpse me again – it won't work this time, I'm much too focused,' says Cathy.

'You know your lines yet?'

'Of course. And you?'

'Naturally, word perfect, my dear. Coming for a drink afterwards?'

'Maybe, but I don't want to be late. I need to sort out my clothes for tomorrow – I've got a funeral to go to.'

'I'm sorry to hear that – anyone close?'

'The sister of a friend. I'm there in a supporting role.'

Barry strides forward from the back of the hall at that point.

'Right – let's get back to sodding scene 4, top of page 95, where we were so rudely interrupted previously by this ageing romantic lead.'

'So, was that a yes to the drink?' asks Andrew, ignoring Barry, as Cathy gets up from her seat.

'If we can make it a quickie,' she says.

'Marvellous. I love a quickie,' Andrew replies in a voice that's directed at the rest of the cast and leaves Barry, out of earshot, wondering what the joke is.

* * *

Dorothy's funeral is, inevitably, a low-key affair. Mavis has invited the only people she can, which amount to a few close neighbours and the Generation Club girls. Whilst her sons have all sent flowers, distance and their own commitments prevent them from being there in person.

Last to arrive at the crematorium is Sally, who has stayed behind to get the food organised at Mavis's house. She slips into the chapel at the last moment, just ahead of the coffin procession, and sits next to Jo, who has come armed with a pack of Kleenex in case nobody else thought of it and grief breaks out all around her. In the event, Jo's tissues aren't needed at the funeral. There's a quiet sadness about Mavis, but she is stoical about her sister.

'Dorothy's quality of life was very poor,' she says to Karen as they walk away from the chapel towards the cars. 'I really believe she's better off now, wherever she is.'

Karen links her arm through Mavis's.

'I wondered if Stephen might make it over from Italy, as he's the nearest.'

'He would have come, but he had a job interview in Milan and he and his partner were going together and taking a few days holiday too. But the boys have all been on the phone to me, and they all got flowers to the funeral.'

'Have you said anything – about going to see them?'

'Not yet,' says Mavis. She gives Karen's arm a squeeze. 'But I'm determined to do it. I'll need a bit of help though, I've never planned anything as big as this before.'

Karen pats her hand. 'That's OK, I'll help you – we can get it all booked on the Internet. Or Cathy might be able to help us, she's in the travel business. Just say when you're ready to get started.'

Mavis stops by the funeral car and turns to look at Karen.

'How about tomorrow?' she says.

Later, back at the house, Sally unwraps the food she's prepared, including a plate of small apple pies.

'Mum wanted to make these for you Mavis. I don't know what they'll be like – she hasn't baked in years and it took her ages. But she insisted on having a go.'

The girls have decided jointly not to bring along their dependants. As Sally put it, 'At their age they go to quite enough funerals – and they'd actually only met Dorothy a couple of times.'

Mavis is touched by Queenie's generosity, also the flowers that Don and Stella have sent jointly. Karen hasn't mentioned the funeral to Bill, although he did remark when she said goodbye to him that she was dressed 'a bit gloomy'. She has left him in the care of one of the allotment people, poring over seed catalogues, and knows that soon she must leave and get back home.

Queenie's pastry turns out to be a triumph and only Sally knows the effort and determination that went into producing it, and the first batch that went into the bin. No sooner has she passed the plate around for the second time than the doorbell rings and Mavis goes out to the hall with her mouth full of apple pie.

In the lounge they hear a small shriek from the hallway, and the room falls silent. After what seems like several minutes but can actually be measured in seconds, the door flies open and Mavis, flushed and tearful, bursts in followed by two young men.

'Look everyone,' she announces, 'this is my son – this is Stephen, and his partner Richie.'

And Jo, whose forward planning has paid off for once, finds that her tissues are in demand after all.

* * *

It's the middle of August, a couple of weeks after Dorothy's funeral, and the GenClub girls are on their way to Karen's house. She has arranged a circle of garden chairs out on the patio, and Bill is pottering about, fussing over his containers and dead-heading the annuals. Karen has asked him to put the sunshade up but he's already forgotten about that and even when she reminds him, will have no idea that he was supposed to be doing it.

Cathy and Sally arrive together and Jo shortly afterwards. They are just getting settled into their seats when the side gate clicks again and they look up to see a new Mavis coming towards them. There are gasps all round.

'Wow! You look fantastic!' says Sally.

Bill, picking up on this compliment, even manages a wolf-whistle that surprises everyone including himself.

Mavis has had a make-over. Urged on by Karen, she's had her hair cut and highlighted and started using a bit of make-up again. It's taken ten years off her.

'Karen and I had a day in Tunbridge Wells,' she explains. 'We had a lovely time, didn't we?'

'Yes we did,' says Bill, and they all turn in his direction. 'We had lunch somewhere, but I couldn't say where exactly.'

'You had roast chicken, Bill, and chips – remember? And then apple crumble and custard. '

'No sitter,' says Karen in a low voice, and Sally and Jo both say together 'You should have asked...'

'Mavis wanted to surprise you,' explains Karen. 'So we all went. And it really perked Dad up, going out like that.'

Bill is wandering off in the direction of the shed by now although Karen still keeps her voice down.

'A change of scene, you know? It wasn't exactly a boy's day out either, but he seems to have enjoyed it just the same. We were in and out of shops half the day and he didn't mind at all.'

The result of the shopping trip is obvious in Mavis' chic new trouser suit, shoes and handbag.

'I've never brought home so many carrier bags,' says Mavis. 'It was such fun, girls, I can't tell you. And that's not all...'

Mavis rummages around in her handbag and produces a glossy paper wallet with a flourish.

'Flight itinerary!' she says, waving the folder across the table. 'I've booked the first part of my trip and I'm off to Chicago in four weeks.'

Spontaneous cheers ring out and Bill, poking his head out of the potting shed, manages another wolf-whistle. The mood remains up-beat for the rest of the afternoon as Mavis talks them through her itinerary, with the August sun cooling a little as it slips lower in the sky.

With the esprit de corps at its height, Karen slips in neatly with her request.

'I've got an old friend coming down next Tuesday afternoon,' she says. 'Any chance of one of you sitting with Dad?'

'I can do it, no problem,' offers Mavis. 'I'll bring round my family photos and the atlas and we can talk about my trip,' she adds, since right now she is unable to think of anything else and wants to share it with anyone who will listen.

'An old school friend, is she?' Mavis adds, and Karen fends this off with a vague explanation about someone she met through work. This is accurate in as far as it goes, but she fails to mention the gender error. 'She' is of course Graham, and Karen is looking forward to several hours of quality time with him at the out-of-town Sundowners Hotel, a prospect that has her smiling radiantly out of all proportion to the gossipy lunch and shopping trip the others are imagining. She deflects any further speculation by moving the conversation along in an entirely unrelated direction.

'How's your play coming along, Cathy?' she asks.

'Not bad, thanks. We'll be ready in time, although the way things went at the last rehearsal it was scary to think that we open in less than three weeks time.'

Cathy has seen it all before. She knows it will all come together and Barry won't actually boycott the opening night, as he has threatened to do. It's his usual threat at this stage of the proceedings, and only first-time performers take the slightest notice of him.

'We should come along to support you,' says Jo suddenly, backed up by an enthusiastic chorus of agreement.

'No, no...you won't want to watch us stumbling through ninety minutes of Barry's latest masterpiece,' Cathy replies, completely wrong-footed by the thought of the GenClub girls gazing up at her from the front row. 'Anyway,' she adds, 'there'd be nobody left to act as sitters.'

'Then we'll all come,' says Sally. 'It'll be good for them to get out and if I remember rightly that hall has good access so there won't be a problem. It'll be a treat for them, don't you think?'

Before Cathy has a chance to protest any further, arrangements are already being made for who's going to pick up who, when, and will Queenie or Stella need wheelchairs? She can see there's very little chance now of the GenClub girls backing down on this one, so goes instead for damage limitation.

'Well don't come to opening night, give us a chance to settle down a bit. What about Friday? I'll see how the tickets are selling. Or there's a matinee on Saturday afternoon…'

'No, let's give them a night out. It's a lovely idea.'

'They'll need all day to get ready for it, anyway. Mum will have to change several times before she feels just right.'

'And it'll take me all day to explain to Dad – if I do it the day before he'll have forgotten what's going on by the time we get there.'

'It's something for them to look forward to, and just the kind of outing we said from the start we'd try to do,' adds Jo, putting it beyond all possible doubt that this trip will happen.

Then Mavis cuts in with her offer, and it's sealed.

'I'd like this outing to be on me – well, on Dorothy, to be strictly accurate – since I'll be leaving you all very soon afterwards.'

There's a slight dampening of spirits when she says this, but everyone agrees it will be a fitting leaving do for Mavis.

* * *

It's only by chance that later that evening Cathy checks the email address she set up with Sally at the start of the GenClub experiment. As far as they know all the postcards they put up have now expired and there haven't been any genuine enquiries for months, although an occasional spammer still gets through to the inbox. There is some junk to clear, and Cathy wonders if she should just close the address down, but isn't sure how to do that.

As she's scrolling through the emails she comes to one, and pauses, her finger hovering over the delete button. It's not the name that stops her – it's as likely to be a spammer's pseudonym as any of the others on the list – but the subject, 'dependants', is not the usual junk fare. Now it's true that all of the men who have contacted them – and several claiming to be women – have been bordering on the pervy, but that's no reason to assume this one will be too. So she opens the email, and this comes up:

Saw your postcard ad and am interested in making contact. Have elderly dependant mother and would appreciate the kind of support network you suggest.

Tony Lane.

It's odd, but when they set it up she and Sally had never envisaged a man in the GenClub. But why not? Cathy wonders if it might be a good thing in some ways; handling wheelchairs isn't all that easy and a man could be a real asset at times like that. And why should he be any less deserving of group support than another woman?

So Cathy forwards the email on around the group, and their replies come back to her in fairly short order and are in complete agreement. Tony Lane needs them. Of course it's also entirely possible that they may need him, at least some of the time, but this does not come out in their replies to Cathy. No, the poor man has come to them for help and there is not a GenClub woman who would deny him that. The logical conclusion is that he should be invited to their next meeting.

The merest hint of concern comes from Jo, who wonders if they should meet on neutral ground first, somewhere public, as she has heard this is the advice given to people on Internet dates. They ponder this, but not for long. There are four of them after all, five if Mavis wants to come along, and only one of him.

What can possibly go wrong with odds like that in their favour? Even if he turns out to be an axe-murderer they should be able to deal with him provided they stick together. They decide to meet at Cathy's house, as they did originally, in a few days time. Tony is invited to attend, without his mother initially, and he accepts.

The GenClub is about to move into its next phase.

CHAPTER 8

HIGH HEELS AND HIGHER HOPES.

They look each other up and down.

Karen, immaculately dressed as always, is the first to comment. She can't help but notice that Cathy's wearing something from one of Marks & Spencer's new ranges. And it looks great on her.

'You should wear purple more often – it really lifts your skin tone. Gives you a lovely glow,' she says.

Cathy plays this down, not wanting to let on that she's wearing the outfit for the first time or that her make-up has been rather more carefully applied than usual. She glances across at Sally and Jo, and it's obvious that they've also made more than the usual effort with their appearance. Jo has pinned her hair up – something the others haven't seen before. It suits her and shows off her small features to good effect. Sally has dug a pair of heels out from the back of her wardrobe and is wearing them with straight-leg jeans and some attitude.

'Well,' says Karen into the guarded silence that has settled, 'if this doesn't impress him, the man's got no taste.'

They laugh a bit self-consciously then Cathy's cat saunters in and they try not to let it leave hairs on them while they make a fuss of it. After a few minutes there's a ring at the doorbell and Karen is the only one who doesn't stand up. Sally and Jo immediately feel silly and sit down again, and Cathy goes out into the hallway.

She comes back with a man in tow. Small, weedy and with mad ginger hair frizzing across his head and peeping out from his ears and nostrils, he looks embarrassed, manages a weak 'hello' and raises one hand in greeting. A correspondingly feeble response ripples around the room. Sally can't help wondering now why she bothered with the high heels, which are killing her anyway as her feet are unused to such harsh treatment.

'This is Derek from next door,' says Cathy. 'He can't get out of his drive.'

There is a moment's pause and a collective sigh of relief, then Jo giggles.

'The red VW,' says Derek apologetically. 'It's just *slightly* over my drive and I could maybe manage OK, but I wouldn't want to clip it. Sorry to be a nuisance. Wouldn't normally matter but it's my wife's choir practice this evening,' he says. 'Christ Church,' he adds, as if this makes a difference.

Sally realises suddenly that it's her car causing the problem and lunges into her handbag for her keys.

'I'm so sorry,' she says. 'I never do that, can't think what's got into me.' She jumps up and heads for the door and Derek trails out behind her, apologising again.

Several moments of muffled laughter follow before Sally reappears, looking pink and flustered.

'Everyone, this is Tony,' she says. 'We met at the front door.'

She steps aside to let the next man in to the living room.

'That's more like it,' says Karen under her breath, so softly that only Jo hears.

Tony Lane is a different kettle of fish entirely to Derek; bigger, louder, and altogether more attractive.

Cathy, who feels that Sally has taken charge of a situation which should rightly have been hers to control in her own house, steps straight in front of her and sticks out her hand.

'Cathy Lawson,' she says smiling broadly and shaking Tony's hand. 'Lovely to meet you, do come in.'

She introduces each of the others in turn, purposely leaving Sally till last. Completely oblivious to the somewhat charged atmosphere, Tony chooses to sit in the empty chair next to Sally. She doesn't dare look at Cathy, but cannot suppress the ghost of a smile as he sits down. Karen and Jo both notice this, but Cathy is too busy prattling on about the weather and re-arranging her long legs to best advantage.

'Well,' says Tony, looking around the group, 'there are certainly worse ways I could spend an evening – thank you for inviting me along.'

Sally extends a stilleto-heeled foot, and laughs disarmingly. Karen waves his comment away and smiles her best smile, and Jo, who's not sure what's expected of her in this unfamiliar situation, looks down at the carpet and says nothing.

'We should start by telling you a little about ourselves and our dependants,' says Cathy, anxious to regain her Head Girl status. 'Jo, will you go first?'

Jo looks up at Tony like a rabbit caught in headlights.

'I look after my father...' she manages, in a small voice.

Karen thinks this is mean of Cathy, and jumps in to help Jo out.

'He used to play saxophone in a dance band,' she says. 'He was quite famous in his day.'

'And now he's writing a book about it,' says Sally, picking up on Karen's initiative. 'You'd like Don,' she adds, 'he's a real character.'

'I'm sure I would,' says Tony beaming at Jo, who has gained a bit of confidence thanks to Karen and Sally's interventions. 'He must have some stories to tell about his dance band days. I played the trumpet for a while in the school band – pretty badly now that I think about it.'

'He suffers from emphysema, and asthma, which is a bit of a worry,' says Jo. 'Writing the book has been a lifeline for him.'

'And for you too, I expect. I presume from the tone of your advert that you're all...er...on your own?' asks Tony.

'Oh yes...' they chorus, rather too quickly.

'Completely,' adds Cathy.

'Ah,' says Tony, in a voice which could mean anything. 'Me too. Divorced, actually. With a mother who looks set to outlive me but can't cope with life on her own. It's a dilemma, isn't it?'

Still good-looking, and obviously in good shape, Tony is the kind of man it's hard to believe could be on his own. For a start, his clothes co-ordinate and someone has ironed his shirt expertly – maybe his mum, thinks Karen. He's got attractively greying hair, and it's been cut properly, not just left to its own devices or hacked at with kitchen scissors. He seems completely genuine and already, should it be put to a vote, every one of the GenClub girls would opt to embrace him into the group – or indeed out of it, come to that.

'So,' says Cathy, 'That's Jo and her dad. Let's go round the rest of us first, then you can tell us about your mum, Tony. Karen also lives with her father – Karen?'

'My Dad has different problems to Don,' Karen says. 'He's in good physical shape but he's got early stage Alzheimers, and his short-term memory is almost non-existent. But ask him any gardening question and he can probably drag the answer up from years back. He's like a filing system of everything that's ever featured on Gardener's Question Time.'

Karen rakes her fingers through her hair a couple of times. She's just had the highlights re-done, so what with that and her pearly nail polish she's looking her sparkling best today. Jo feels drab next to her, as she always does.

They talk a bit about Bill, and Tony listens quietly and takes it all in. Then before Cathy gets a chance to move things on Sally jumps in and drags the organiser's role over to her corner.

'You go next Cathy. Tell Tony about Stella.'

Cathy has no option then but to launch into a description of her aunt. They had agreed previously not to get into their own personalities, but Cathy seems to have forgotten this.

'One of my biggest problems,' she says, leaning back in her chair, 'is to fit everything in around my commitments to my drama group. It's so difficult keeping all the balls in the air.'

It's on the tip of Karen's tongue to say something sharp to Cathy that will cut her down to size, but she thinks better of it and instead brings the topic back to the general arena rather than the personal.

'Yes, well we all have commitments, as I'm sure you do too Tony, and we've had to find different ways of managing our time effectively. I'm a graphic designer and because I'm freelance and working from home I can work in the evenings after Dad's gone to bed, but that's obviously not possible for everyone.'

'Wouldn't work for me,' says Tony. 'I run a building firm and once the light goes so do we. Not that I'm on the tools any more, I gave that up years ago. And once it became obvious that Social Services weren't going to be much help to me and Mum, I took another step back and left my partner with most of the day-to-day running.'

'Sort of sleeping partner now, are you?' asks Karen, raising her eyebrows and smiling wickedly.

'Right,' says Sally briskly, 'Well, I think that only leaves me and my Mum,' and she tells Tony all about Queenie and along the way drops in the fact that she's divorced and has a daughter at university.

'Do you have children?' she asks Tony.

'Three, but I never see them. They've grown up and moved away, and with a poor opinion of their Dad, thanks to my ex.'

'So no help with Grandma?' asks Cathy.

'Never see her. She's probably forgotten all about them now. She's a bit like your dad, Karen, perfect health for her 85 years, but very forgetful and she can't be left to manage anything much on her own. I have to do all the cooking because she'll never remember if she's left a pan on the stove and we've had that many incidents the Fire Brigade wanted to adopt her as their mascot.'

'Really?' says Jo, the first thing she's said for ages.

'No not really, just a joke,' says Tony, and Jo immediately feels stupid and blushes scarlet, but when she looks up again he's smiling at her in a nice, warm way, so she doesn't feel quite so bad.

'So as I said, Social Services weren't much help and something had to be done so I sold my house, built a granny annexe on Mum's, and moved in with her a year ago. Now I make sure she takes her pills when she's supposed to, and go around behind her putting right the things she's had a go at.'

'I know that feeling,' says Karen.

'The other day I found a used tea-bag and some toast crusts in her coat pocket.' Tony laughs, not unkindly. 'Poor old Beryl,' he says. 'Her house used to be her pride and joy, but now she keeps forgetting where the dusters are kept and the Hoover frightens her. It must be so frustrating.'

The room falls quiet and they absorb this for a moment. It is frustrating, and it's something they all share, oldies and YoungGens alike.

'But they all keep cheerful, somehow.' Cathy says the very thing they were all thinking.

'I try to make sure Mum has something to laugh about every day, and that helps to keep me sane as well. Nothing like a good laugh to take away the tension,' says Tony.

Sally remembers the day she wore her slippers out to lunch with Queenie and Cathy. It's a story she might tell Tony one day, but this isn't the right time or place to be going into footwear when she's trying to give the impression that she wears killer heels as an everyday matter of course.

'It's good that you've kept the group small,' says Tony. 'More intimate that way, everyone gets to know everyone else.'

'That's just the way we like it,' Karen says, giving him a smile and a little wink. Jo turns to look at her and wonders why she can never think of anything to say in this kind of situation. Then she remembers that she's never in this kind of situation normally.

Cathy feels Mavis should be mentioned as Tony's likely to meet her at the drama group evening if he wants to become a part of the group.

'There were five of us at the start, but Mavis has dropped out now and in any case she's going away soon.'

Tony is nobody's fool, and picks up on this straight away.

'Death in the family?' he asks.

'Her sister. She's actually got all our oldies round her house this evening – I think they're watching a film together,' Cathy explains.

'That's a good idea – you've really got this thing together, haven't you?' says Tony, and then smiles a little ruefully. 'But I can see that you might not want anyone else crashing in on the group now.'

There's a rush as everyone jumps in to dismiss the idea.

'Well, if you can bear to have us, I'd certainly like to be a part of it, and I'm sure Beryl would too,' says Tony. 'But you don't have to say anything now, you'll probably want to have a chat amongst yourselves and then you can give me a ring.'

Cathy looks around at the rest of the girls.

'I think we've already made that decision, Tony. Welcome to the Generation Club.'

***

Mavis arrives at Karen's house just before midday, armed with photos of her sons, an atlas and a book about Chicago, where her world travel adventure will start.

'I thought we could walk along to the 'Dog and Duck' for lunch,' she tells Karen, who agrees this is a good idea. She's never thought about doing it herself, but knows full well how little outings like this perk Bill up. It's a cloudy day, not nice enough to sit out in the garden but fine for Bill to potter for a while after they get back. The afternoon will fill up OK, Karen is sure, so she puts Bill out of her mind and allows herself the luxury of concentrating on her own afternoon. A little thrill of anticipation rushes through her, and she's sure it must be written all over her face. But Mavis doesn't seem to notice anything out of the ordinary.

'Have a lovely time, don't spend all your money and for goodness sake don't rush back,' she says as Karen heads for the front door.

'You're an angel, Mavis. I'll be home by five,' she says.

And then she's free. It's as if the day has suddenly become brighter, and everything in it is hers for the taking. She drives to the Sundowners Hotel singing along to the car radio and feeling almost light-headed with joy. She stops just once, at a small supermarket, to buy a bottle of wine and some sandwiches.

She picks up the key from reception, and finds the room. There is nothing to distinguish it from any other hotel room, but to Karen it looks quite perfect.

She pulls a black lacy top and skimpy skirt out of her bag and lays them on the bed, smoothing out the creases. Alongside these she puts a pair of stockings and suspender belt, then she takes the bag into the bathroom and fixes her make-up and hair. She's already wearing her sexy black lingerie – the set Graham's seen so many times already – so when she's finished in the bathroom she only has to slip into the rest of her clothes and she's ready for him.

After these preparations Karen is practically on fire with anticipation, but she takes a few deep breaths, puts the kettle on, and tries to settle herself down to wait for Graham. The room overlooks the back terrace, with no view of the car-park, so she can't see when he drives in. The kettle boils, and she makes herself a cup of coffee.

By the time she's finished her coffee there is still no sign of Graham and she's beginning to think about calling his mobile. He is now 45 minutes late, which is unusual. She finds her mobile in her handbag and looks for his number. Normally a call to him is out of the question in case he's with somebody else at the time, but today he'll obviously be in the car on his own so it's OK to risk it.

Then just as she starts to punch in the numbers there's a light tap at the door and Karen practically throws herself across the room to open it.

'I was getting worried about you, you're not normally late,' she says, holding her arms out and then pressing herself against him. Graham looks uncharacteristically harassed. He's pulled his tie open and the top button of his shirt is undone. His normal laid-back persona seems to have disappeared today.

'Terrible traffic,' he says into her neck. 'Hold-ups all the way here.'

'You should have phoned me, my imagination was running wild.'

'I didn't want to stop, just kept going hoping it would get better,' says Graham, moving out of her embrace and into the room. 'Anyway, I'm here now.'

"Well, we've got the whole afternoon, isn't that great? So what can I get you?'

'You look fantastic,' he says by way of answer. 'What are you offering?'

' Well, let's see. There's coffee, wine or me – you choose.'

'Probably all three, but not necessarily in that order. Come here.'

His kiss is fierce, not the tender greeting Karen had hoped for, but then it's been a long time and there's a hunger inside her, which is obviously the same for him. He moves his hands under her top.

'You're in a hurry,' she says, smiling up at him and slowly pulling his tie undone.

'It was only the thought of this that kept me going all the way here.'

He unclips her bra, and she starts to undo the rest of his shirt buttons. But this is not quick enough today for Graham, who steps away from her and starts tugging his shoes and clothes off, leaving them scattered across the floor.

'I can't keep up with you,' says Karen, and she laughs softly although she's actually feeling rushed and a bit cheated. This was an afternoon she wanted to glide through in slow motion so she could savour it over the weeks ahead and now it's turning into a frantic gallop to the finishing line. She'll be lucky if she can remember much about it at all.

She starts to say something, but Graham kisses her long and hard and next thing she knows she hasn't even had a chance to pull the bedspread back and already they're churning it up into uncomfortably hard ridges.

A sweaty five minutes later, with Graham panting in her ear, Karen has the disconcerting feeling that somewhere along the line things have changed between them. His breathing slows down and just as he's about to doze off a mobile phone rings and after a few seconds he realises it's his.

'Shit.'

He sits up and starts looking around at the trail of clothes on the floor to see if he can locate it, but the ringing is coming from Karen's side of the bed and she reaches down to pick the phone up.

'Sorry, forgot to switch it off,' he says.

She passes the phone to him and he takes one look at the caller display then clicks it off and drops it onto the floor on his side. Karen has good eyesight and in the second or two before Graham took the phone from her she could easily read the name Sarah. She hasn't met Graham's wife and he's never said much about her, but she does know her name is Debra, so it's not her. She imagines Sarah is someone from the office, his secretary perhaps.

Karen struggles to get the afternoon back on track.

'I bought sandwiches – do you want one?'

'No thanks, I had something on the way here. Wouldn't mind a coffee though.'

Karen gets up to make the coffee, and she's thinking, How come he ate something on the way here? He said he hadn't stopped. But she can imagine him needing petrol at some point and every garage in the land sells food these days, so she tells herself it's no big mystery.

They lie together in bed, drinking their coffee, and Karen tells him about the GenClub girls, how they're so supportive and about Mavis who's with Bill this afternoon. Graham listens but doesn't add much, tells her he's in the final at the squash club and has started playing golf again. He makes her laugh with a few funny stories about people he plays with, and goes into lengthy and amusing detail about the recent golf club dinner. He says a bit about the project he's starting on soon at work, gets technical and loses her completely but is oblivious to her lack of response and keeps going regardless.

Karen relaxes, snoozes a bit in his arms while he's talking.

'How long have we got?' he asks suddenly. Her heart sinks.

'I said I'd be home by five.'

'I'll need to be away long before that, I've got to go back via Tunbridge Wells so I can drop in to a client there.'

'You never said – Graham, this was our afternoon, just for us.'

'I know, I'm sorry babe. I didn't know myself until I was on the way here. Tracey rang me from the office, it's quite important and I could hardly say no, could I?'

'Who's Tracey?'

'My secretary. What's the time now?' He leans across her to look at his watch on the bedside table, and sees the disappointment written all over her face.

'I'm really, really sorry Karen. First I show up late, then I go early. I know it's hard for you to organise time off and goodness knows we don't get much time together.' He kisses her, tenderly, with more of the old Graham about him, and wraps her into his arms.

Karen can think of a few things she should be asking him at this point, but he's running his hand up her thigh now and whispering softly in her ear. She'd still like to know who Sarah is, but before long he's sliding inside her again, taking her more slowly this time, and she knows she won't ask him today, possibly never.

* * *

It's almost five when Karen pulls the car up on her driveway. She lingered a while at the hotel after Graham left, had a shower then drove home slowly to fill in the time. They never even opened the bottle of wine and she left it and the sandwiches in the room. A lucky bonus for the chambermaid she thinks.

When she opens the door the house is very quiet and Mavis calls out to her from the living room, where she's been reading a magazine. Through the French doors she can see Bill hoeing one of the flowerbeds and the lawn mower is standing by.

'Had a good time? Oh, I thought you'd come home weighed down with carrier bags,' Mavis says, disappointed because she was looking forward to seeing the things Karen had bought.

'There was nothing I wanted to buy – just wasn't in a spending mood today I guess.'

Mavis gives Karen a funny look, but doesn't comment.

'How was Dad?'

'Fine, we had a nice lunch in the pub – I think he enjoyed going along there for an hour. How was your lunch?'

'Erm...we didn't have much really,' says Karen, thinking of the sandwiches they never ate and realising suddenly that she hasn't eaten since breakfast and she's quite hungry now.

'Well, I daresay you had plenty to gossip about,' says Mavis, but she's thinking that this doesn't sound like much of a girly day out.

Karen pops out to say hello to Bill, and Mavis gathers up her bag and jacket and follows her out into the garden.

'I'll give you a lift home, Mavis. It's the least I can do, I'm really grateful to you for today.'

'Oh, it was a pleasure. We had a good afternoon, didn't we Bill?'

Bill is animated and quite chatty.

'Oh, yes, and a lovely pub lunch. I had – what was it I had Margaret?' he asks.

'You had steak pie and a glass of shandy.'

'That's it, steak pie and mash. I don't think I'll be needing much for tea,' he tells Karen.

Karen is unusually quiet on the way back to Mavis's house and when they pull up outside she seems eager to get away so Mavis doesn't press her to come in.

'It's in a bit of a mess anyway, what with all the clearing out I've been doing, and getting things ready to pack. Do you know, I can't remember the last time I got away from this place.'

'I envy you, Mavis. All that freedom,' says Karen.

'It's a bit scary actually, but exciting too. I can't wait to see them all. But I'll miss you girls – you've been my second family, you know. I can't imagine what I'd have done without you lot.'

'It works both ways. Thanks for today, Mavis, it was really great of you.'

They hug briefly, then Mavis gets out and walks to her gate. She turns round to wave to Karen and sighs as she remembers the look on her face when she got home today.

Hope she doesn't let the bastard break her heart, she thinks.

Karen waves back, and Mavis is suddenly struck by how sad and vulnerable she looks. There's nothing she can do if Karen won't confide in her, but in that moment she knows this won't end well.

BILL

Now you see this photo, this was taken when we were on holiday somewhere. Karen was just a little girl at the time – see how small she is there next to those other kids. I don't remember who they were, people we met on the caravan site I expect. That old car in the background was ours. It took us all over the place, that car did, holidays and trips out to show gardens. All over the place...

This was my Maureen, soon after we got married. Karen's the image of her, same eyes, same smile... that's why I worry so much about her, in case the same thing happens to her as happened to Maureen. They never found the driver, you know. Never found him. He just drove off and left my darling girl at the side of the road. He just left her – how could anyone do that? I miss her every single day, you know. But I still have Karen, my little girl. She's just like her mum...that's why I worry about her when she goes out. Sometimes I look at her and she could be my Maureen.

Now this is a picture of the garden when we first bought this house. Karen was about nine then and she was so excited to be moving here because before that we lived in a little house that didn't have much of a garden. It wasn't far from here – I can't remember the name of the street but I know we didn't move far. Where those silver birches are now, that was all overgrown and you couldn't even see how far away the back fence was. It was wonderful, having such a big garden to plan and cultivate. We spent a fortune on this garden, me and Maureen. Every weekend we were out there, hacking back the brambles and weeds and turning the ground over till we had it all cleared and ready to start again. There wasn't a thing left by the time we'd finished, it was like a blank canvas just waiting for us to put the picture of our ideal garden onto it.

I don't know what I'd do without Karen. If she left it'd be like losing Maureen all over again. She gets cross with me sometimes when I forget things. I can't help it, it's just hard for me now to remember everything. She wouldn't leave her old Dad though, would she?

I don't blame her for getting cross with me because I get cross with myself, too. I couldn't bear it if she left me here on my own. Or if she found somewhere for me to go – a home, somewhere like that, and then left me with a lot of strangers. I try not to forget things, so then she'll stay and I won't have to go to a home. She's a good girl, my Karen. Looks just like her mother.

I just want to stay here, in this house, with my garden and Karen. That's all I want, really.

CHAPTER 9

HAPPY FAMILIES

Tony has invited the GenClub to his house, to meet Beryl.

'She'll be happier on her home ground,' he explains, 'as it's rather a lot of people for her to get to grips with in one go. But I've explained about the group, and she's all for it.'

Everyone, including Mavis, is going, and rather than turn up mob-handed they decide they'll all make their own way there, except that Karen has offered Mavis a lift so she'll arrive with her and Bill.

Tony lives in a rather posh suburb of Horsfield, full of 1930s detached houses with mock Tudor facades, and large one-off villas dating back to the Edwardian era. The side roads are quiet and tree-lined, with not a hint of lippy lads on bikes racing along the pavements or teenagers hanging around street corners. There's the occasional whine of a lawnmower but apart from that it's a quiet, undisturbed neighbourhood.

Sally and Queenie are the first ones to arrive. Sally drives slowly along the road looking for the right number, except that she can't see any of the numbers mainly because Queenie keeps getting her head in the way but also there don't seem to be too many numbers to see. Finally, they find the right house and stop outside, sitting there for a moment to take it in.

It's obviously been an in-fill house, built in next door's garden. More modern than its neighbours, number 78 is a chalet bungalow with a green-tiled roof, dating from the 1950s, thinks Sally, of the sort she remembers from her childhood storybooks. She had a book with a house in it just like this one – the storybook father smoked a pipe and had Brylcreemed hair and a neat moustache, and the mother was pretty with red lipstick and a gingham apron. They smiled a lot and their children were lively, rosy-cheeked and obedient. There was a small, bouncy dog and a ginger cat. Sally's thinking all this as she looks out at Tony's net-curtained windows, till Queenie cuts in on her daydream.

'Well,' she says, 'I can see I'll have to mind my Ps and Qs round here. I hope they aren't going to be stuck-up.'

'Tony certainly isn't, so I see no reason why Beryl should be. Let's not make any judgements before you've even met them, Mum.'

The front garden is neat, with a low wall and a wooden gate. There'll be a big back garden with an old apple tree and a swing hanging from it, thinks Sally, still inside her storybook.

She gets out, then gets Queenie out, and they make for the front path. Sally unlatches the gate and a small, bouncy dog immediately comes racing round from the back of the house, yapping at them. It's white and brown with a perky little face, and it dances around a bit on the spot in front of them but makes no attempt to jump up. This is a relief to Queenie, who can't stand dogs at the best of times and these days is afraid of being knocked off balance.

Sally says something encouraging to the dog, who stops barking, wags its tail and trots along beside them to the front door gazing up at her all the way. As she pauses to ring the bell she spots a ginger cat curled up asleep on a sunny window ledge, and wonders for a moment if she hasn't just passed through a time warp and stepped inside a 1950s storybook without realising it. But then the door opens to them and it's OK because it's Tony and not the pipe-smoking father standing there.

'Sally! Good to see you again,' he says, 'and you must be Queenie. Come in and meet Beryl. Not you, Gnasher, go round the back – go on!'

'You called this sweet little dog Gnasher?' says Sally, laughing.

'I was brought up on The Beano and the Dandy,' says Tony. 'What else would I call him? He's Gnasher the Fourth.'

The dog immediately gets off the front step and heads for the back garden, looking back fondly at Sally as he goes.

'He's fallen in love with you,' explains Tony. 'He likes women. He'll fall in love with each of you in turn.'

Tony opens the door to the front lounge and steps aside for them to go through, where they find themselves alone. It's a brown and beige room, and although none of the furniture is recent it's all in perfect condition. The three piece suite looks comfy and someone has plumped up all the cushions, positioning all the small ones neatly on point, and a couple of high-backed fireside chairs stand ready for this afternoon's high volume of visitors. There's a smell of lavender furniture polish lingering in the air and a cut glass vase containing carnations has been centrally placed on the windowsill with family photos on either side, including an old wedding picture.

Queenie takes all this in, and approves. It's her kind of room, although she's never actually had one as big or uncluttered as this. On a footstool there's some blue knitting rolled up with both needles poking through the ball of wool, and joy of joys! There's a copy of *The People's Friend* on the coffee table. Sally sees this and nudges Queenie but she's already spotted it.

'Last week's,' she mutters to Sally. 'Not a particularly good one.'

So there's evidence of Beryl's occupation of this room, but so far no sign that Tony lives here. Sally hears him call out to his mother, and soon after he joins them again, filling up the lounge just by being in it.

'Sit down, please. Beryl's just fixing her hair and lipstick, back in the boudoir, so we might not see her for a little while. She spent most of the morning polishing the furniture in here, hence the smell of lavender. Hope we don't all start sneezing.'

Sally has given up on the stiletto heels today, as her feet still haven't recovered from last week's assault on them. Instead, she's moved the battlefront up a few notches, and is sporting a low-necked tee-shirt. Sally and Queenie sit together on the sofa, and she looks around again at the room.

'It's lovely,' she says. 'This house is so ...'

'1950s?' Tony prompts. 'My parents had it built,' he says, pointing in the direction of the framed wedding photo on the windowsill, 'and my brother and I grew up here. I never expected to be coming back for more than a visit, but there you are – life puts these interesting diversions in your path, doesn't it? This room has hardly changed over all those years – it's Beryl's lounge and she likes it this way.'

'So what about the granny annexe you built? If Beryl's not in it does that mean you've become the granny in residence?' says Sally.

'No, she's in it – it's just a bedroom and bathroom so she can stay downstairs. We share the kitchen and the dining room and I have the rooms upstairs. I've got them a bit more 21st century than this,' adds Tony.

The door opens and in comes Beryl, small, neat and white haired, with half-moon glasses and a smile that could light up the dullest room on the bleakest day. She looks the very essence of everyone's favourite grandma, thinks Sally, then remembers Tony saying she never sees his children. Maybe her other son has a family, she thinks, and hopes so because it's such a waste of good grandma material otherwise.

'Ma,' says Tony, 'come and meet two of the latest ladies in my life,' and Beryl chuckles a bit and taps him on the arm as if to make him behave himself.

Tony introduces Sally and Queenie and then the doorbell goes again and Gnasher starts barking and the whole scene is repeated twice more as the room starts to fill up. Beryl smiles a lot and shakes people's hands and everyone talks all at the same time until Tony says, quite loudly, 'Jo's late.'

'I wonder if she's got the time wrong?' says Cathy.

'I'll just go out to the gate in case they're looking for us,' says Tony, and after he leaves the room it goes quiet for a bit until Stella leans forward to ask Beryl if she has other children.

'Another boy,' says Beryl. 'Tony's twin. He lives in America.'

This starts Mavis off on her favourite topic, which everyone but Beryl has heard to death by now, but they sit politely through it again anyway. Except that is for Bill, who yawns loudly once or twice until Karen pokes him in the arm and shushes him. Tony comes back, and announces that there's no sign of Jo and Don.

'My Daniel lives in Beverley Hills,' says Beryl in an unintentional piece of one-upmanship that Mavis doesn't even try to match.

Well, thinks Sally, so much for the other set of grandchildren – don't suppose she sees any of them either. Safe to assume then that the knitting isn't destined to be worn by any of the kids, especially not the Beverley Hills set.

'Is he in films?' asks Stella, and Beryl laughs and shrugs as if to say that she doesn't know what Daniel gets up to in his free time, so it's left to Tony to explain.

'No, he's in teeth – he's a dental surgeon doing mainly cosmetic work so he must be making a fortune there. Can't see him coming back to Horsfield, somehow – it wouldn't be quite the same clientele.'

'You don't see many people with buck teeth these days,' says Queenie, thoughtfully, and that seems to kill that particular conversation.

'Maybe I'll give Jo's mobile a quick ring,' says Cathy, reaching into her bag. 'It's not like her to be late.'

Tony insists that she must use their landline so then they both disappear out into the hallway. Meanwhile, Karen tries to bring Bill in to the conversation as he hasn't opened his mouth, except to yawn, since they arrived.

'Have you got a big garden at the back, Beryl? Dad's a great gardener and he'd love to have a look at yours sometime, wouldn't you?' she says, turning to Bill with feigned enthusiasm.

'D'you grow your own fruit and veg?' he asks Beryl loudly and abruptly, who's taken aback by this and has to think about it a bit.

'There's an apple tree,' she says, putting her hand to her mouth and frowning with the effort of giving Bill the best answer she can.

I knew it! thinks Sally, although she's not optimistic about the swing. Maybe there was one once, maybe little Tony and Daniel squeezed onto it together, giggling loudly until ...

Her daydream is interrupted as Cathy comes back into the room.

'They're not far away. Poor Jo, she's been driving up and down Marlborough Crescent instead of Marlborough Close. Tony's keeping an eye out for her and they'll be here in a minute.'

'Cookers or eaters?' Bill barks out suddenly, and Karen sighs deeply, looks across at Cathy, and wishes she'd never started down the garden line of conversation.

Cathy raises her eyebrows and says 'Locarno?', not really knowing if it's appropriate or not, and then Stella saves Karen from further embarrassment by describing a delicious apple dessert she used to make. Just then they hear voices in the hall and the lounge door opens to admit Jo and Don.

Jo's looking flustered at what she sees as her stupid mistake in mixing up the road names, and apologises far more than is necessary. She's got her hair loose again today, but as she flicks it back Karen notices that she's wearing pearly pink nail polish, and she can't remember seeing that on Jo before.

But it's Don who turns everyone's heads and Bill even produces a wolf-whistle that makes them all laugh. Don has come up trumps today. He's wearing a dark blue bow tie with tiny white dots on it, and a light beige linen jacket. The creases down the front of his navy trousers are as sharp as a razor, and his shoes have been polished to within an inch of their lives.

Beryl gets to her feet, as if she's just about to be presented to the mayor.

'Well, well,' says Tony, 'I think you'd better go to your room Mother. I saw the look you gave the gentleman in the bow tie, you little flirt.'

Beryl laughs, and sits down again. Don, not at all embarrassed by this, steps forward, and kisses her hand. As he straightens up Stella glares at him and only Cathy notices the huge wink he gives her.

'Great to meet you, Don. I want to hear all about this book of yours,' says Tony. 'But first, I'll bring in a couple more chairs and then get some tea.'

It's Tony who organises the tea out in the kitchen and brings everything in on an old wooden trolley, but Beryl's the one who officiates, slicing the cakes up with a steady hand and pouring tea into bone china cups. Tony leaves her to it, now relegated to being the one who passes everything round, and Beryl is indeed the mistress of her own lounge.

Before long, the conversation turns to the proposed outing to see Cathy's play.

'Mavis insists on treating us all, including you and Beryl if you'd like to come, Tony,' says Sally. 'We decided on the Friday evening.'

'I'm definitely free,' says Tony. 'Mother might have a hot date though... shall I get your appointments diary, Ma?'

Beryl puts her hand to her mouth and giggles.

'It's kind of you, Mavis, but I can't let you pay for us – we've only just met,' he adds.

'Oh yes you can,' says Mavis. 'This will be my GenClub leaving do, and I'm jolly well going to treat everybody. I had a bit of a windfall,' she explains.

Arrangements are made for travelling to the village hall, Cathy says she'll make sure there's enough disabled parking space near the main doors, and Jo offers to pick up Stella on the way there. All in all the afternoon turns out to be quite lively, and Tony makes sure he has a chance to talk to Don about his Mecca dancehall days. Beryl doesn't say much, but laughs a lot during the course of the afternoon, and everyone takes to her immediately.

'I like Beryl, she's a dear,' says Cathy to Stella on the drive home.

'And Tony's very good with her,' Stella replies. 'They'll be great people to have in the club. I hope you won't find it a little off-putting having us all there at the play,' she adds.

Cathy's been wondering about that herself.

'I'm a bit apprehensive,' she says, 'but I'm sure it'll be fine once we get started. No backing out now, anyway...'

* * *

It's Friday evening, and Sally's waiting for her daughter to arrive home for the weekend. This is an unscheduled visit, and because Eleanor has been using her summer holidays to work full-time Sally hasn't seen her since the end of May. She was edgy and a bit distant then, and the weekend didn't go as well as Sally would have liked, so she's hoping for a more relaxed time with her daughter now.

It has always seemed strange to Sally that when Eleanor comes home now it's to a place she's never actually lived in. She'd already gone off to university by the time Sally moved into her mother's house, and although her bedroom was relocated more or less as it had been in the family home, it's not the room she grew up in. The furniture's the same, the curtains were adapted to fit, and the carpet's as close as they could find to the original but there are no memories in this bedroom, for Eleanor or Sally. Selling the family home hit Eleanor hard, harder than her mother, whose memories of it were by no means all happy. Now, as she waits to hear her key in the lock, Sally knows her daughter will not be comfortable spending a weekend in what, to her, will always be Grandma's house.

Queenie doesn't look at it in quite the same way, and in her heart of hearts she's glad she wasn't the one who had to move into Sally's house. It worked out the right way round to suit her, but she can't see it from Sally or Eleanor's point of view.

There'll come a day when they have to sell the house, and move to a flat or a bungalow, when Queenie can't manage to get upstairs any more. Sally's dreading this. Prising Queenie away from her house will be traumatic for both of them, and it's a topic that's not mentioned and never will be until the stairs defeat her entirely and she has to give up the struggle. Sally had the guided tour of Beryl's granny annexe while they were there, and it would be a neat solution here as well, although she doesn't think they could raise the money. But Queenie didn't want to take a look, as if to do even that was in some way committing herself to a different future – one that she doesn't want to think about.

Queenie is very proud of her granddaughter, and loves having her in the house. In her eyes Eleanor can do no wrong. Their relationship crosses the divide between the generations, and they have a closeness that Sally envies and cannot quite come to terms with.

It's almost six o'clock by the time Eleanor arrives, and as she calls out from the hall Sally is coming downstairs. She gets to the bottom step at the same moment Eleanor turns around from closing the front door.

'Hi Mum,' she says, moving towards Sally with her arms outstretched.

But Sally is rooted to the spot, the smile of greeting frozen on her face. Eleanor is, obviously, pregnant. About five months, Sally thinks, at the same time as a lot of other thoughts clatter into her head.

Eleanor's arms fall back to her sides.

'Mum, I'm sorry about the shock. It would have been worse to tell you on the phone, and I didn't know the best way to do it.'

Sally is unable to think of anything to say, so Eleanor carries on.

'We'll need to talk later,' she says, picking up her bag. 'Where's Grandma?' and she sails off into the living room.

Keep cool, keep cool, Sally thinks as she follows her. Queenie is sitting in her usual chair in front of the television, but the sound has been turned down in anticipation of Eleanor's grand entrance. By the time Sally gets into the room Eleanor already has her arms around her grandmother.

She can't have failed to notice, thinks Sally, and she's right.

'Did you know about this?' Queenie asks Sally, accusingly, over Eleanor's head.

'No,' says Sally. 'I didn't.'

'Mum, don't start. I need to have a shower and sort myself out a bit before we get into all this,' says Eleanor, with a degree of defiance that Sally finds perplexing. So far she hasn't made a single comment and already Eleanor's getting belligerent and Queenie's implying there's been a conspiracy to keep the truth from her. As if, thinks Sally. She can't remember the last time Eleanor confided anything in her, never mind something as important as this. Queenie is still holding on to Eleanor's hand, as if to protect her, and Sally starts to feel she's the one on the outside.

'Fine,' she says. 'You go on up to the bathroom and I'll get back to the kitchen.' Where I can be of some use, she adds silently to herself.

Eleanor bends to kiss her grandmother, then walks past Sally and off up the stairs.

'Don't be too hard on her,' says Queenie. 'These things happen.'

'Yes, well thank you Mum. I'll certainly bear that in mind.'

Queenie then picks up the television remote and fumbles about with it to get the sound back up several hundred decibels to the level she usually has it, and then fiddles with her hearing aids so as to turn them down a bit.

Sally sighs, and marches out of the lounge and back to the kitchen. There's plenty she could do. Dinner to finish preparing, some ironing on the worktop, a bit of washing-up left from lunch. Sally does none of these, choosing instead to sit at the kitchen table, staring at the back door handle, which is just the kind of inanimate object she needs to focus on right now – something that won't answer back or try to make her feel negative about herself. Her shoulders seem to have crept right up under her ears, and she makes a conscious effort to let them drop.

I will not let things get out of hand, she thinks. I'll be calm and understanding. We'll sort it out together, as a family. Then the phone rings, making her jump, and her shoulders shoot back up again.

It's her ex, Ian, making one of his infrequent calls, which always coincide with Eleanor's visits. Normally they are able to exchange pleasantries before Sally hands the phone over to Eleanor. Today, she can't be bothered.

'She's in the shower,' says Sally, abruptly.

'Ah, that'll be why she isn't answering her mobile. Tell her to ring me back. Any time this evening, I'm not going out.'

'Oh, shame,' says Sally. 'Don't suppose I will be either. Too busy deflecting blows from the rest of my family.'

Ian doesn't speak for a few seconds.

'Hello? Oh, I thought I'd lost you for a moment,' Sally says into the silence.

'What's going on there?'

'Nothing much. Our daughter's pregnant.'

'Yes, I know.'

'What? You know? You *know*? I didn't know, Ian. I didn't know until ten minutes ago when she arrived here, and even then she didn't think to mention it. But you already knew – how was that then?'

Sally is getting worked up. Calm and understanding seem to have gone out of the window and the pitch of her voice has gone up several notches.

I was OK all the time I was in contact with that door handle, she thinks. It's just people that make me lose my cool.

On the other end of the phone, Ian has a go at smoothing things over and inevitably makes them ten times worse.

'She needs a bit of financial help and she had to give me a reason for wanting the money. Sally, I know it's a shock and naturally you're disappointed – so was I at first. But it's not such a big deal these days, there are plenty of single parents doing a great job of bringing up their kids.'

'Yes, so my mother tells me. Am I the only one who thinks there's a tiny bit of a problem here? What will happen to her university degree? Where's she going to live, and what will she live on? Social security? Oh no, of course, you're bank-rolling her, aren't you?' Sally's getting into her stride now.

'And what about the father? You're probably going to tell me now that you've already had a cosy chat with him over a pint and a game of darts down at the local. And I bet he's a great chap.'

'Now just calm down, Sally, you're getting carried away. I don't know who the father is, actually. I haven't asked, it's none of my business.'

Sally's voice rises a bit higher.

'It may be none of your business, but it's bloody well going to be my business. Ian, she's not yet twenty and now she's buggered up all her future hopes. And ours too, well mine anyway. You don't seem too bothered.'

'Of course I am, how can you say that? I'm very concerned about Eleanor's future. Why do you think I was giving her the money, if not for her future?'

Sally is suddenly aware of someone else in the room. She turns to see Eleanor standing in the doorway. She's washed her hair and it's hanging wet around her shoulders, and without make-up on she looks a lot younger than her twenty years. Sally wants to hug her and make it better, like she could when Eleanor was little and had a cut finger or a grazed knee. But a sticking plaster won't be much help in this situation and there's a look on Eleanor's face that stops her in her tracks, even before she's made a move.

'I'll call you back,' she says abruptly into the phone, and places the receiver back more carefully than she expected to be able to.

'Was that Dad? I missed his call on my mobile.' Eleanor comes into the room and sits down at the kitchen table. 'There was no need to give him a hard time, Mum, it's not his fault.'

'Let's not go there, Eleanor, that's between him and me. You might understand that one of these days, when you're a parent, and that's the thing we need to be discussing right now.'

'I didn't intend for this to happen.'

'Well, that's something I suppose. Have you thought about what you'll do?'

Sally doesn't want to mention adoption, and she's clearly past the termination stage, but her mind is racing ahead already. A picture pops into her head – a baby in the house, the washing line full of tiny clothes, and a pram in the hall.

A baby! Suddenly, it doesn't seem such a disaster. They'll manage. Sally will be there to help and it'll work out OK. She starts to think about re-visiting the granny annexe option again and wonders vaguely if Tony could give her some advice about extending the house. It would certainly help to keep them all from under each other's feet. Yes, a granny annexe downstairs, and a nursery – a nursery! – upstairs.

'Dad didn't say? I thought he might.'

'Say what?'

Clearly, plans have been made, and Sally's off the loop again.

'I'm not staying here Mum. I'm going with a friend to live with his family in India. They've got a hotel and leisure centre at a resort in Goa and it sounds really wonderful.'

Eleanor's face has lit-up with the excitement of this enterprise.

'I'll be able to work there and there's accommodation on site plus it'll be a great place to bring up a child,' she says. 'Dad's paying for the flight – I have to go before I'm seven months or I can't fly then until after the baby's born.'

Sally's head feels like it's going to burst open. India? That's halfway round the world. She'll see even less of her daughter than she does now, and her grandchild will think of her as a stranger. The washing line in her back garden is suddenly empty again, the baby snatched away from her.

'Who's this friend? The baby's father?'

'No, just a guy I met – he's been over here on a gap year, working in a bar in town.'

'Is that all you know about him?'

'No, I know all about his family, where they live, what it's like there…Mum, he's OK, just an ordinary guy.'

'Nothing more between you two?' asks Sally, as she struggles to prise scraps of information out of Eleanor.

'Hardly.' Eleanor points to her bump. 'This kind of scuppers anything like that,' she says. 'Even if either of us wanted a relationship, which we don't,' she adds.

'And what about the baby's father? Doesn't he get a say in all of this?'

Eleanor looks a bit shifty and starts examining her nails, then picking at them. Sally has obviously touched her on a raw nerve.

'No say, no involvement. Mum, it was just a fling. We won't be contacting each other again.' She flicks her damp hair over her shoulder and lifts her head to look at her mother.

Sally sits across the table from her daughter, looks at her pale but defiant face, and wonders if this is all just a bad dream. But when she looks up again the rest of the world that is her kitchen seems perfectly normal, so she assumes it must really be happening.

'But these people in India, they won't just give you free board and lodging, surely. I can understand it if you're working for them, then it would be part of the package, but there'll be quite some time when you won't be able to work – what happens then? How will you support yourself – and the baby when it arrives?'

'Dad says he'll send money over.'

There's a niggly pain starting just behind Sally's left eye. So it's a done deal. Damn Ian and his bloody chequebook.

'There's no need for any of this, Eleanor. Come home, have the baby here and together we'll work it out. If Dad still wants to support you he can do it by sending the money right here, and if he doesn't then we'll find another way. You can work or go back to college, whatever you want to do, and I'll look after the baby. I don't see what's to be gained by going across the world.'

'Oh *Mum*!' says Eleanor, raising her voice.

'What? Now what have I said? You've got to be practical, Eleanor. There's going to be a baby – and that baby has got to come first in whatever plans you make.'

Eleanor gets up from the table and heads for the door.

'That's what I'm doing,' she yells. 'I'm putting the baby first, ahead of you. What makes you think the best thing for either of us is to stay here? With you, Mum, organising my life for me, because that's what you really want to do, like you always have. You're such a control freak. I bet you've already got the pram parked in the hall and picked out the paint for the nursery.'

There's a heartbeat's moment of silence.

'Don't be ridiculous,' says Sally, forcing herself not to shout. 'That's not fair.'

'Isn't it? Why do you think I chose a university as far away as I could get? Well, you're not going to control the rest of my life. I make all my own decisions now, and I intend to carry on doing just that.'

Eleanor marches out of the kitchen and upstairs to her bedroom. Her arrival there is signalled by the slamming of the door. Sally puts her head in her hands and sighs deeply.

'I don't think you handled that very well,' says Queenie from the hallway, and Sally takes a leaf out of her daughter's book, wrenches the back door open and slams it behind her.

Outside in the garden she snatches up some sprigs of mint and parsley, and mutters quietly to herself,

'Locarno...Locarno...bloody Locarno...'

CHAPTER 10

LEADING LADY

Tony and Beryl arrive at the community centre with plenty of time to spare. He has already suggested that they round off the evening by going along to the Jolly Sailor, and in view of this it was decided that Queenie and Stella should hire wheelchairs. Jo thinks the walk to the pub will also be too much for Don, but she knows he won't go in a wheelchair so she's prepared to take the car along there and risk the chance of finding a parking space.

Tony has picked up the wheelchairs and has them folded and stowed in the back of his car, and Cathy has, as promised, made certain there are enough parking spaces at the front of the hall for unloading. Tony gets the first wheelchair out of the car and opens it up so he's ready for whoever arrives first. Jo has arranged to pick up Stella, Mavis is coming with Karen and Bill, and Sally is bringing all their tickets. Everything that can be pre-arranged has been. So it should all go swimmingly.

* * *

Backstage, Cathy is quietly nervous. She's not one for the overt display of nerves that some of the other actors exhibit, instead she sits on her own by a clothes rail and practises deep breathing.

Around her is the usual detritus of community halls. There's an old darts board leaning up against a tea urn, a Tombola drum on some broken chairs, and over by the fire exit is a pile of jigsaws left over from a jumble sale. What they're using as a props table is actually made up of an old notice board on a trestle, and the props lady is just checking that it's stable enough to last out the night. There are a couple of notices still pinned to the board. One of them is a poster for a review the drama group did years ago, and the drawing pins have rusted into the paper.

Barry is fussing around them all and issuing last minute reminders.

'Carol, don't forget to go on at the start of Act 2 *with* the bottle of wine tonight. And David, try not to trip over Steve's feet again – one prostrate actor is quite enough for this plot.'

'Be nice if the telephone rang at the right time tonight,' remarks Andrew, mildly, because last night's sound effects cock-up didn't really faze him at all, just gave him a comic opportunity he wasn't expecting. A master of the ad-lib, Andrew coped magnificently and gained an extra ripple of applause for his improvisation.

'Yes, well I'll tell George – yet again. Cathy, are you OK?' asks Barry.

Cathy opens her eyes and smiles up at him.

'Fine thanks, Barry. Just relaxing.'

Andrew sits down next to her, takes her hand and strokes it.

'Run away with me,' he says. 'Let's leave this rabble behind and go somewhere we'd really be appreciated, my darling.'

'Where might that be?' asks Barry. 'Afghanistan?'

'New York…Paris…or Croydon,' says Andrew, kissing Cathy's hand.

'Bugger off, Andrew, you're ruining my meditation.'

'OK, dear heart. See you on stage.'

Andrew stands up and blows a kiss at Cathy, who waves him away from her but can't suppress a smile. He can be irritating, but underneath all the flim-flam he's been a good friend over the years and she's genuinely fond of him.

She closes her eyes again and takes a deep breath.

***

The hall is filling up nicely. Tony has wheeled first Stella, and then Queenie in, and set them up on the aisle side of the back row, as instructed by Front of House.

'We won't see a thing here,' Queenie moans to him. Behind Tony, Sally lets out a sigh.

'Yes you will,' she snaps. 'The stage is quite high and you're not that many rows back. It's not exactly the London Palladium.'

Queenie sniffs and turns her face away from Sally. Then she starts messing about with her hearing aids.

Tony turns to say something to Sally, thinks better of it, and manoeuvres Queenie's chair a little to the right of the man in front of her.

'Get him to take his hat off if it's in your way,' he says to Queenie.

'He's not wearing a hat,' she replies, mystified.

'Well there you are then. Things have improved already,' he says. Stella, who won't see much wherever she sits, is perfectly happy where she is. She laughs a bit, then Queenie joins in although she's not sure she sees the joke.

Queenie has never been to a London theatre, although when Sally was growing up the family always spent Sunday evenings in front of the telly watching the weekly parade of stars that was Sunday Night at the London Palladium. It was an opportunity for Queenie to see how the other half lived, and one that she enjoyed hugely, without any aspirations herself to join them in the audience. Tonight, she's dressed as if she has finally made that social leap, in a dusky blue dress and jacket she bought from Sally's catalogue for a family wedding last year. She's giving her new shoes an airing – the ones she bought at Barkers when they had lunch there with Cathy – and earlier in the day Eleanor washed and set her hair for her. This is something she never lets Sally do, preferring instead the little hairdressers on the corner of their road, but Eleanor has a way with rollers so she got the job, and the tip that went with it.

Sally is right – the Community Hall has nothing much in common with the London Palladium except that both have a stage. There's no tasselled red velvet curtain here though, it's heavy black cotton and there's a small rip at the top on one side. But the lighting rig is quite impressive, the result of a European Community handout, and it's quite cosy in a ramshackle sort of way. The audience is fairly mixed, although it's safe to say that Queenie is better turned out than anyone else at this performance.

Stella, who has been to the Community Hall many times before, hasn't made such an effort, looking more casual, and consequently more in tune with the rest of the audience. When they arrived Mavis told Queenie how lovely she looked, which pleased her no end.

'Luckily, I talked her out of the tiara,' whispered Sally, and Mavis laughed but not unkindly as she's had a soft spot for Queenie ever since she made the apple pies for Dorothy's funeral.

The rest of the GenClub group has seats in row D, centre block. They could have had the front row, but this was more than Cathy could handle so she told them D were the best available, and everyone seemed pleased enough with that. The bell has rung, and they're getting themselves settled in their seats when Don turns round and sees that most of the back row is empty, including the seat next to Stella.

'I think I'll go back there and keep the girls company,' he says, as he gets to his feet again.

'Oh, *Dad*!' protests Jo, and half of Row D has to get up and flatten themselves back so that Don can shuffle past them and into the aisle. This leaves him a bit short of breath and he stands for a moment, holding on to the aisle seat, wheezing. Jo had got herself safely tucked up in the middle of the row between Don and Karen, but now she starts to get concerned about him, so then everyone has to get up again so that she can squeeze past too. Eventually she's out in the aisle with him.

'I'm alright,' he says, but she helps him along to the back row anyway and gets him settled next to Stella.

'You were better off down there,' says Queenie, and there's a whistling as she starts to fiddle with her hearing aids. 'Can't see much from here.'

Jo gets back to Row D and finds they've moved along to close up the gap in the middle so that now she has to sit on the end, next to Tony. This makes her feel uneasy and a bit vulnerable. Jo remembers going to pantomimes as a child, and getting picked on once to help with card tricks and stunts because she was the one sitting on the aisle. She's never liked it since.

Tony turns to her.

'Everything OK back there?' he asks.

'Yes, I think so. Thanks,' she says. The house lights dim, then lower slowly into blackout, and Jo starts to feel more secure. In the back row, Don reaches for Stella's hand.

At the tech desk, George starts the opening music, then fades it out as he brings the stage lighting up. It's a very good set, and it gets an enthusiastic round of applause, then Andrew wanders in through the French doors at the back and *Bring Me That Horizon* is up and running.

* * *

Cathy's first scene is not one of her solo ones, which is a relief to her because having another actor on stage with her helps to calm her nerves. Stella's often been to her plays, but this is the first time Cathy's had a whole crowd of friends in the audience and she's more jittery than she expected to be.

Carol, who's acting opposite her in this scene, is even more nervous than Cathy. This play is her first time on stage and she didn't have a good opening night. Not only did she forget to bring on a crucial prop, she fluffed her lines more than once. Tonight she's got to forget the mistakes of the night before and somehow get her confidence back. But she's a bag of nerves, and it's not long before disaster strikes. Carol forgets where she is on the script and jumps a whole page, and Cathy has her work cut out just keeping them both on track. In the wings, Barry listens tensely, wondering if the audience will still be able to follow the plot. Thank God she's on with Cathy, he thinks.

But all this concentration and quick thinking does at least mean that Cathy soon forgets about the GenClub sitting en masse a few feet away from her. She gets into her stride and by the time her first solo scene comes up she's lost her nerves and is performing to her usual standard.

In the interval they all meet up at the back row, clustering around Don, Stella and Queenie. Tony takes orders for tea and coffee.

'Jo, come with me – I'll need some help,' he says, and the two of them break away from the rest of the GenClub and head for the back of the hall.

'This was such a good idea,' Tony says to Jo. 'They're having a great time. Mum's stayed awake so far, so that's a good sign, and Bill seems to be following what's going on.'

'Dad's enjoying himself amongst the ladies,' says Jo.

She still feels a bit shy with Tony, but she's getting more used to him being around, and he has a way of making Jo feel valued. He could have asked any one of the others to help him get the drinks, but he asked her. If Jo stopped to think about it, she would probably say it was just because she was standing next to him at the time, but she'd be wrong.

They join a long queue in front of the serving hatch. Behind it, two ladies in aprons are trying to cope with the rush without getting flustered. Only one of them has succeeded.

'We should do this more often,' says Tony.

'I think they only put on a play twice a year,' says Jo.

'I didn't mean that,' says Tony, and Jo realises she's got the wrong end of the stick again and assumes he means outings in general, so she rushes in to cover up her embarrassment before he can say anything else.

'I did have another idea, actually,' she says. 'The BBC Big Band is playing a gig up in Tunbridge Wells next month. I haven't said anything to Dad yet but I know he'd love to go, and I thought maybe some of the others…'

'Yeah, why not? It sounds good,' says Tony, 'so you can count us in for that one. You'd better mention it soon though, Queenie will have to start shopping now for another outfit – I hope Sally can stand the strain.'

'She seems a bit tense tonight. I think her daughter's home for a few days. Three generations of women in the same house…'

'…and the same kitchen. No wonder she's tense, poor girl.'

Then they're suddenly at the front of the queue, and it's all down to getting the orders right, making sure it all fits onto two trays and seeing that everyone has a biscuit in their saucer.

* * *

Backstage, Carol has gone to pieces. The youngest of the group by about fifteen years, Carol's stage debut is not proving to be a happy one.

From the first day she joined the Horsfield Players Carol has made it patently obvious that she fancies Andrew, in spite of the difference in their ages. Taking on this role was more an attempt to impress him than a real desire to act, and now she can see that it wasn't a particularly good move. Andrew is unmoved by anything Carol says or does, in fact he hardly seems to notice her, and as if that wasn't bad enough she now realises she's entirely unsuited to acting and she should have kept to scene painting.

Barry does his best to calm her down but he's clearly not up to the challenge.

'I don't think I can walk out there again,' she wails. 'Jenny knows all the lines, she'll have to take over.'

'How can we do that?' asks Barry, spreading his arms out in a gesture of helplessness. 'We need Jenny on Prompt, and anyway the audience will be totally confused if a different actress suddenly comes on in your role.'

'No, it'll be OK – she can wear my clothes,' Carol argues, as she tries, not very convincingly, to sell the idea to him.

Andrew, who has been following this real-life drama quietly in the background, steps forward decisively.

'Carol,' he says, 'come with me.'

And he puts his arm around her shoulders, kisses her, and takes her out through the stage door.

Cathy looks at Barry.

'He wouldn't,' she says. 'Would he?'

'I have no idea what you've got in mind,' says Barry. 'But he might.'

'Well, let's just hope it works.'

* * *

The bell rings for the start of the second act, and the GenClub splits up again. The house lights dim and music floats through the hall. When the curtain goes up two actors are already on stage, and then Carol walks in from the doorway stage right. There's a slight spring in her step now, and when she says the first line her projection is much better.

'She seems to have got over her nerves,' Tony whispers to Jo. He gets his head right up close to hers to say this, and his chin brushes her cheek. Jo gets a slight whiff of after-shave, and doesn't dare turn to look at him. She can feel herself getting hot, and yet again she's glad of the darkness.

The bag of sweets Mavis brought with her goes down row D again, the action moves along, and before long they're in the run-up to the final scene.

Cathy and Andrew are playing this one together, and it's the only occasion in this play where Barry has them on stage at the same time. Cathy has to get really mad at Andrew, which she finds surprisingly easy to do tonight. When she gets right up close to him she can see that there's a faint smudge of lipstick on his cheek. It could be Carol's, she thinks, in fact it most probably is hers.

'You self-centred *bastard*!' she spits at him. 'You don't care for anybody but yourself!'

Andrew catches her wrists as she goes to strike him. 'I care for you,' he says.

In Row D, Mavis is completely lost in the action, gazing up at Cathy and Andrew with her mouth open. Karen glances at Bill on her right. A tear is slowly streaking down his cheek. She can't begin to guess what this scene has sparked off in Bill and she wants to take his hand and squeeze it, but doesn't like to break the spell for him. She looks back to the stage where Andrew now has Cathy in a clinch. Either they're really enjoying this, Karen thinks, or they should be up for an Academy Award.

The action isn't over yet. Barry doesn't write endings where people fall into each other's arms and live happily ever after, so Cathy and Andrew have a fair bit of emotion still to get through. But now they have the audience in the palm of their hands.

The telephone rings abruptly, jolting everyone in their seats. George has had the timing spot-on all the way through this evening's performance, and this final ring is bang on the button. Backstage, Barry allows himself a small smile of satisfaction, and Cathy delivers the last few lines. The curtain comes down.

Mavis knocks the sweets off her lap with the exuberance of her applause and as is traditional in the community hall at such times, the foot-stamping starts. With their hands linked, the actors line up at the front of the stage to take their bows, and when they come up for the second time Cathy finally allows herself to look down into Row D. And the GenClub responds by cheering loudly.

* * *

123

Down at the Jolly Sailor, they're in luck. A big group of girls out on a hen-night has just vacated several tables on the back terrace and swept past them in a flurry of feathers and pink cowboy hats. The tables have already been pushed together, so all they have to do is choose their seats and move the empty glasses to one side.

It's been a sunny day and the night is fairly mild, although September is creeping in with a nip to the mornings and evenings. In anticipation of this the pub has lit the patio heaters, and the Old Gens get themselves snugged-up under the nearest one. Mavis goes off to buy drinks, with Karen providing back-up to carry them through. The talk round the table is all of *Bring Me That Horizon*.

'I told you she was good,' says Stella proudly.

'And you were right. Best of the bunch,' Tony agrees.

'And that man who played Philip, he was very good as well,' says Queenie. 'I couldn't take my eyes off him,' she adds.

Sally wants to jump in and say, Aha! So you didn't have trouble seeing the stage after all! But she holds it in.

Mavis and Karen appear in the pub doorway, carrying glasses and a bottle of champagne, and at exactly the same time Cathy arrives to a round of applause from the GenClub.

'How did it look from down there?' she asks. 'I hope you enjoyed it, we did go wrong a couple of times.'

'Well it didn't show,' says Jo. 'You were great, Cathy. Well done.'

Mavis pours the champagne and toasts are drunk – to Cathy, to the Horsfield Players, to Mavis and to the GenClub. Because the majority of the group are either driving or on medication, not much of the champagne is actually being drunk. Mavis, however, doesn't fall into either category and she's in party mood, so she ends up drinking most of it herself.

'I just want to say,' she says, getting to her feet and swaying just a bit, 'that I'll miss you lot. You've been the best friends any girl could wish for. So you've got to carry on now, looking after each other.'

'Mavis,' says Karen, 'Anyone would think you were emigrating. You'll be back in a couple of months.'

'Yes, I know,' says Mavis. 'But it won't be quite the same then, will it?'

There's a bit of a silence after that, while they all digest Mavis's remark and then Bill steps in with a stage whisper to Karen.

'Who is that woman?' he asks.

'It's Mavis, you know her,' Karen replies, putting her hand on Mavis's arm as she sits down again.

'No not her. *Her*,' he says and points across the table. 'I've seen her before somewhere. Recently.'

'That's Cathy,' says Karen, and laughs. 'She was in the play. She was the one in the red dress. That's where you've seen her.'

One by one they all laugh, then Bill joins in, throwing his head back and roaring with laughter. Mavis tips the last of the champagne into her glass and raises it again.

'Here's to you, Bill,' she says, and blows him a kiss across the table.

'Let battle commence!' he replies.

The evening has been a huge success. As they reach the car park at the community hall and goodbyes are echoing around the empty space, Cathy leans across to Sally and says, 'This is just how we imagined it, right back at the start – remember?'

'It's how you imagined it,' Sally replies. 'My imagination didn't reach as far as yours. I'm not much good at that.'

And there's just something about the way she says it that leaves Cathy puzzled and more than a little concerned.

'I'll ring you in the morning,' she says.

DON

I don't think there was ever a time when I didn't want to play music, right from when I was a little lad in the Boys Brigade and one of the older boys put a bugle into my hands and let me have a blow. Mind you, that was a tuneless instrument – but you get my drift.

And music's been good to me over the years. See all these LPs? I'm playing on most of them. Session musician, you see – I earned more money like that than I ever did on the Mecca circuit, and I got to play with some of the biggest names of the day. This one here, this is Lita Rosa, very big singer in the Fifties, and this is one of Dickie Valentine's. Nice bloke, he was, and a real professional. I even recorded with some of the visiting Americans and was picked to go on tour with Sammy Davis Jr. – that would have been some time in the Sixties. We had a ball on that tour. I'd never seen so much booze in my life.

At first, after Jean went, I couldn't see how I would be able to work and look after Jo. She was only four years old and it seemed impossible. But actually, it worked out OK, better probably with me being a musician than if I'd had a regular job, and you wouldn't think that, would you? You see, in the school holidays I always tried to get on a tour, and take Jo with me. There was a girl singer in every band in those days, and they generally fussed over Jo and looked after her if I wasn't around. We used to treat these tours as our holidays. The rest of the time I only took jobs in London so I didn't have to stay away from home, and my neighbours were very kind and between them they had the babysitting covered. I was home in the daytime so I was always there to take her to school and fetch her home after, and of course I didn't work every night. Then as she got a bit older I'd sometimes take her on gigs with me.

The Mecca management never paid their bands very well, but it was regular work with some of the best in the business. Not challenging, like the session recordings, but there was an esprit de corps in the dance bands that you'd go a long way to find these days. And that's why I'm writing this book. It's a testament to all the musicians and the many friendships that were forged in those Mecca dance bands, and it's been great finding some of the guys again. Not that many of them play anymore, well a few do of course but most, like me, have had to give it up on health grounds. I used to find it very frustrating – and there are times when I still do. I get my old saxophones out of their cases and clean them up, make sure all the valves are still working properly and give them a bit of a polish, and I'd love to just have a blow. But I can't do it now. It's the breathing, you see, not enough puff.

Those girl singers I mentioned – well naturally there were occasional romances. And in the dance halls it wasn't difficult to attract the attention of a pretty girl when you were one of the musicians. There was a regular clientele at most of the ballrooms so after a while you got to know some of them and … well, one thing generally led to another. But Jo always came first with me, and the last thing I wanted was for her to be let down by another woman. It was bad enough when Jean left us, she didn't need to go through it all again with someone else – and neither did I. So I made sure there was never anything too serious going on. To be fair, most of them wouldn't have wanted to take on a little girl or a stroppy teenager anyway and a musician's life isn't what you'd call normal.

I've got no complaints about the way my life turned out. I was lucky enough to be doing a job that I loved, surrounded by friends I admired, and there were occasions when I got a sniff at the big time. You can't ask for much more than that – but if I could have one wish now it's this; just to see my Jo and her mother together as friends. That would make me a truly happy man.

CHAPTER 11

LOOSE ENDS

The party – or at least the play – is over. The GenClub girls (and guy) take their oldies home, and step back into their everyday lives after a welcome bit of respite and escapism.

It's about 11.15 when Sally gets in and Eleanor is still up, watching a stand-up comedy show on television. This is a late night for Queenie, so she foregoes her usual cup of Horlicks for once and just calls out goodnight before making the long, slow haul upstairs and then to bed. Sally joins her daughter in the lounge.

'How was the play?' Eleanor asks without taking her eyes off the TV screen. Her hands are clasped across her bump, and every so often she rubs it gently. Sally sits down opposite her.

'Very good, Cathy was great. We had a drink in the Jolly Sailor afterwards.'

'Did Grandma enjoy herself?'

Sally stops to think before replying. She's beginning to edit her remarks to Eleanor first instead of just coming right out with them, like she would with anyone else. Like she used to with Eleanor. What Sally's actually thinking is that Queenie was a misery some of the time but on the whole behaved quite well. She's also wondering what her mother's like when she's out of her company. Maybe they're both better apart.

'Yes, she had a lovely time,' she tells Eleanor, as she imagines this is what she wants and expects to hear.

'I'm glad,' she replies, yawning and rubbing her eyes.

'You should go to bed if you're tired, Eleanor. What time are you planning to leave tomorrow?'

'The 10.30 train so I'll be back at the flat by 4pm. Dad's coming next weekend to collect my stuff. I rang him tonight, he was cool.'

Sally's thinking that Ian has been much too cool over this for her liking, but she says nothing.

'The flights are booked for ten days time. I spoke to Ben earlier.'

Sally's heart sinks. It's really happening.

'Give me the address and a phone number where we can contact you,' she says, leaning over and reaching for the address book she keeps in the sideboard drawer.

Eleanor keeps her eyes firmly fixed on the television.

'I don't have them right now.'

'Well when you get back to your flat, then.'

Eleanor doesn't comment.

'You do have the address, don't you?' persists Sally, knowing she's moving onto precariously dodgy ground by taking that tone.

'Not exactly. Mum, don't nag.'

'I'm not nagging, but naturally I want to know where you're going. You weren't just planning on disappearing into the blue, I take it.' Sally takes one step closer to blow-up territory.

'That's ridiculous. Of course I'll get you the address – you don't need it tonight though, do you?' Eleanor looks across at her mother for the first time in this particular conversation, and puts on her defiant face. Everything is now in place for another flare-up. Fearlessly, Sally pushes on.

'So – let me see if I've got this right, Eleanor – all you actually have so far is the phone number where this Ben's living in the UK. Is that it?'

'Mobile number, yes. Well what else do I need at this stage? I'm not planning to write to the family, I'll be seeing them in a couple of weeks.'

Sally takes a step backwards in retreat, but her mind is working overtime. In the morning she'll talk to Ian, see if she can get some sense out of him.

'Mum, I'll be fine. It'll all be fine. And once I'm settled you and Dad can come out and see us. Bring Grandma.'

Sally can think of nothing worse than a long haul flight in the company of her mother and her ex-husband, but this is not the moment to say so. On the other hand, she can't quite summon the energy to sound enthusiastic about the prospect either.

'Well, we'll see. One step at a time I think. Now I don't know about you, but I'm off to bed.'

Eleanor heaves herself up from the depths of the sofa and heads for the hall.

'Night,' she calls over her shoulder.

Sally clicks the TV remote off, picks up an empty mug and the biscuit tin from the coffee table and switches off the lounge lights. She goes down the hall towards the kitchen and there's a heaviness in her heart that stays with her all night as she watches the hours tick by on her bedside clock.

In the next room Queenie snores the night away in untroubled sleep.

* * *

Jo parks in their allotted space and walks arm in arm with Don to the main door of their apartment block.

'Dad, would you like to go to the Tunbridge Wells Assembly Hall to see the BBC Big Band?'

'Would I? You bet!' Don stops in his slow shuffle to turn to Jo, and in the glow from the outside lights his eyes shine. 'That would be great, really great. Just us?'

'No, I thought another GenClub outing if the others are interested too. Tony thinks it's a good idea, but I haven't had a chance to mention it to anyone else yet.'

'He's a nice bloke, that Tony, I like him a lot. If I'd had a son that's just how I'd have liked him to turn out,' he says as they reach the front steps. 'He might have made a good pianist too, with those fingers,' he adds.

Jo's wondering why she's never noticed Tony's fingers, since Don finds them worth remarking on. Must take a look next time I see him, she thinks.

'So when's this gig?' Don asks, as Jo opens the door to their flat.

'The 28th of this month, that's almost four weeks away. I'll have to move on this if we want to get decent seats.'

Jo turns back from closing the door and finds Don standing in their hall looking at her.

'What?' she says. 'What's the matter?'

'It's the day Jean arrives.'

A sliver of ice cuts through Jo's heart. She's been putting Jean's visit to the back of her mind, but now there's no getting away from it. Her mother is coming.

'Then you'll have to make a choice, Dad, only don't wait too long before deciding what you want to do.'

Jo walks past him to the hall cupboard, hangs her jacket up and holds her hand out for Don's anorak.

'She won't be coming here on the 28th, that's the day she flies in to Heathrow. I suppose she'll go to her brother's house first of all. We haven't made any plans beyond that,' he says, following Jo down the hallway and into the kitchen.

'Then there won't be a clash with the gig, will there?' Jo fills the kettle and switches it on, reaching into the cupboard above for coffee and mugs.

'I could go over to Essex to see her, if you don't want her coming here,' Don says.

'Don't be daft! You can't go all that way on your own, Dad. If you do that I'll have to come with you so it defeats the object, doesn't it? I'll still end up seeing her, whatever happens.' She folds her arms and leans her back against the worktop, looking defensive and cornered.

'Jo, if you're really not happy about this I'll just tell her to forget it. It's as simple as that.'

The kettle boils, and Jo makes them each a coffee. She puts the mugs on the kitchen table, pulls out a chair and sits down.

'Then you won't get the chance to see her either, and I'd feel guilty about it. Though I can't really understand why you're so keen on it, Dad, after what happened. What she did to us.'

Don sits opposite Jo. He reaches across the table for her hand.

'Water and bridges, Jo – it was all a very long time ago. OK, we suffered a bit at the time, but in the long run we probably came out of it better than she did. We had each other, but she passed up on the chance of having either of us. And look what she missed all those years.'

Don stops to have a good cough, and Jo gets him a glass of water, before he can pick up his theme again.

'Maybe we'd have split up anyhow, you know what it's like being married to a musician – you've seen enough of it with others. Then you'd have been bounced backwards and forwards between the two of us. What you and I had was a lot better than that, wasn't it?'

Jo nods and gives his hand a squeeze.

'Yes, I know all that…but what's the point in seeing her again now? You're not hoping to get her back, are you?'

'Of course not! But aren't you just a little bit curious? I am! I want to know what she's like now, how her life turned out – and I want her to see how *you* turned out, Jo. We can't turn the clock back, and I'm not sure that I'd want to anyway, but for a while she was the centre of my life, and the start of yours. You can't just wipe that out. And one afternoon together might heal some of the wounds we both carried around for years.'

All this talking has made Don very wheezy, and he coughs a bit and gasps for air.

'You need your puffer, Dad,' says Jo, getting up to take one from the cupboard. 'Here you are.'

While Don's inhaling, Jo thinks about what he's just said. She has to admit she *is* a bit curious. She has very few memories of her mother, mostly because she made a conscious decision not to remember her. There are one or two ancient photos that she hasn't looked at in years and that's about all – no small souvenirs, no empty scent bottles, no hand-knitted dolls clothes, nothing. Just a feeling that Jean must have been a heartless bitch to walk out on her four-year-old child, and even that gets weaker with the passing of time. Maybe Dad's got the right attitude, Jo thinks – although the thought of actually confronting Jean turns her stomach to ice. She begins to realise this is something she has very little chance of avoiding, so she might as well face it on her terms.

'I'll tell you what, Dad,' she says. 'You arrange for Jean to come here one day, and I'll make sure I'm home to meet her. I'll be civil and pleasant, but I can't promise any more than that. And if it gets to be too much for me I'll go out for a walk and leave you to it. Is that a deal?'

Don lays his puffer aside, then pretends to spit on his hand and they shake on it, like they used to do when she was a kid and they made deals. He smiles at her.

'That's my girl,' he says, and then he starts to sing a few breathy lines to her before he has to give up and have a cough; '"You're the cream in my coffee, You're the salt in my stew, You will always be…"'

'"…my necessity, I'd be lost without you."'

When she was little Don used to make up daft words like "You're the froth on my Guinness," or "You're the flake in my ice-cream" and he never seemed to run out of ideas. Sometimes the things he came up with made Jo laugh so hard her sides hurt. She remembers one day when, desperate to make up her own line, she sang back to him 'You're my Dad and my Mum' and knew straight away that it wasn't any good because Don didn't finish the song. He just gave her a big, long hug, and they didn't sing any more that day.

Jean was never around to hear them sing together, and that, thinks Jo with some satisfaction, is one more thing she missed out on.

* * *

'Bye…take care…see you soon!' Mavis risks upsetting her neighbours by calling out a fond farewell to Karen and Bill as they drive away from her house. She waves till they've turned the corner, then unlocks her front door and goes in.

The hall is silent and feels cold. She's never really liked this house and will be glad when it's sold and she can move on. People have started looking and the estate agent is confident he can find a buyer without too much difficulty, although he's nailed her right down on the price. Mavis just wants to be rid of it and settled in a little flat somewhere, so she hasn't dug her heels in over this.

She walks through into the kitchen. Whoever buys will have to spend a packet on this, she thinks. Nobody in their right minds would want these awful units and worktops, she decides, as she clears up the remains of her last-minute snack earlier in the evening and wipes a J cloth across the surfaces. Mavis would have liked a new kitchen herself, but she never had the cash, and Dorothy would have hated the upheaval, so it was never an option. She makes herself a strong coffee – she's not used to drinking champagne and it's left her with a bit of a swimmy feeling in the head – and wanders through to what used to be Dorothy's bedroom.

There's no trace left there of Dorothy. The old bedroom furniture has been cleared, although not before Mavis had a good look in every corner and under the mattress in case of a further stash. She's had the old wallpaper stripped and emulsion put on the walls, and the dining room table, chairs and sideboard have been moved in. A cheap, new carpet and some bright curtains complete the makeover. The agent approves, telling her it adds considerably to the appeal of the house, and Mavis, who never thought the house had much appeal in the first place, can only agree with his assessment.

She's currently using the room as her packing HQ, and the table is piled up with things she needs to take with her. Her new suitcase, half filled already, lies open on the floor, alongside a matching cabin bag. She's taken to checking her tickets, passport and currency at regular intervals each day, leaving nothing to chance.

Most of her holiday clothes are new, the result of several shopping trips with Karen, and as she sits with her hands cupped round the coffee mug she turns to look at a line of carrier bags containing shoes and clothes. Sadie the cat comes in, announcing her entrance with a loud miaow, and sticks her head in one of the bags. The tissue paper inside rustles a bit as she noses around.

Aware that something's up, Sadie has taken to mooching about the house calling in a monotonous tone and getting on Mavis's nerves in the process. It's possible that she's missing Dorothy, Mavis thinks, but more likely it's just that her peaceful life has been disturbed, first by the decorators and now by all this packing. Although she doesn't realise it, Sadie also has a holiday coming up – at the West Point Cattery, where Mavis will be taking her in a taxi tomorrow morning. Now, she reaches down to stroke Sadie's black head and is rewarded by a throaty purr.

'I'll only be a few weeks, old girl,' she says. 'It's high time we both branched out and saw something of the world outside this house – and you've got our Dorothy to thank for this opportunity.'

Unimpressed, Sadie wanders off to take a look in another carrier bag.

* * *

11.20pm, quite late for Bill to still be up and about, but relatively early for Karen. She packs Bill off to bed, goes into her study and switches on the computer. She's got plenty of work to get on with but that's the last thing on her mind right now.

As the emails drop into her inbox, Karen's eyes are fixed on the screen, waiting for something to come through from Graham.

There's nothing. Karen sighs, and switches off. She feels tight and prickly inside, as if all her nerve endings are straining. She doesn't know what to do next – text him, email (again) or risk phoning. The possible consequences of each course of action chase each other around in her head until she can't think straight any more. In the end, she decides it's now too late to do anything more about contacting him tonight, switches off the study light, and heads for bed.

* * *

By half past eleven Cathy has her make-up off, her pyjamas on and her bed turned down. It's been a long day, with the prospect of three more performances ahead. Tomorrow there are both matinee and evening shows, with the last one on Sunday evening. There'll be the usual cast party afterwards and Cathy's working on Monday morning so she needs to get as many hours sleep in tonight as possible.

She switches off the light and snuggles down under her duvet. Almost immediately the phone rings.

Cathy's heart pumps furiously. Her first thought is that something's happened to Stella, but she knows she was perfectly fine when she dropped her off less than half an hour ago, so what could possibly have gone wrong in that time? And if Stella's had an accident or been taken ill, who would be ringing her? All this, complete with full-colour graphics, races through her mind in the two or three seconds it takes her to switch the light back on and pick up the phone.

'Cathy, it's Andrew.'

'God, you had me worried. What are you phoning me for at this time of night? I only saw you an hour ago. I was just dozing off.'

'I did try you earlier, but I expect you were with your friends. Sorry if I woke you.' He doesn't sound sorry, and Cathy's concern for Stella and her subsequent relief has now turned into a peevish resentment.

'How do you think it went tonight?' Andrew asks, conversationally.

'Not bad,' she snaps, 'better than last night – except for Carol's freak-out, that is. Amazing, though, the change in her after the break. Look, can't this wait till tomorrow, Andrew?'

'I'd rather not,' he says. 'Not with everyone else around.'

'Why? What's so important? Or so secret?' asks Cathy, although she's beginning to guess.

'Well, I can't help thinking that there may be some gossip tomorrow, about Carol and...er...me. I just wanted to explain...'

'There's really no need, Andrew. What you do, and with whom, is none of my business. Anyway, well done for getting her back on stage,' says Cathy. 'Whatever it took.'

'Ah, yes, well...just wanted to clear that with you,' he says. 'I wouldn't want there to be any confusion, or any bad feeling between us, Cathy.'

'Why on earth would there be? Listen, I really have to get some sleep in, Andrew. I'll see you tomorrow at the hall.'

Cathy smiles to herself as she replaces the phone and switches the light off again. Andrew sounded rather put out, she thinks, a bit of a turn-up for the books. She rolls onto her side and stretches.

I wonder, she thinks sleepily, whether the on-stage magic between us would go if we tried a little magic off-stage? And would that matter anyway, in the long run? Cathy smiles again at the thought this conjures up, and then lets herself sink down into a sleep that is beset by some pretty wild dreams.

CHAPTER 12

A QUIET NIGHT IN

Tony's suggested contribution to the next GenClub
meeting is heroic.

'I'd like to cook dinner for you all,' he says,
by email, to the group. They discuss this amongst
themselves before they get back to him, and come to
the conclusion that it's not a good idea. After all, he's
just a man.

'He'll never find something all the Old Gens will
eat,' says Karen, and it's a good point. 'They've all got
something they're either not allowed, it upsets them,
they can't digest it, or they just don't fancy it.'

'Anything foreign is out of the question,' adds Sally.
'And he won't want to make a roast, which they'd
probably all go for, because it's too fiddly. And there
are ten of us – that's far too much work to expect
anyone to do.' Sally's thinking that if they start down
this road sooner or later she'll have to take a turn
herself, and it's a thought that fills her with horror.

'It's a nice idea but I really don't think it's fair to
let him. I bet he hasn't realised what he'd be taking on
trying to cater for us lot,' says Cathy.

'No, he won't have thought it through,' adds Sally.

'Typical man!' laughs Karen.

Only one voice is raised in Tony's favour.

'But if he wants to do it I think we should let him.
He'll feel totally rejected if we just tell him not to
bother,' says Jo.

They think about this for a bit. Maybe Jo's right. Maybe it's not fair to dismiss it out of hand if this is something Tony wants to do. After all he might enjoy the challenge, men like that sort of thing. And although nobody says it in so many words because it seems unlikely on the face of it, they're all wondering if he might actually be a pretty good cook, perfectly able to cope with a dinner party. Sally thinks, privately, that he's almost certainly better at it than she is. But there are ten in the group, the Old Gens will definitely be difficult to cater for, and it would mean an awful lot of work. It's a tricky one.

It's Jo who comes up with a solution.

'I know – why don't we suggest that he cooks just for us four, and then we can put all the oldies together somewhere else for the evening, Stella's flat for instance.'

'Brilliant!' says Karen. 'We could cook for them at lunchtime and then leave them with sandwiches or something for later. That would work. Well done, Jo!'

Jo glows as she soaks up their praise. It's not often she comes up with such a good idea – or at least it's not often she feels she can voice an idea and risk getting it dismissed as daft.

So, it's decided. Tony is happy to fall in line with this suggestion, and Stella is happy for the Old Gens to congregate at her flat. As soon as an evening is chosen he starts looking through recipe books, and the girls start looking through their wardrobes. And when Jo is out, Don – never one to miss an opportunity – struggles down onto his hands and knees and ferrets about in the back of the sideboard where he remembers an unopened bottle of rather good sherry is lurking.

* * *

The day Sally has been dreading arrives. As arranged, Ian has already collected Eleanor's boxes from university and dumped them all in her bedroom at Queenie's house. Now, on the afternoon of her departure, the plan is for him to meet her off the train in London and drive her to Heathrow. Sally is meeting them there.

She leaves the house with a heavy heart. Queenie doesn't want to go with her and has opted instead for the afternoon with some of her neighbours, old friends who will let her go on about Eleanor without trying to focus her attention onto something else. So on the journey to the airport Sally has nobody to talk to, nobody to take her mind off the imminent parting, nobody to tell her everything will be all right. She puts the radio on, but doesn't hear a thing. The traffic is heavy and she has to concentrate on signs and lanes, but in spite of this all she can think about is losing her daughter to another continent on the other side of the world.

Eleanor's flight isn't until the evening, but she's already made it clear she doesn't want them to wave her off from the terminal building. In fact she doesn't really want them there at all as goodbyes are not her thing, but Ian was a necessity for carrying her luggage from the train onwards, and Sally just plain insisted.

Sally is first at the airport. They've arranged to meet at the check-in desk, and she paces up and down waiting for them, unable to sit down, unable to do anything much. She watches in a detached way as the cross-section of the human race that gathers in such places passes before her eyes, hardly able to believe that in a few hours Eleanor will fly away from her for ... how long? Months? Years? Forever?

It's all starting to catch up on Sally, and she can feel tears pricking at the backs of her eyes. Don't start, she tells herself. Don't let her go like this. Things are bad enough as it is, without you making them worse. She gulps it down, and blinks several times, rapidly. Her eyes clear, and she sees Ian and Eleanor coming across the concourse in her direction, so she takes a deep breath, puts on a smile and steps out in front of them.

'Hi Mum, knew you'd be early,' says Eleanor, giving her a quick kiss on the cheek. She's glowing. She looks happy and excited and more like the old Eleanor than Sally has seen in a long time.

Ian parks the suitcase and cabin bag side by side, neatly lined up. Sally can see he's struggling with this as well, and doesn't dare meet his eyes right at this moment.

'Shall I get coffees?' he asks. 'Or something to eat?'

Poor Ian, thinks Sally. Poor us.

'Nothing for me Dad, I'll get dinner on the flight.'

'No, me neither,' says Sally.

'Well, let's find somewhere to sit then,' says Ian.

There are plenty of empty seats, so it's hardly a question of finding somewhere. They gravitate towards the nearest bank of chairs, where naturally they have to sit in a line as the chairs are unmoveable. Eleanor sits at one end and Sally at the other.

'What time is Ben arriving?' asks Sally, across Ian.

'About an hour's time,' Eleanor replies.

'So late? He'll be cutting it fine for departure. I was hoping we'd at least have some time to chat with him before we went,' says Sally.

There's a sigh from Eleanor's end of the line.

'Mum, I'd rather you didn't stay much longer actually. I'd rather you went before Ben gets here.'

'Don't you want us to meet him? Or is it the other way around?'

Ian turns to Sally and gives her a sharp look.

'What was that for?' she asks him.

Eleanor sits forward on her seat and faces them both.

'I just don't want to drag this out,' she says. 'You'll only get upset Mum, and that won't do either of us any good. Dad, tell her will you?'

Drawn in against his will, Ian clears his throat and turns back to Sally.

'Eleanor has a point,' he says. 'If she doesn't want us to stay...maybe it's best to go before they're called through. It'll only get worse, the longer we're here. There's no easy way to say goodbye.'

There. He's said it out loud. Goodbye. Something snaps in Sally, and she drops her head. A hot tear splashes onto her hand, then another.

'Eleanor...' she starts, before her voice cracks.

'Oh, Mum,' says Eleanor, and reaches across Ian for Sally's hand. 'You see what I mean? None of us can really do this sensibly.' She stands up abruptly. Sally wipes a finger under each eye and looks up at her daughter.

'Now, I think you should both go. I'll be fine right here. I'm near enough the check-in desk to see when Ben arrives and he'll take my suitcases across there for me. I'll phone you first thing tomorrow morning, as soon as we've landed and got our luggage clear of the airport.'

Now Sally and Ian both stand as well. Eleanor leaves them no chance to protest, giving each of them a hug and telling them not to worry, that everything will be just great.

Now that it's come to it, Sally can think of nothing to say. She fights the tears back, hugs Eleanor again and stands back as Ian does the same and says all the things she supposes are right for this situation. Eleanor puts both hands to her lips then turns her fingers towards them. Sally backs away slowly, and her throat is so tight she knows only a good cry will relieve it. Then Ian takes her by the shoulders, turns her around and they walk away together.

It's only later that Sally realises she didn't even say goodbye.

* * *

Sally glances at her watch as she puts her key in the door.

They'll be boarding soon, she thinks.

She goes into the kitchen and puts the kettle on, then sits down at the table. She feels tired and empty. She'll have to call round to the neighbours soon and get Queenie back home, but at the moment she doesn't feel able to do anything. The kettle boils and she makes no attempt to get up. She's still got her jacket on, but can't summon the energy to take it off even though it's warm in the kitchen.

Her mobile phone bleeps at her from the bottom of her handbag and she rouses herself sufficiently to dig it out. Cathy has sent her a text:

How did it go?

I don't know, she thinks. Awful, I suppose. I don't know.

She flips the phone closed and drops it back into her bag. Ten minutes pass. Sally looks at her watch again and imagines Eleanor getting into her seat, doing up her seat-belt, smiling, chatting, adjusting the overhead vent and taking the in-flight magazine out of the pocket in front of her. She can see it all, except for Ben of course, who's just a shadow in the seat next to Eleanor.

Her mobile bleeps again and this time it's Ian.

Chin up. She'll be fine.

Yes, she thinks, she will be fine. It's only me who won't be. Not for a while yet.

Sally gets up wearily, and decides to go and get Queenie while she's still got her jacket on. She's almost at the door when the phone in the kitchen rings, and makes her jump. And for a moment after she answers it, the world whizzes round in reverse.

* * *

'What?' shrieks Queenie. 'What?'

They're on the doorstep, two houses down, and the neighbours are standing behind Queenie not knowing whether to bring them into their house or get them along the road to their own.

'He's dumped her,' says Sally, a bit louder. 'At the airport.'

'Better she goes on her own, then, if that's what he's like.'

'Mum, she can't go, there are no tickets. The whole thing was a con,' says Sally, adding, 'Eleanor's in a real state, she's completely devastated.'

And she's not the only one, thinks Sally, whose emotions have been all over the place today to the point where she can't figure out how she feels about anything anymore. They make the short walk back home.

'I've got to ring Ian. He's nearer than me – he'll have to go and fetch her,' she says to Queenie as they close the front door behind them.

By the time Ian answers his phone Sally is furious.

'You've just paid for a complete stranger to travel home,' she shouts at him, 'or buy a new computer or whatever else he might have done with the cash. And Eleanor is distraught. How *could* you have just handed over the money, without asking any questions...'

'Because I thought Eleanor had already asked all the questions. There's no point in going into this now, I'll get off to Heathrow and bring her back to your place.'

Sally slams the phone down.

'I could kill him,' she says fiercely to Queenie.

'Hardly Ian's fault,' says Queenie. 'These con-men are very plausible.'

Queenie has read something recently in a true-life magazine. 'They look for a weakness, and then work on it,' she says, authoritatively. 'Eleanor's weakness was she wanted a way out of her dilemma, and he came up with the solution, you see. What about the police?'

'I don't think there's much to be gained from getting them involved, he'll have disappeared by now. She hasn't been able to contact him, of course. All we can do is put it down to experience. Ian's lost his money, and Eleanor will certainly have lost any remaining faith she had in men.'

'And what will she do now? Go back to university?'

'I don't know. I doubt if she'll want to face them all again, to be honest. And there's still the baby to consider. We'll have to talk about it tomorrow,' says Sally, who doesn't dare think ahead herself and knows Eleanor won't want to either after this set-back.

And she's right. A few hours later Ian turns up with Eleanor. Going on recent experience, Sally has been expecting her to be belligerent, defensive and withdrawn. She's none of those things. When Sally opens the door Eleanor falls into her arms and sobs.

'It's OK, it's OK sweetheart,' Sally says, stroking her head. 'You're safe, that's all that matters.'

'I was such a fool,' Eleanor bawls through her tears. 'But he showed me the photos, Mum...his family...the chalets...the dogs...'

'Never trust a dog round a baby,' says Queenie. 'It's definitely for the best if there are dogs there.'

This seems to start Eleanor off again, so they decamp to the kitchen where Sally gets her settled at the table, fetches a box of tissues and then makes tea. While Queenie holds Eleanor's hand and asks her a few insensitive questions, which – surprisingly – Eleanor doesn't seem to mind, Sally takes Ian out to the hallway.

'Her boxes from university,' she hisses at him. 'You just dumped them in her room – she won't even get into bed with all that lot there.'

'I'll go and move them,' says Ian, glad of something to do. 'Where to?'

'One or two can stay there but the rest will have to go on the landing, there isn't anywhere else. She's not going to feel like sorting them out for a while, I don't suppose.'

Ian stops on the stairs and leans over the handrail.

'Sally, I'm sorry about all of this, I feel so responsible for encouraging Eleanor. I thought I was doing the best thing by giving her the money, and that's the truth. And how was I to know, or Eleanor if it comes to that? Con-men are very plausible.'

Sally sighs. 'Yes,' she says, 'so my mother tells me. Just do me a favour, Ian, keep your chequebook to yourself in future unless it's something we've discussed together. This whole episode has been very traumatic for all of us.'

From the kitchen comes the sound of Eleanor blowing her nose again.

'And I've no idea where we go from here,' she adds.

* * *

By the end of the week Sally has regained her composure enough to contemplate Tony's dinner party. Meanwhile, Eleanor is quietly brooding on Ben's defection, and spends most of her time mooching aimlessly around the house. Tonight she'll be on her own for the first time, since Queenie is all set to spend the evening at Stella's flat with the rest of the Old Gens. So far she hasn't shown much interest in what her mother and grandmother are getting up to this evening, and is already settled in front of the TV with a bar of chocolate and a cup of coffee when they leave the house. To Sally's relief the worst of the shock and disappointment seems to have passed.

'Don't wait up,' Sally calls to her. 'Don't know what time we'll get back.'

'Drive carefully,' says Eleanor. 'Have a nice evening,' and Sally feels this is progress of a kind if she's started thinking about others.

They are the first ones to arrive at Stella's. Cathy has made sandwiches – enough for an army by the look of it, thinks Sally – and Karen's bringing a cake. When Jo and Don arrive, he's carrying a large plastic carrier bag.

'DVDs,' he explains. 'And a box of chocs. Why should you lot have all the fun?' He laughs, which makes him cough and starts Jo off worrying.

'I'll be fine,' he says. 'We'll all be fine. We've got Tony's phone number if there's a problem.'

'Which there won't be,' adds Stella.

Karen and Bill have stopped off at Tony's house to pick up Beryl, and they arrive last of all. Beryl seems glad to be in the company of the others again, after her first encounter with Bill she's a bit wary of him, but tonight even he's on good form. Karen takes her coffee and walnut cake through to the kitchen, then she, Sally and Jo all leave together.

'Be good!' Don calls after them.

'And you lot be careful,' says Karen, as Stella closes her front door.

They stand in the hallway for a moment and look at each other.

'Well, let's go then,' says Karen.

'I hope...' Jo starts.

'Don't even think about it,' says Karen. 'They'll have a great time. And so will we, if we ever get there.'

'I'll drive,' says Sally. 'No point in taking three cars,' and they make their way out of the main entrance and across the forecourt to where Sally's parked her car.

From Stella's lounge window, the Old Gens watch them drive away.

'Now then,' says Don, reaching into his carrier bag.

* * *

By the time they arrive at Tony's house, having turned the wrong way at the end of his road because Sally wasn't concentrating, Cathy is already there. Apart from Tony everyone's driving tonight so the wine is strictly of the non-alcoholic variety, but he's got the cut-glass out and the dining table looks smart and elegant with everything matching and set out correctly. The Gen Club girls sweep a glance over it, and approve.

Tony is a perfect host, settling them all down with a drink in Beryl's lounge and refusing all offers of help. He goes out to the kitchen to check on progress, and comes back with Gnasher the dog in tow.

'He's not normally allowed in here, so I've told him it's one strike and he's out.'

Gnasher pauses at the door, then without looking to right or left makes a beeline for Jo and sits in front of her, gazing up into her eyes.

'This dog is very fickle in his affections,' laughs Sally.

'Well he doesn't get that from me,' says Tony. 'I brought him up to be steadfast and faithful.'

Unused to being the centre of attention, Jo doesn't know what to say or do, but she reaches down and strokes Gnasher behind one ear. This brings forth a tiny yelp, the force of which makes his body jump back a little, and his tail starts an attempt at wearing a hole in the carpet.

'He's moving in for the kill now,' says Tony. 'Look out for the paw.'

And right on cue, Gnasher lifts one paw and places it on Jo's leg.

Just then the kitchen pinger grabs Tony's attention and while he's out of the room Gnasher moves closer and snuggles up on top of Jo's feet.

'I don't usually like dogs,' she laughs, 'but this one is pretty cute.'

She leaves Gnasher reluctantly, when Tony calls them through for dinner. Cooking is obviously something of a hobby with him. Each course is imaginative and nicely presented and there's even a choice of pudding. Cathy thinks the profiteroles might be Marks & Spencer's, but what the hell, she thinks, who on earth makes their own profiteroles these days? It begins to look as if he probably could have managed dinner for the ten of them after all.

'Now girls, I want you all to come upstairs with me,' Tony says, smiling.

'You'd never cope with us all,' says Karen.

'We're having the coffee and cheese in my living room,' he continues, ignoring the laughter. 'And you're quite right, Karen, I wouldn't,' he adds.

So they all troop up behind him, carrying trays and coffee pots, to what was formerly two bedrooms and has now been knocked into one huge room and converted into Tony's personal hideaway.

'Wow!'

'Just look at this!'

On the wall facing them is a huge plasma screen, linked to a hi-fi and home movie system. It's sleek, black and something that none of them has ever seen before outside the pages of a magazine. Tony picks up a remote, clicks a button and music softly floods the room.

They gaze around. There are leather sofas on a pale, wooden floor, with blonde wooden side tables and shelves. The paintings Tony has hung on his walls are vibrant splashes of colours, textured and abstract, and one huge canvas dominates the wall opposite the windows. This room is so different to where they've just come from it's hard to believe they're under the same roof.

'I think it's important we both keep our own identities,' he says. 'I'm not ready for Mum's chintz and polished oak just yet, and she'd be uncomfortable with this lot around her. But this way it works for both of us.'

'And you kept this quiet,' says Cathy, her hand on the top of a guitar case resting up against the wall. 'Are you taking lessons?'

Tony laughs. 'No, you know what they say about old dogs and new tricks. I used to play in a rock band, many years ago. My aim in life was to sound like Eric Clapton.'

'And did you?'

Tony shrugs. 'Well, I like to think I ran him a close second,' he says, smiling, and pouring out coffee. 'We played in local pubs and village halls. I still play every so often, but only on my own – I don't know what happened to the rest of the band, and anyway I'm too old for that scene now.'

'Eric Clapton's still at it.'

'I think he's got rather more pulling power than I have, Sally.'

'Dad said you'd make a good pianist,' says Jo. 'You've got long fingers.' She takes the cup he's holding out to her, paying careful attention to his fingers.

'Did he?' Tony spreads his hands out in front of him and they all look. 'Maybe he's right. Bit late to take it up now though.'

'Oh, I don't know,' says Karen. 'Never too late, Tony. Look at Don with his book.'

They relax into this new atmosphere and then Tony wants to know what everyone's been up to since they were last together. There's a bit of a pause here. The other girls know about Eleanor, but whether or not Sally's ready to pass the details on to anyone else yet is a moot point. Surprisingly, she doesn't hold anything back.

'I'm a bit out of my depth with pregnant daughters,' Tony comments, getting up from his seat to stop the CD that's playing and replace it with something that's got a bit more edge. 'Mine was only twelve the last time I saw her. But in your situation I imagine I'd want to kill someone.'

'I don't know how we'll manage when the baby arrives,' says Sally. 'That house won't hold us all,' she adds, thinking longingly of the granny annexe downstairs.

'Before long she'll probably want her own place,' says Cathy. 'And she'll go straight to the top of the council lists. Not that you might want that for her,' she adds, seeing the look on Sally's face.

'Not if it's on the Westbourne estate,' says Sally, stirring her coffee furiously.

'One of the Horsfield Players lives there,' says Cathy, thinking of Carol. 'I don't think it's all as bad as the paper makes out.'

There's a silence, because they're not convinced. And Sally's intuition is correct here, if Eleanor gets a council flat it will probably be on the Westbourne estate, where there's a rapid turnover of tenants. She doesn't want to dwell on this much.

'Well, we'll just have to see what comes up. So, what's the next show, Cathy?' she asks.

'Well, the pantomime goes into rehearsal next month, but I'm never involved with that. The next play will be in the spring, and we'll be looking at suggestions for that quite soon. I might not be in it, of course.'

Karen slices off a sliver of cheddar. 'That Andrew's a bit special, isn't he?' she asks, popping the cheese into her mouth.

'You could say that,' says Cathy, in as neutral a way as she can muster. 'Good actor.' By way of a diversion, she gets up and cuts herself some cheese, hoping nobody's going to remark on how authentic their on-stage necking looked. It's been said before, often, and she's always been able to laugh it off in the past. Suddenly, that doesn't seem so easy to do. But she's in luck because Tony is shifting the focus away from her now.

'And what's new with you, Karen?' he asks.

Karen rakes her hand through her hair and fluffs the fringe up. She still hasn't heard from Graham and he's on her mind the whole time now, eclipsing everything else in her life.

'Nothing much to report,' she says. 'Oh, I've had a postcard from Mavis...' She looks around for her bag but it's downstairs. 'Well, I'll show you later, but anyway she's having a ball from the sounds of it.' She leans forward again to retrieve her cup.

'Have you done any more about this Tunbridge Wells gig?' Tony asks Jo, who's been waiting for an opportunity to bring it up.

'Yes, I've got the ticket prices so now we can think about where we want to sit. Dad would probably choose the front row – as close as he can get to actually being on stage, but I don't think we really want that,' she says. 'I'm told they play a lot of music from the 40s and 50s, plus some modern stuff, so I'm sure everybody would enjoy it.'

Then Jo does something she'd never usually do. She talks about herself.

'It's the same day my mother arrives in the UK, actually.'

This comes as something of a surprise to everyone except Cathy, who has picked bits of the story up from Stella. Nobody wants to push Jo, so they wait a little, leaving her plenty of space, and slowly the rest comes out until she's up to date, with Jean's visit pending.

'What you said to your Dad was absolutely the right thing, Jo. Life is all about compromises,' says Karen, who knows a lot about meeting people halfway.

'Yes, you're right to do it on your terms, and keep an open mind,' says Cathy. 'Just see what happens. Go with the flow.'

Jo nods, finding herself glad of the opportunity to talk this through. 'I've got cousins somewhere, too. We haven't met since I was four,' she goes on, now into her stride. 'There are some I've never met.'

'Then this might be the chance to find them again, if you want to,' says Karen. 'You could do that through your mother.'

'It would be nice to have relatives, I suppose. I don't really know anything much about them.'

'I could say the same about most of mine, and I've met them all,' says Tony.

Sally takes her hand.

'Families are the most important thing in the world,' she says, and for a moment it looks as if she might start crying.

Someone needs to break the silence that's building up.

'More coffee anyone?' asks Tony.

* * *

By the time they get to Stella's it's well past midnight.

'Mum will probably be asleep by now,' says Sally, as she rings the doorbell.

Stella opens the door, at the same time as a gale of laughter bursts out from her living room.

'Come in, come in!' she sings out, and they follow her into the living room, where every face turns towards them smiling and rosy-cheeked.

'Have you been drinking?' asks Karen.

'Just a small one,' says Don, and Beryl giggles.

'Looks like several small ones to me,' says Sally. 'You know you're not supposed to Mum, with your medication.'

'Oh, piddle,' says Queenie, which makes Beryl giggle some more.

Jo picks up the sherry bottle standing on the table, now plainly empty.

'*Dad!* What on earth were you thinking of?'

'Having a good time, dear. How about you? Nice dinner?'

Bill slaps his knee and laughs, but Karen isn't laughing.

'Come on Dad,' she says, urging him to his feet. 'We've got to drop Beryl off first, you know. And then if I have to put you to bed it'll be the early hours before I get any sleep myself.'

Stella fetches their coats.

'We've had a lovely time, haven't we?' she asks nobody in particular, as she hands out jackets and anoraks.

'Lovely,' agrees Queenie as she gets to her feet and then falls back down into the chair. 'Lovely cake, Karen. Lovely sandwiches.'

Sally takes her mother's elbow, hauls her up again and then gets her into her tweed jacket.

'Goodnight, sweetheart...' Don sings to Stella, as he plants a kiss on her cheek. Bill puts his arm round Beryl's shoulders as Karen ushers them out of the door.

'I don't know what your son's going to say when he sees you,' she says to Beryl, who smiles up at her engagingly and replies, 'He'll probably say, "Go to your room you naughty old thing!"'

Behind them, Stella laughs as she closes the front door.

BERYL

I can't quite remember how long I've lived in this house, but I could probably work it out because the twins were about four when we moved in. My husband was in the building trade, and his parents gave him the land because it used to be a part of their garden – huge, it was – and he had this house built. Up till then we'd been living next door with my in-laws until our house was ready to move into. It hadn't changed much over the years, just a bit of decorating now and then, until Tony put my little extension on the back and then did up the kitchen and his room upstairs. But it feels just the same to me, it's a comfortable house and I'm comfortable in it.

When the boys were small they were such good friends for each other. Most of the time they didn't need other children around them, they just liked playing together. But then later on they seemed to grow apart. And now Daniel's living over there in Beverley Hills of course they never get a chance to meet up. It's a shame really.

Tony's wife didn't like Daniel. I think that's what started it off. I always thought she was jealous of him because the boys were still very close in those days. She had a temper on her and I know Tony often got the rough edge of her tongue. She didn't like his music, didn't like him being in the band, didn't like his motorbikes. It's a wonder they got married in the first place really. I don't know where she is now, or those three lovely little kiddies. They never get in touch with their Dad and I know it upsets him, though he doesn't say.

Then after the divorce there were other girlfriends. Some he brought to see me, and I suppose there were others that didn't last long enough for that. There was a singer, Fran, and that was quite serious for a time.

She was in a band with him, and they lived together for the best part of a year. I didn't take to her much. She was too hard for my liking, so I wasn't sorry when that came to an end. And after her there was lovely little Susie, a tiny thing, nothing of her. She used to eat like a sparrow, but she loved champagne. They often used to bring a bottle over here when they came to visit, and she'd say, 'Go on Beryl, join me in a few bubbles.'

They were together for a couple of years and when they split up he was more upset then than he had been by the divorce. So was she, actually. One day I'd have one of them here crying on my shoulder, and the next day the other one. They decided it wasn't going to work out for them, Susie wanted babies and Tony didn't, well she was quite a lot younger than him. It was a real pity, but better to find out then than later I suppose.

Last Christmas Daniel sent me a DVD of the family. They've got this big house and lots of dogs, and two of their children are getting married next year, so their boyfriends were on the film too. They all sound so American, even Daniel. I couldn't believe they were really my family, it was more like watching one of those American shows on the television. I won't get over there to see them now, and they all sound very busy with their work and everything so I can't imagine them coming back here. Tony gets cross about it, but what can you do? They've got a life there now, why would they want to come back here?

I'd like Tony and Daniel to be friends again, it's not natural for twins to be so distant with each other. I don't know what I can do to make it happen though, I think it's just something they've got to work out for themselves.

Tony's very much like his father, not only in looks but in his manner, too. He's very kind, generous and easy-going, it takes a lot to get him upset or angry, and he makes me laugh all the time. Sometimes he'll just say something, or look at me in a certain way and it reminds me of his Dad so much. I know he worries about me, I'm a bit forgetful these days it's true to say, but I've always tried to be independent and not worry him. It was his idea to move in here, I wouldn't have pushed him into a decision like that. And it is lovely having him in the house, not that we're always together by any means. But just knowing he's there, it's a comfort.

CHAPTER 13

MOTHER LOVE

Tony has the bright idea of hiring a mini-bus for the trip up to Tunbridge Wells.

'I'll drive,' he says. 'I'm used to driving a van so this won't be problem. And it means the rest of you can have a drink if you want and not worry about getting stopped on the way home.'

'Let's not get the Old Gens anywhere near a bar,' says Karen, 'not after the other evening.'

Jo apologises again for Don and the illicit sherry.

'It wasn't your fault, Jo,' says Cathy. 'Anyway, there was no harm done and once in a while I don't suppose it matters too much. Stella had more fun that night than she has done for years.'

'You didn't have to put her to bed, though. Dad was incapable of sorting himself out, he was all silly laughter and rubber limbs. I don't think I want a repeat of that.'

Karen still can't see the funny side of it. She's been very prickly lately, they've all noticed it though nobody has commented, either to her or to each other. The girls are wondering if it's her hormones. Tony has other ideas, which he's keeping to himself.

'Well, I'll sit with the oldies in the coffee bar, and you four can booze away with a clear conscience,' he says with typical good humour.

'How much does it cost to hire a minibus?' Sally is finding it harder to manage now that Eleanor's home. Her shopping bills are inevitably higher, and her daughter can't contribute anything herself at the moment. She's also aware of all the things they need to buy for the baby, too. Ian will help, of course, but money is much on Sally's mind right now and she's already had to fork out for their tickets to the show.

'Oh, don't worry about that,' says Tony, who sees a good deal more than he lets on.

'But I do worry – we'll all have to pay our share, and I'd just like to know how much we're talking about.'

'It's my treat,' he says.

'Again? You treated us to dinner the other night,' says Sally, now feeling awkward about being the only one to raise the subject of money.

'Oh, that was nothing. Anyway, who's counting? Sally, just leave it all to me, end of story. OK?'

'Well, if you're sure…'

'We'll take care of it next time,' says Cathy, quickly. She's anxious not to make a thing of this if Tony's happy about it, knowing as she does that Sally is finding things a bit tight at the moment.

'Dad's so looking forward to this,' says Jo. 'He's been in touch with a couple of old mates who might also get along, so it'll be a bit of a reunion for him as well.'

'Can't see him staying in the coffee bar for long, then,' Karen remarks, but nobody takes this up.

* * *

They make a jolly party, travelling up to the concert. Tony concentrates on the driving, the girls have a gossip at the back and the oldies seem to have a lot to laugh about. The evening at Stella's flat has certainly been a bonding experience for them, and they're unrepentant about it. Don is as excited as a schoolboy about this outing, and Jo keeps an eye on him from the back of the bus in case he gets too out of breath.

Queenie has been baking and brings out a Tupperware box, which she passes round the bus.

'You'd think we're going up to the Liverpool Arena, not just the Assembly Hall in Tunbridge Wells,' Sally whispers to Karen, 'but she insisted. She seems to like an opportunity to get back into the kitchen every so often and Eleanor thinks we should encourage it. I'll have to make sure that box stays on the bus or she'll be handing them out in the foyer during the interval.'

Karen laughs.

'My mother,' says Sally over her shoulder to Cathy and Jo, 'is on a mission to feed the world.'

'Congress Tarts,' Queenie announces. 'These were Sally's favourites when she was little. I haven't made them for years.'

Stella, mindful of her diabetic restrictions, especially after the forbidden sherry and chocolates of last week, takes a rueful look in the box and then waves them away with a sigh.

'I would if I could,' she says. 'They look lovely.'

Bill, with his mouth full, confirms this. 'Very nice indeed,' he says, spraying pastry crumbs, and then helping himself to a second one as the box goes past him again on its way back to Queenie.

'*Dad*!' says Karen, crossly, and tuts.

* * *

Unlike their last theatre outing, there are clear lines of distinction this time as they take their seats. Without a word being said, the Old Gens cluster together immediately, leaving the rest of the party to organise themselves in their wake. Not wanting to get stuck with the aisle seat again, Jo nips in front of the other girls to end up sitting between Beryl and Cathy. Two seats along from her, Don keeps fidgeting and turning round, hoping to spot his old chums, but the moment the lights dim and the musicians file onto the stage a smile lights up his face, and stays there for the duration.

The first number blasts out at them, Queenie fiddles with her hearing aids, and everyone starts tapping their feet. Stretching his legs out into the aisle, Tony is mildly surprised to find that he's enjoying it. Not his kind of music at all, he nevertheless enjoys watching musicians at work, and can appreciate their skill and professionalism. And on a different level, this trip has made Don happy, which has made Jo happy, which pleases him.

In the interval the girls rush off to the bar and Tony gathers up the Old Gens. He's just leading them through to the coffee bar, when a voice rings out from behind them;

'Don Taylor, you old bugger!' and Don is hi-jacked by two elderly men who are soon joined by a third. Knowing there's no way he's going to stick with them now Tony calls back over his shoulder, 'See you back in the seats after the interval.'

But there's no sign of Don by the end of the break and when the curtain goes up again he still hasn't returned and Jo is getting agitated in case something has happened to him. Stella leans across Beryl to whisper to her.

'He'll be fine, Jo. If anything had happened we'd know about it by now. He was with at least three other people, not on his own, so don't worry.'

But in spite of this, Jo can't relax and she spends the rest of the concert with her mind somewhere else. It's something of a relief to her when it comes to an end, the rehearsed encore has been played, and the house lights go up. All over the auditorium people are starting to leave the theatre, and the GenClub stand about in the aisle, wondering where to look for Don and hoping he'll come shuffling down to meet them at any moment. Then Tony suddenly attracts Jo's attention.

Up on stage, where a few of the musicians are still gathering up their music and instruments, stands Don, chatting to the tenor sax player. In spite of herself, and more from relief than anything else, Jo bursts out laughing.

'He just can't keep away,' she says. 'I bet he wangled it so they could watch the second set from the wings.'

'Hoping for an opportunity to get on and have a blow,' says Tony.

'Which is what he'd like more than anything in the world,' she adds.

They make their way down to the front, and call up to Don. One of his chums is also on stage now, standing with the lead trumpet player and pointing to something on his music. He looks up at the sound of Don's name and peers down to the stalls below.

'Which one of you's little Jo?' he calls down, and Jo gets pushed to the front and waves up at him, less embarrassed than she would have been before the interval drink.

'Jo, you remember Lionel, don't you?' says Don. 'He used to come roller skating with us that summer in Bournemouth!'

Far from being fed-up with them, the members of the band seem to positively enjoy having Don and his friends to chat to and are in no apparent hurry to get on the road. The GenClub doesn't want to prise Don away as they can see he's in his element, so they decide to sit down in the front row and just wait until he's ready to go. It's another half an hour before they actually get away and climb back into the mini-bus.

'Well, no need to ask if you enjoyed that,' Stella says to him as they settle down in their seats.

'Who'd like another tart?' asks Queenie, prising the lid off her Tupperware box again, and at the back of the bus Sally raises her eyes to heaven while the other girls stifle their laughter.

* * *

Don spends the next few days on a mad round of emailing, as his pals around the UK and further afield get to hear about the gig in Tunbridge Wells, and then come back to him with their various questions and comments. He hasn't mentioned Jean again, and Jo wonders if he's forgotten about her in all the excitement, or even better, given up on the idea of getting her down to Horsfield. But her hopes in this direction are misplaced, and a phone call kicks them into touch for good.

As it happens Jo is out when Jean rings, which is a relief, so Don has to make decisions without consulting her.

'She's coming down on the train tomorrow so it'll be lunchtime when she gets to us. I told her to take a taxi from the station.'

The following day is Saturday, and one of Jo's customers has arranged to come to the flat at some time in the morning to collect an evening dress on which she's just done extensive alterations.

'I'll have to wait in till the dress has gone, so I won't be able to go out shopping. She'll have to take pot-luck with what's in the house for lunch so let's hope she's not expecting me to put on a show,' she says.

'I shouldn't think so,' says Don. 'Actually, she asked if she could stay over. It's quite a long way to travel for just a few hours,' he goes on, a bit hesitantly.

'Well she can't stay here,' says Jo.

This is undeniably true, even if Jo wanted her to. Their spare bedroom is now Jo's sewing room, and at the moment she's got yards of midnight blue satin spread over her cutting table, waiting to be transformed into a bridesmaid's dress. Now that the evening gown is finished and will be on its way tomorrow, Jo really wants to get on with her next assignment. She's been hoping to make some headway with it over the weekend, but that's not looking very likely now although she can at least get started on it this evening.

'Nobody used that spare bed for years before we got rid of it, now all of a sudden it seems we need one again.'

'I told her that. She understands we can't put her up and she said did we know of anywhere? I was wondering about the motel. What do you think?'

Neither Jo nor Don has ever been inside the Horsfield Traveller's Lodge but it's been there for years so logic tells them it must be run to an acceptable standard.

'It's only for one night, Dad. How bad can it be? Let's just make the booking for her. It's so close to the station she won't even need a taxi on Sunday for her train, so that's a point in its favour.'

Jo makes the phone call to reserve a room at the motel, and then starts nervously trying to imagine what she'll say to Jean when they meet again for the first time. In her sewing room, she folds and smoothes the blue satin before pinning on the pattern pieces.

Hello Mum? Hello Jean? What have you been doing the past fifty-three years? Have you missed me? How many times did you think of me? At the moment, Jo can't imagine herself saying anything at all to Jean. Everything she thinks of sounds really daft and inadequate for this situation. If she could get a picture in her head of her mother, it might help with the difficult process of working out how to start off that first conversation. She wonders if Jean will be slightly cantankerous, like Queenie, or sweet and cuddly like Beryl. Or maybe she got herself a university degree in New Zealand and she's brisk and analytical, more like Stella. The problem is, Jo's got nothing to go on – no photos, background or information.

She checks the pattern pieces, takes her shears and cuts into the satin. It strikes her suddenly that Jean doesn't know what she's going to be like either, or Don, if it comes to that. In fact, she realises, she's got two of us to face, whereas we can stand side by side and face her together. So she's probably just as nervous about this meeting as I am. Well, in a couple of days it'll be over, she thinks, just one weekend and we're home and dry. Now, how difficult can that be?

* * *

Saturday morning passes in a haze. As luck would have it, the evening dress client calls quite early to collect and pay, so Jo does have a chance to get to the supermarket after all.

It's packed. In every aisle there are couples having rows, children causing rows, and single people like herself getting impatient and side-stepping rows. Jo battles her way through the crowds and picks up some salad things and a quiche, then on a whim goes almost all the way back to the entrance for blackberries and a pot of cream. The queue at the checkout is long and slow-moving, which gives her plenty of time to keep looking at her watch as the minutes tick on towards Jean's arrival time at Horsfield station. Finally, Jo ends up running back to her car so she can get home before the dreaded taxi dumps her mother on them.

None of the pictures Jo's had in her mind's eye come even close to the reality of Jean, and nothing Don has ever said could have prepared her for the first sight of her mother in fifty-three years.

Jean, as she climbs out of the taxi, looks weirdly eccentric. Her hair is bright red, and when she turns around after paying off the taxi driver a slash of scarlet lipstick makes a startling feature in her pale face. She seems at first to have a bandage around her head, but as she gets closer it's obviously a long scarf tied Red Indian fashion across her forehead with the ends dangling down onto one shoulder. On a twenty or thirty-something in the 1960s this would have looked attractive. On Jean, fifty odd years too late for both the fashion trend and the appropriate age, it simply looks mad. She's wearing a black raincoat and white tights, is as thin as a stick, and slightly stooped. She's pulling behind her a large, red suitcase. She is not what they were expecting.

Standing in the lounge looking out of the window, Don mutters 'Bloody hell, girl.'

Jo is rooted to the spot. The bell rings twice before she can force herself out into the hallway to open the door, and in the event none of the things Jo considered saying to her mother as an opening gambit are needed. Jean takes the initiative, and hangs on to it.

'Well, just look at you! Josie, you'll never know how glad I am to see you after that beastly journey. Come here and let me hug you.'

Jo is enveloped in a hug that she doesn't want. She feels herself stiffening and pulling back as her mother's bony frame presses itself upon her, arms locked around Jo's back. It's a strange sensation, and not a pleasant one. It seems to last a very long time. Finally, Jean releases her, takes half a step back and scrutinises her carefully.

'You look very much like your father, Josie. Well, never mind. I know I have no claims on you, looks or otherwise.' She holds up a hand. 'No...don't try to tell me anything different, I understand perfectly how it is with us and I've only got myself to blame.'

Jo, who hasn't said a word up to now, is thinking that it's a good thing she has taken after Don. She backs away, pushes open the lounge door and steps to one side for Jean to go through. The red suitcase is standing where Jean abandoned it just inside the front door. Jean takes her raincoat off and hands it to Jo, revealing a white blouse and black skirt, with a black velvet waistcoat. There's a ring on her right hand that, if it's a real diamond, has cost serious money.

Don comes forward to greet Jean with a kiss to the cheek. She accepts this coolly, and with no attempt at any reciprocal contact, far less the intense hugging Jo has had to endure. In those few seconds, Jo can see it all. She's only come to see me, she thinks. Poor Dad, she's not really interested in him at all, he was just the means of getting to me.

'You're looking peaky,' Jean says to Don. 'I hope you look after yourself in this awful climate.'

'It's the emphysema,' says Don. 'Too many years in smoky nightclubs, breathing in second hand smoke.'

'And smoking yourself, if I remember rightly.'

'No, I gave that up donkey's years ago, when Jo was still a baby.'

'I can't remember ever seeing you smoke,' says Jo, the first time she's opened her mouth since Jean arrived.

They sit down, and Jean looks around the room, unwinding her head bandage as she does so and then patting her hair into place.

'This is a nice flat, Don,' she says. 'Small, but you've got it very snug for the two of you. Too small for visitors Josie, is that right?'

'We don't have a spare bedroom now, it's my sewing room.'

'You father told me that. You clever girl! I'm dying to see these dresses you make! Will you show me?'

'There isn't much to see at the moment, the ball gown I was altering was collected this morning and I've only just started cutting out a bridesmaid's dress. You can look at that if you want.'

'I do want! There's so much I want to know about you, Josie.'

You could make a start by getting my name right, thinks Jo, but doesn't say so.

She excuses herself and nips off to the kitchen to organise lunch. This reunion is turning out to be quite different to the way she's imagined it. For a start, it begins to look as if a little of Jean will go quite a long way, but that's not all. Her attitude towards Don is aloof and distant, and given the circumstances of their parting all those years ago, Jo reckons he deserves better than that.

I can't leave them alone together for long, Jo thinks. Poor Dad will never be able to cope with her. In a panic, she sets the table at a furious pace and puts out the food, thinking that if they can just get this visit over with, as quickly as possible, then Jean will go and life can get back to normal again. Her mind wanders back to the suitcase in the hall. I'll get her down to the Lodge as soon as it's decent to do so, she thinks. From the lounge, she can only hear Jean's voice, Don doesn't seem to be contributing much to the conversation. She calls them through for lunch.

'Oh, you darling girl, you've gone to so much trouble. And I'm such a poor eater, you know. Still, I shall try everything here,' says Jean as she perches on one of the dining chairs. Don has insisted that they have a bottle of wine, on the basis that it'll help to break the ice. He reaches into the fridge for it.

'Still drinking, Don? You didn't give that up with the cigarettes then?'

'Once in a blue moon,' says Don, amiably. 'And I thought as this was a special occasion…'

'Oh, it is, it is. You're so right. Very, very special.'

Don fills their glasses, and half-fills his own. He's about to propose a small toast, something about reunions, when Jean cuts in on him and hijacks it for herself.

'Here's to you, Josie. Good luck in everything you do and all your adventures. I hope you do have adventures?' Jean sips a little wine and takes a tiny amount of salad and a piece of bread. Jo's hoping they aren't going to hear too much about Jean's adventures, whatever they may be, but is saved from replying about her own.

'Jo has a very full life,' says Don, and is all set to start telling Jean about the Generation Club, but he's too slow off the mark and she slips in with a story of her own.

'Beastly long flight from New Zealand,' she says. 'But I had the good fortune to sit next to a very interesting man, Kiwi of course, born and bred. Now, he was telling me …'

Jo and Don eat their lunch. Jean talks, and uses the bread to push a few bits of lettuce around her plate, then later manages a blackberry or two. Jo makes coffee and puts chocolates on the table. Jean has seven of them and several refills of strong, black coffee.

'Now you'll want to see my old place in Auckland,' she says, getting up to go into the lounge and rummage in her handbag for photos. Jo and Don look at each other while she's out of the room.

'No, I don't think we do,' mutters Don, wheezily. 'Sorry, sweetheart,' he adds, reaching across the table for Jo's hand. She smiles back at him, and sighs.

'Here we are,' says Jean, bringing in two albums, and Jo can tell there'll be about a hundred photos in each. She clears some of the things from the table and prepares for a long session.

Jean's house – owned or rented, she doesn't make this clear – is an impressively large mansion with a swimming pool in the grounds and a circular drive at the front. There seem to be a lot of people of varying ages in every photo taken at this place, some of whom appear to be living there with her, although the relationship between any of them or their connection to Jean is not mentioned. She simply gives their names as she goes through her narrative. 'This is Daphne again, with John and Anne-Marie...' Jo's wondering if it's a commune of some sort. The photos become more general as they go off into the bush with Jean, on various holidays around both islands and then into the city of Auckland.

They finally reach the last photo, after at least an hour, and Don says something about how interesting it looks over in New Zealand.

'Well, yes, it is. And one has one's friends there now, so many of them. It's quite a social life, you know. Different to England, of course, but that's a good thing in my view.'

'I think we should be getting you down to the Traveller's Lodge, to check in,' says Jo. 'We don't want to lose the room, and they do get quite busy there.'

'We think you'll be very comfortable there,' says Don.

'And it's right near the station, so you won't need a taxi tomorrow to get to your train.'

Jean looks up at Jo in surprise.

'Tomorrow?' she says. 'Oh my dear, I'm not leaving you that quickly. I haven't come all this way for just one afternoon. A few days at the least, maybe a week – I suppose that will be all right with the hotel?'

There is a moment's silence.

'Well, you'll have to ask them,' Jo manages, weakly. She glances at Don, who has his arms crossed over his chest, and is blinking rapidly.

'We didn't realise that was your plan, Jean. There are things we're already committed to during the week,' he lies.

'No matter, Don,' Jean laughs. 'I can amuse myself for a few hours, you know. I managed to come all the way here on my own, after all.'

Jo drives Jean to the motel, takes her suitcase in for her, and they wait together in the reception area. Finally, someone attends to them and sweeps Jean off towards the lifts, but not before she's had time to kiss Jo and give her another bony hug.

'This is so nice,' she says, 'getting to know each other at long last, Josie. Maybe tomorrow you could show me the sights of Horsfield, just the two of us, eh?'

'There aren't any sights,' says Jo, 'it's just an old market town.'

'Well then, the shops. Let's go shopping together – they tell me most of your shops open on a Sunday these days. And we could have coffee somewhere and watch the world go by. Wouldn't that be fun?' Jean claps her hands, and Jo's heart sinks a little further.

She makes a dash for it when the lift comes, and doesn't look back.

Back at home, Don is listening to the CD he bought at Tunbridge Wells and picking over the remains of the box of chocolates. He offers them up to Jo as she comes in, but she shakes her head.

'You finish them, Dad. I think she had all the best ones anyway.'

'Mmm, we're only left with the creams,' says Don, squinting at the little menu, but he pops one in his mouth anyway.

Jo sits next to him on the sofa and puts her head back. She's still got her coat on with her hands in the pockets. She sits up and turns to look at him.

'Are you all right Dad? You look exhausted.'

'I am exhausted. Aren't you?'

'I've got a headache,' Jo admits.

'I've got earache,' says Don, and laughs a wheezy laugh.

'Was she always like this?'

'Not that I remember. I'm sorry Jo, I never expected that she'd turn out to be so eccentric and full of herself. There was no hint in the emails.'

'That's the trouble with emails, they're just shorthand messages. You'd have been able to tell more from letters I expect.'

They fall silent, both thinking about the rest of the week that lies ahead.

'Any ideas?' says Don.

'Not really. We've just got to get through it now. She wants me to go shopping with her tomorrow.'

'Oh dear. Can you face that?'

'I'll have to try.' Jo sighs and leans back again on the sofa. 'I think I'll go for a walk Dad, try to clear my head. Are you OK for a bit? I'll get supper later, if you want something.'

'I might just go to bed,' says Don. 'Or maybe a lettuce leaf to wipe round a plate?'

They laugh, co-conspirators, on the same side again. Jo kisses the top of Don's head, and leaves the flat.

She walks briskly, in the opposite direction to the Traveller's Lodge, just in case Jean has a room facing the street and spots her below. She heads for the park, and cuts through to the Old Town and the parish church.

The trees are turning colour, and already there are crunchy leaves on the paths and the pavement beyond the park. It's the time of year Jo likes best, but this afternoon she's really not enjoying it to the full.

I should have stuck to my guns, she thinks. I should have followed my gut instinct and refused to see her, no matter how persuasive Dad was.

Jo rustles up some leaves as she walks, and hardly notices anything else round her. She knows Don has been hoping that the two of them would be able to connect on some level, that the blood tie would, in the end, overcome decades of estrangement. Even if Jean went back to New Zealand and they never subsequently saw each other again it would be enough for Don to know that they'd closed the circle. But Jo has never had any realistic hopes of that. She just wants to know why Jean went, to understand what drove her mother to go in such a bizarre fashion.

As it is, Jo is completely unable to relate to Jean in any way, and this is bewildering to her. All the evidence points to the fact that she's nothing like her mother. But that can't be right, she thinks, surely everyone takes something from both parents. It's as if the woman who arrived at their flat today isn't the real Jean, but a caricature, or an impostor. Don says she wasn't overbearing and self-centred fifty years ago, although the warning signs must have been there when she walked out, which probably answers the long-standing question of why she walked out.

Jo's mind is in overdrive. On the one hand she's trying to come to terms with the reality of Jean, and on the other hand she's trying to think of a way of getting her mother out of town and out of their lives again. She's shaken from this absorption when a car stops opposite and the driver calls across the road to her. She looks up and sees Tony waving at her.

'I thought it was you,' he says, as she reaches the car, 'so I turned round and came back – how's it going?'

Jo pulls a face. 'Don't ask,' she says. 'Pretty bad. I'm walking off a headache.'

'Hop in,' he says, 'and tell me about it.'

They park alongside the church path, and Jo describes her mother to Tony, and the way the afternoon has turned out. It begins to look less desperate as she tells the story, as if putting it into words for someone else's benefit takes the sting out of it. There are parts that even start to seem funny.

'I'm trying to figure out now how I can get rid of her,' she says.

'You could inject cyanide into the chocolates,' says Tony. 'Go for the hard centres.'

'That had crossed my mind.'

'Or just tell her it's not working, thanks for coming but now it's time to move on.' But Jo shakes her head, and he knows she wouldn't be capable of doing something as bold as that, even though Jean sounds like a woman with skin as thick as shoe leather, who's hardly likely to take offence.

'OK, then. Here's a short-term solution that might save your sanity,' he says. 'Why don't you both come over to us for dinner tomorrow evening, tell her it's a long-standing arrangement you can't break.'

'Well,' she says, turning the idea over, 'that's a thought. I could suggest it to Dad.'

Tony makes a show of adjusting the rear mirror. 'And if Don doesn't want to come out there's no need for Jean to know that, and you could come on your own,' he says, casually. 'As long as he'd be OK for a couple of hours.'

Jo's tries this scenario out in her mind. She pictures Tony's streamlined living-room, with the cream leather sofas and the hi-tech equipment that she wouldn't even know how to turn on. She tries to visualise herself in the picture without the GenClub girls around for moral support and finds, surprisingly, that she can do it with ease.

'What do you think?' he asks.

Secretly she's thinking that this variation on Tony's idea is the one she likes best. But back in the real world, she's still the same old Jo.

'I'll mention it to Dad and let you know tomorrow.'

'OK. How's your head now?' asks Tony.

'Better, thanks.' Jo goes to climb out of the car, but Tony puts his hand on her arm.

'I'll drive you back,' he says, but he doesn't rush to get her there.

CHAPTER 14

BRING IN THE WELCOME MAT

It's 10am, and Jo's just thinking of setting off for the Traveller's Lodge, when the doorbell rings. She has a horrible suspicion it's going to be Jean on the other side of the door, and it is, complete with the same scarlet lipstick that matches her hair and today's special surprise – plenty of blusher and iridescent green eye-shadow.

'Good morning, lovely girl,' her mother shrills at her. 'I couldn't remember what time we agreed, but this seemed about right.'

Jean breezes into the flat, straight past Jo and into the lounge.

'Father at church?' she jokes, laughingly.

'In the bathroom,' says Jo, thinking, and he'll stay there if he's got any sense.

'No matter, we'll get off to town. Let's not waste a second.'

Jo calls out to Don.

'See you later, Dad. If you need me I've got my mobile.'

Jean waltzes off and waits for Jo by the main door. Jo ducks back into the flat to call softly to Don through the bathroom door.

'If I'm not back in two hours I'll need rescuing, so call me, OK?' then she joins her mother and they head for the car-park.

The town is busy for a Sunday. Jo finally finds a parking space and they walk towards the shops, Jean hanging onto Jo's arm and Jo hoping not to see anyone she knows. In the shopping precinct there's a crowd watching some street theatre, with a man on a unicycle weaving expertly in and out of the people on the fringes and whipping up enthusiasm for his mates at the centre of attention. A couple of overhead banners remind Jo that this is an annual event organised by the local arts centre to raise awareness of live theatre in the town, and an alarm runs through her as she realises that Cathy will probably be involved somewhere. If they run into her there's a strong possibility that Jean will hi-jack any conversation they might have and take complete control of the situation. Plus, Jo doesn't really want to be seen with an eccentric old dame in a bandana and pantomime make-up. She cringes at the thought and steers her mother quickly in the direction of the nearest shop, which turns out to be Bellingham's, an up-market jewellers and the most expensive shop Horsfield runs to.

Once inside, Jo makes a show of looking at trays of rings thinking that once a decent amount of time has elapsed she can move Jean on into the department store next door.

'Which one's your favourite?' asks Jean, leaning in over the glass cabinet and getting her head up close to Jo's.

'I don't know – I never usually wear rings.'

Then to Jo's horror Jean calls an assistant over.

'We'd like to look at some rings,' she says.

'No,' says Jo, 'we wouldn't.'

'Well, I would,' says Jean and the young man obligingly takes out the trays Jean points to and places them on the top of the display unit. 'The topaz – there – and that one also.'

He takes both topaz rings out and puts them on a black velvet cloth. Jo doesn't move.

'Try them,' says her mother. 'It's your birthstone, you know. November – topaz.' She holds out her own hand and the ring she's wearing winks up at them. 'April – diamond,' she says. 'That's right isn't it?' she asks the young man, who nods and gawps at the size of the stone in her ring.

Jo freezes. There's no way she can afford to buy anything in this shop and she's beginning to panic now. Jean picks up her right hand and tries to force one of the rings on but it's too small to go over her knuckle.

'Oh, shame. How about this one, darling? Ah, that's better. That fits you perfectly. Not such a pretty setting though, in my view. What else have you got?'

The assistant replaces the original two and then goes off to find more rings. Jo turns to Jean.

'I don't want a ring,' she says, 'especially not from here. They're much too expensive for me.'

'Josie, your birthday's coming up in a few weeks. I've missed far too many of them but now I can make up for it. I want to buy you something you can keep and this would be perfect.'

'No,' says Jo, who's now feeling embarrassed by the whole unfolding episode. 'I don't want it. There's no need for anything.'

'But *I* want it *for* you. Ah, now what have you found for us.'

Three more rings are tried on Jo's unwilling fingers, and discarded by her mother on the grounds of either style or size.

'Pity about the first one, that was actually the best stone and setting by far,' says Jean. 'I wonder if they can get it enlarged.'

'No,' Jo says firmly. 'It's not something I would ever wear. Let's just leave it.' She strides away and walks out of the shop, with Jean in her wake, and leads her into Barkers next door, where they find themselves initially in the accessories department.

Jean tries on a pair of red leather gloves and looks at the price tag. Then she selects a matching bag.

'Bit old-fashioned in here,' she says to Jo, looking around at the oak panelling, 'but quality goods.' She goes to the nearest desk and slaps her purchases and credit card down on the counter.

'There's a queue, madam,' the assistant says.

'I thought I *was* in the queue,' says Jean, and Jo walks away as she hears the assistant say, 'We don't normally queue that way.'

'Well how would I know?' asks Jean in a shrill voice that carries across the sales floor. 'I'm from New Zealand.'

Further purchases are made in the coat, lingerie and knitwear departments, all stuff that Jean will have to get back to Auckland somehow. Jo points this out.

'Oh, I'll worry about that when the time comes. Excess baggage if necessary,' she says, airily.

The source of Jean's apparent wealth is unknown to Jo, who can only speculate. Maybe a rich second husband, she wonders, not that there's been any hint so far that she married again after Don divorced her. And apart from the diamond ring, nobody looking at her would guess that she had money. It's a mystery.

'I can smell coffee,' says Jean, her nose pointing up and sniffing the air. 'Time for a little break from shopping, I think. Come on, dear, my treat.'

They take the lift up to the second floor and into the restaurant, where Jean buys an expresso for herself and a cappuccino, 'for my daughter,' she announces in a loud voice. Jo tries to blend into the wall behind her and steals a furtive glance at her watch. They've only been out for just over an hour, although it feels longer.

'I'll need to get back home to get lunch for Dad,' says Jo, priming her mother well in advance.

'He doesn't seem to do much for himself,' says Jean. 'What did his last slave die of?' she laughs.

'He's a very sick man,' says Jo. 'It's bad enough having the asthma, but his lungs are in a dreadful state. Emphysema is a killer, you know.'

'Well, if you let it get you,' says Jean dismissively. 'You have to fight these things, not give in to them.'

Jo can feel her hackles rising. She's had about as much as she can stand for one day and this isn't the way it was meant to be. It was Don who wanted to see Jean, not her. She was the one who said she'd walk away if things got to be too much for her, and leave them to it. But Jean has made it clear she's got no interest whatsoever in Don, and like a limpet she's attached herself firmly to Jo. There doesn't seem to be a way to shake her off at present.

They finish their coffee and Jean gathers up her carrier bags.

'Where to next?' she asks.

'The Traveller's Lodge,' says Jo firmly. 'I'll take you back with your shopping then I must get off home.'

Jean protests, but Jo's not giving in now. They make their way out of Barkers and past the jewellers again.

'Pity about that ring,' Jean says, ignoring the fact that Jo has already said she doesn't want it. 'I might just pop back in right now and see about them altering it...'

But Jo is too far ahead to hear any more, and because Jean doesn't fancy walking all the way to the Lodge with her shopping bags, she's got no option but to trail along behind her back to the car.

The room in the Traveller's Lodge is better than Jo expects. It's light and airy, with bright furnishings and a nice bathroom, all spotlessly clean. Jo's plan was to leave her mother at the door and drive off, but Jean has insisted she come in for a moment.

'I've got some photos you might want,' she says, on the way up to the room.

She produces a manilla envelope from the bottom of a cabin bag, which matches the red suitcase, and puts it in Jo's hands.

'I had copies made of these,' she says. 'So you can have the originals.'

Jo opens the envelope and takes the pictures out. There are four of them, black and white in various sizes. Each photo shows Jo and her mother together, and the person behind the camera was presumably Don since they all seem to be holiday snaps. The first one is on a beach somewhere. Jo is a little blonde two-year-old in a ruched swimsuit, sitting in the sand waving a spade in the air and laughing wildly. Kneeling behind her is Jean (although it hardly looks like the same woman), wearing a smart one-piece swimsuit and sunglasses. She has one hand shielding her eyes from the sun and the other tucking her hair behind her ear.

The next two were taken around the same time and it looks as if the first one may actually have been clicked by mistake. They're in a field somewhere, with an old black car parked behind them. There's a picnic rug on the grass, and in the first picture Jo is lying on her tummy, propped up on her elbows and looking straight into the camera lens, with a teddy bear on its back at her side. Jean sits next to her on a picnic chair, legs stretched out and crossed neatly at the ankles. She's reading a magazine.

The second photo in the same place has Jo sitting up and cuddling the teddy to her chest. Jean has put her magazine down and this time they're both smiling at the camera.

The last photo is on a merry-go-round, of the sort that used to be in children's playgrounds before Health and Safety saw them off. Jo's maybe a year or so older, wearing shorts and a cardigan and is holding a gigantic candy floss with one hand, and the safety rail with the other. Her laughing face shows how excited she is. Her mother is sitting on the next seat to her, with a rail in between them. Jean has a headscarf on and dark glasses. She's facing away from the camera, looking at something else completely.

Jo puts the pictures back in the envelope.

'You're not touching me,' she says, quietly.

'What?'

'In none of these photos. You aren't holding my hand, cuddling me, or touching me at all. You look as if you didn't really want to be there. Is that right?'

Jean hangs her coat up and crosses to the dressing table mirror. She messes about with her hair for a moment before she replies.

'It was very difficult for me, Josie, with your father...' she starts.

'My name's Jo. Nobody has ever called me Josie.'

'I used to,' says Jean.

'That was more than fifty years ago – I don't remember that and I can't remember you, if you want to know, because you went out of my life so quickly. And what do you mean, it was difficult with Dad?'

'You know what musicians are like,' she starts. 'He was out till all hours, and I was left at home with you night after night. No help at all with nappies or feeding, or anything else if it comes to that.'

'He was a musician when you married him, you knew he'd be working unsocial hours.'

'I couldn't go on tour with him, not once you arrived. So there was nothing at all to do but be a *housewife*.' Jean says the word as if it's tantamount to *servant*. 'It was different in those days, Josie. Women put up with that kind of life, if they could stand it.'

'Most did stand it, for their children, and some loved it. It depends on the woman. Anyway, you could have got divorced. You didn't have to disappear.'

Jean carries on, as though she hasn't heard Jo. 'And frankly, dear, though one didn't want to have to say this, sex is non-existent when one's husband is out every night. I mean to say, who wants it in the middle of the day, with a toddler running around?' Jean sighs deeply. 'And that was when it was still a possibility, before the *other women*.'

'What did you say?' Jo can't believe what she's just heard.

'Oh, those girl singers in the bands, the little songbirds. They were a prey on weak men, and your father was always one of those.'

Now Jo's getting really mad.

'He's not weak, he's gentle. There is a difference, you know.' Jo's thinking, ask her now, do it now or the moment will be lost forever. There's a heartbeat of a moment's silence.

'So why did you leave *me*?' she says.

Jean doesn't hesitate. It's as if she's been waiting for this.

'Single mothers weren't the fashion then. I had no means of supporting myself, let alone a child,' she says briskly.

Jo stares at her mother, unimpressed. Jean tries again. 'It wouldn't have been fair to take you away from your father and your home.'

Jo says nothing, but her grip on the brown envelope is getting tighter.

'I wanted my life back, surely you can understand that.'

Jo puts the envelope down on the bed.

'I don't want these. They don't show me anything of my childhood that I could possibly want to keep. My childhood, the one I remember, was happy and filled with love and fun, and it didn't need you to make it complete. It already was.'

Jo makes for the door. 'I'm sorry you didn't feel I was worth sacrificing things for. Fortunately, Dad did. He gave up good job offers and tours that would have led to better things, and he did that gladly because at home he had a small child who needed him. Now he needs me, and I think he's worth it, too.'

And then, right on cue, Jo's mobile rings. She gets it out of her bag and sees her home phone number on the display.

'I'll be home in five minutes, Dad,' she says.

She's got the door open now, and Jean's staring back at her with her mouth open.

'Please don't come round the flat again. You're not welcome there.'

And then she's outside. She's shaking, but there's a feeling of lightness about her and she's proud of herself and of Don, and as she walks to the car she's got her head held high.

* * *

Back at home, Don is anxious to hear how Jo got on with Jean.

'It was dreadful,' she says. 'She wanted to buy me a ring – in Bellingham's of all places – and we went into Barkers for coffee. I was terrified of running into someone I knew. Then when I got her back to the Lodge she had some photos she wanted to give me.'

'Not more of Daphne in Auckland?'

'I'd have preferred that, I think,' says Jo. 'No, these were photos of her and me taken on holiday. You must have been the one who took them.'

Jo goes on to describe the photos, and her reaction to them.

'How arrogant is that?' she asks. 'She actually thought I'd want to have them as a keepsake.'

'She obviously had time... to take them out of the photo albums before she went,' says Don, wheezing badly. 'So it wasn't... wasn't a spur of the moment decision, as she told me once.'

'I asked her why she went. I had to know, Dad. She wasn't very nice about you, I'm afraid. And that's when I got cross.'

Jo gives Don a blow-by-blow account. They've never had secrets from each other, and Jo reckons this is no time to start. Don's a mild mannered man, but now he's angry, mostly on Jo's behalf.

'She said *what*?' says Don, coughing on the last word.

'Little songbirds, she called them. And she wanted her own life back – that was how she put it. That's what it all comes down to Dad – we weren't enough for her so she went off to find something better.'

'That's ... an awful thing to say ... to your ... your own daughter,' says Don, forcing the words out between gasps. 'Jo... can't breathe...'

Jo rushes off to get his oxygen. It's a long time since he's needed this, and she fumbles with it in her haste. Don is now hyperventilating quite badly.

'Oh, Dad, I shouldn't have told you and let you get upset by this,' she says, getting the mask over his face and doing her best to quieten him down. 'Now, just stay calm and try to breathe normally... let's do it together... OK now... that's better.'

But it isn't much better, and Jo's getting frightened, although she doesn't want Don to see this. She keeps him on the oxygen and very gradually his breathing settles. He's deathly white, and Jo can't remember the last time he looked as bad as this.

When she feels able to leave his side, she goes to the phone to call the doctor out. As it's Sunday, there's only a message service and a divert to the emergency phone, but quite quickly a call comes back to them and a doctor they don't know says he'll be round in ten minutes.

Don is sweating profusely, and they're both struggling to stay calm. It's a long ten minutes.

* * *

It's the middle of the afternoon before Jo remembers that she left Tony dangling with his invitation over there to supper, and now she really needs to give him a call and put it off.

'Dad's in bed, he had a bad attack this afternoon. I think it was my fault, although the doctor said if he's been overdoing things lately an attack might have been on the way in any case. Too much stress, he said.'

'Why would it be your fault?' asks Tony.

'I told him what Jean said about leaving us, and he got a bit agitated. Then it started,' says Jo, who's wishing she could go back and replay that particular conversation, 'and it was pretty scary.'

'And how did you leave things with your mother?'

'I told her she wasn't welcome here anymore.'

'Well done!' says Tony. 'Good for you. How did she take it?'

'With her mouth open.'

'Ha! Probably not used to being spoken to like that. How do you feel now?'

'Not the best daughter in the world, to be honest. Glad about her, but wretched for Dad. The doctor says he'll be OK in a couple of days, but he's got to rest. I can't leave him tonight, Tony. Thanks for asking us over, but...'

'But ...I could come over to you, if you like. I want to hear the whole story of your triumph over the wicked mother.'

Jo laughs. 'It was a bit like that,' she says. 'I felt great afterwards, like a huge weight I'd been carrying around had just fallen away. Then Dad started hyperventilating and I didn't feel so good anymore.'

'So... come over or not?'

Jo plays with the phone cable, winding the coils round her finger, contemplating. Then her newly confident self perks up and takes over. Why not? it asks her, and she's got no answer to that.

'OK, yes, that would be nice actually. You can tell me if I said the right things to her.'

'You don't need me to tell you that. I'll see you later.'

CHAPTER 15

MOVING ON

At about the same time as Tony's knocking (quietly, so as not to alarm or disturb Don) on Jo's door, Cathy is settling down to watch the *Strictly Come Dancing* results show with a glass of wine and some peanuts at her side. This week it's being screened earlier than usual to accommodate an international football match, so her Sunday schedule, which normally includes a walk if the weather permits, and a visit to Stella, has had to bunch up a bit. Now she's glad to relax in front of the television, safe in the knowledge that she's got nothing else to attend to and the rest of the evening is hers.

This is the moment at which the telephone rings. Cathy tuts a bit, debates whether to answer or not, then hauls herself over to the phone because there's always the chance it may be Stella. The *Strictly* theme music is just starting and she's in no mood for this call to turn into a social chat, but then she can't imagine any of her friends ringing at this time since they would be doing the same as her. There's someone she's forgotten, though.

'Oh, hello Andrew,' she says, with one eye on the television. It's been a few weeks since she last saw him, at the end of production party, and on that occasion they circled warily around each other, leaving little opportunity for conversation. Carol, of course, had been there, with Andrew very definitely in her sights, and Cathy couldn't help but notice that as soon as he left, she did too. Gossip was rife at the time, with much speculation on the outcome of this unlikely liaison and as there have been no rehearsals or meetings to attend since, Cathy has had no contact with him until now. So Andrew's phone call is both unexpected and, at this particular time, unwelcome.

'Shall I pick you up on my way past?' he asks.

'What? When?'

'About ten minutes?'

Cathy is at a loss. Not only that, but the reprise of the first couple's dance is about to start.

'I've no idea what you're talking about,' she says briskly.

'Play readings? This evening? You wrote the date down, I know.'

It all falls into place with a clang. Cathy has made the classic mistake of writing a date in her diary and not transferring it to her calendar.

'Oh, bugger. Do I have to go?' she asks, glancing longingly at her wine, and beyond that, the samba.

'Well, not if you can't. But you did tell Moira...'

'Yes, yes OK. Ten minutes you say?'

Cross with herself for making this administrative error, Cathy immediately hits the record button, and gulps down a mouthful of wine. By the time Andrew rings her doorbell she's almost ready to go and only has to leave him loitering in the living room for a few minutes.

'It's just as well you rang,' she tells him on the way to Moira's bungalow, where the readings are to take place. 'I'd completely forgotten.'

'Oh dear, that would have got you a detention from Moira,' says Andrew, 'and a nasty growl from HiDog.'

Moira, ex head of drama at a posh private school in her native Scotland, is directing the next play. She has three for them to look at tonight, and several of the group have said they'll go along to the reading. At four feet ten, Moira is what Andrew has described as a pocket battleaxe. Whatever successes she had with her pupils, and nobody has any idea of this, the general feeling is that she probably achieved them largely through intimidation. But they can't deny that she does a good job with the Horsfield Players, and in the four years since she retired to Sussex she's been responsible for some of their most celebrated productions. Her methods are different to Barry's. Rehearsals are disciplined, her directions precise, but she's not without a sense of humour, and she likes working with both Cathy and Andrew. Carol would not get a look-in on one of Moira's plays, as she's not in the business of pandering to people's whims.

When they arrive, Moira has already arranged her dining room chairs in a semi-circle in the living room. Her constant companion, a white miniature poodle, is eating from its bowl in the kitchen, but as soon as Cathy and Andrew enter the bungalow it leaves that, starts yapping furiously and then races up and down the hallway.

'Hi dog!' Moira yells at it, and it trots into the lounge and over to her side. If the dog has a name, nobody knows it. Moira always calls it to order in the same way, and the group (none of whom like the animal) have taken to calling it HiDog in private. Andrew has a particular dislike of the poodle, since the occasion when it nipped him on the ankle during rehearsals. Since then, Moira has tended to have him in her arms most of the time. The only occasions she leaves him at home are on performance nights, and that's only because he ran onto the stage on the opening night of the first play she directed in Horsfield.

'The liveliest part of the whole piece,' Stella said later, which was not so much a criticism of the actors as a comment on the choice of play.

One or two other members start arriving. Feeling mischievous, Cathy leans across to Andrew.

'Is Carol coming tonight?' she asks him.

'No idea.' Andrew replies, dismissing the subject with a shrug.

'Oh, shame.'

He looks over at her, not sure if she means it's a shame she's not coming or a shame he doesn't know. Cathy studies the script Moira has given them all, and her face gives nothing away.

'Well, now,' says Moira, scooping HiDog up into her arms and checking her watch briskly. 'Let's get started.' It's half past seven on the dot.

* * *

Sally and Eleanor are watching *Strictly Come Dancing* together. It's not really something Eleanor would choose, but she's got nothing else to do and there was clearly not going to be any discussion about changing channels.

'If I'm not careful I'll get hooked on this,' she comments, settling herself more comfortably on the sofa. 'Next thing I know I'll be voting. If my friends only knew.'

Sally laughs. 'You don't have to watch it.' But Eleanor stays put.

'What's Grandma up to in the kitchen?'

'Making Christmas puddings.'

'So soon? Will they be OK by Christmas?'

'They have to mature,' says Sally. 'When I was a kid she kept some of them from one year to the next because you can't make up a small quantity. They get better with age.'

'Like Grandma!' says Eleanor.

There's a smell of spices and beer drifting through from the kitchen, where Queenie is laboriously measuring everything out into a huge china mixing bowl. It's been at the back of one of the kitchen cupboards for years and escaped Sally's purge when she moved in, on the basis that one day it might come in handy simply because of its colossal size. It takes Queenie ages to assemble all the ingredients, weigh them out and finally mix everything up, but she's in no rush and is perfectly contented because she can do most of it sitting at the kitchen table. By the time the programme is nearing its end, she's ready to start putting the mixture into pudding bowls.

'Oh, that's ridiculous,' Sally shouts at the television. 'He shouldn't be going out. I think I'll write to someone at the BBC.'

Eleanor rolls her eyes. 'OK, Mum, don't get so worked up,' she says.

The serving hatch flies open, and Queenie's face appears.

'Come on,' she calls through to the lounge. 'You've got to stir the puddings.'

Sally never made her own Christmas puddings, so this is a new experience for Eleanor.

'We have to stir, and wish,' she explains.

Eleanor goes first, turning the dark, aromatic mixture over with a wooden spoon. *Let my baby be all right*, she wishes. She hands the spoon to her mother. 'Your turn,' she says.

Sally stirs. *Let Eleanor be happy*, she wishes. 'Go on, Mum,' she says to Queenie.

Let these puddings turn out OK, Queenie wishes.

There are seven small, white pudding basins lined up on the table.

'Do we need this many?' Eleanor asks.

'Well now,' says Queenie, pointing to each one in turn. 'We need one for ourselves, then there's one each for Cathy and Stella, Jo and Don, Karen and Bill, Tony and Beryl, Mavis because she might be back in time... and... who's the last one for?' Queenie looks confused. 'Have I counted them all?'

'Harry and Joan along the road?' suggests Sally.

'Oh, yes, I forgot them,' says Queenie, who's only known them for fifty odd years, and the GenClub members for six months. 'They'll make a nice Christmas present, little bit of holly and a red ribbon on the top.'

Sally smiles at Eleanor, who has a look on her face that indicates she can't imagine anyone wanting to receive a Christmas pudding as a present.

'I'm sure they'll love them, Mum,' she says to Queenie.

* * *

Don hears Tony's voice in the hall, relaxes, and settles a little further down under his duvet. He's feeling weak, and shaken up by what was a very bad attack, but he's relieved to know that Jo's got other people to lean on these days, especially Tony, who Don has a lot of time for. Partly thanks to the medication the doctor gave him earlier, partly because his concerns for Jo have abated, he drifts into an untroubled sleep.

Although she doesn't realise how far she's come lately, Jo finds for the first time this evening that she can really relax in Tony's company and enjoy it. He listens to her, and makes her feel she's got something to say that's worth hearing. And he makes her laugh.

'I feel I should park outside the Traveller's Lodge all day tomorrow until your ageing hippy mother comes out, just in case you're exaggerating.'

'I promise you I'm not!' says Jo.

'Are you glad it's over? Nothing left unsaid?' he asks.

'Not by me, no. It feels good to be able to close that whole chapter now – no longer any reason to keep looking back and wondering why.'

'What if you get like her when you're old?'

'Shoot me!' laughs Jo.

'No, that'll be very messy. A little toxic mixture from the chemist smeared over the top of the lipstick would do the job with much less fuss.'

'You're obsessed with poisons.'

'I think I must've read too much Sherlock Holmes. I went straight on to that when I gave up the Beano.'

'Gosh, that was quite ambitious for a little boy. Didn't you find it rather difficult?'

'Not really, I was 32 at the time.'

Tony stays for a couple of hours and when they say goodbye he kisses her lightly on the mouth, without making a thing of it, as if it's the most natural thing in the world. Which, of course, it is.

* * *

'I didn't like any of those plays,' says Cathy on the way home.

'No, I can't say I was struck. Of course she might not choose one of them.'

'Bet she will. Bet it'll be the last one.'

They arrive at Cathy's house and Andrew opens the car door for Cathy and then hovers on the pavement.

'Are you waiting for me to invite you in?' she asks.

'Oh, that would be nice, thank you so much,' Andrew replies, locking the car up smartly and taking Cathy's arm as they walk towards her front door.

'I opened a bottle of wine earlier – if it's not too Sainsbury's for your palette you could join me in a glass.'

'Wonderful, nothing in the world I'd like better.'

'No need to go over the top, Andrew,' says Cathy. 'It's only a glass of wine, that's all.'

'Yes, well, we'll see about that m'dear,' he says. 'There were peanuts too, if I remember rightly.'

Cathy laughs. Not much chance of me being cross with Andrew for long, she thinks. But although she's heard something on the grapevine she can't resist the urge to find out from him how things turned out with Carol, so once she's got him softened up with a glass of red wine in his hand she fires off her opening shot.

'It didn't last, then. With Carol,' she says.

Andrew puts his glass down carefully before replying.

'There was nothing to last,' he says, reaching for a handful of peanuts.

'Oh? We rather got the impression that you were having your wicked way with her.'

Andrew laughs. 'The other way round, if anything.'

'Oh, poor Andrew, fighting to keep your honour intact. That must have been a struggle for you.' Cathy picks up her wine glass and peers at him over the rim.

'Sometimes,' he says, picking his words carefully, 'desperate measures are called for.'

'Initially, maybe. But Carol wouldn't have seen it that way, she would have thought there was more to it than that. And you can be very persuasive, you know.'

'I've never managed to persuade you,' Andrew says grimly. 'And in terms of being persuasive she made me look like a complete beginner.'

Ignoring the reference to herself, Cathy ploughs on, like a terrier with a bone now. 'I would have thought you'd make the most of it, Andrew, Carol's hardly unattractive. And so young,' she adds slyly.

'That was a bonus,' Andrew says, rolling his wine around the glass, 'and I'm only human, after all. Anyway, dear heart, why would you care? I seem to remember you telling me it was none of your business.'

Touché, thinks Cathy.

'Oh, just Players gossip,' she says, airily.

'Oh, I see. Well you can repeat this titbit of gossip to any interested parties,' he says. 'Carol won't be coming to the Players again, and I won't be contacting her again. Now are you satisfied?'

Not really, thinks Cathy, but I can see that's all the information I'm likely to get out of you.

'Perfectly,' she says, refilling both glasses, though her mind's still full of unanswered questions. 'Anyway,' Cathy says, making an attempt at moving things on, 'if Moira does choose that last play there's a smashing part in it for you.'

'The charming, erudite fiancé, you mean?'

'No, the lecherous old father.'

'Ha!' says Andrew, 'Fabulous! I might get to play opposite you again, as my loving wife.'

'Not likely – I'd be going for the WPC part, there might be a chance to put you under arrest.'

'Even better – handcuffs and all, one presumes?' says Andrew.

'Now now, just because you got the taste for that sort of thing with…'

'Don't say it,' Andrew groans theatrically, making a show of rubbing his wrist. 'You bring back awful, painful memories.'

But then he laughs, and Cathy joins in, and suddenly they seem to be back on their old familiar footing and they're both relieved to have made it there without bloodshed.

Karen's got a lot of work to catch up on, so once supper's over and she's got Bill settled in front of the television she takes herself off to her computer. It's not something she likes to do as a rule, because it seems mean to leave Bill sitting on his own in the evenings, but lately she's let work slip away from her and now she's got to get a grip if she wants to keep her clients happy.

But before she can concentrate on anything, she can't resist checking her emails again in the faint, and growing fainter, hope that there may be one from Graham. There isn't.

Karen can't understand where it all went wrong. He never said anything to her, and although their last meeting was memorable for all the wrong reasons, she had the feeling they parted on just the same terms as before. Now, there's this ominous silence.

It hits her suddenly that if Graham has had an accident, nobody would let her know and she'd just go on wondering, never really knowing what happened. But inside, in her innermost being, she knows this is fanciful and just a device that allows her to ignore the truth. There's been no accident. Graham just doesn't want to see her again, and can't bring himself to tell her so. There's one other possible scenario, and that's the one where his wife finds out he's been having an affair. This, and the not-quite-abandoned accident theory, are her preferred options because in either case it's left him with no choice. It isn't a case of not *wanting* to see her, more not *being able* to see her, which is easier for Karen to handle than straightforward rejection.

With some difficulty, she chases these thoughts out of her mind, opens the file she's been working on and settles down for a few hours work.

And just at that moment, Bill comes barging into the room.

'Karen, come and look at this! I think we went there on holiday once...'

'*Dad*! I'm trying to work!' she snaps, then seeing his face fall she feels ashamed and tries to make it better. 'I'll come in a minute, just let me finish this.'

'It won't be on in a minute,' he says, 'it's on now,' and walks out of the room and back to the lounge.

Karen groans and puts her hands to her forehead.

'OK, I'm coming now,' she calls out. Late night at the keyboard coming up, she thinks.

By the time she's sitting on the sofa next to him, Bill has forgotten that she was sharp with him. But Karen hasn't, and the guilt niggles at her for the rest of the evening and long into the night.

CHAPTER 16

A TANGLED WEB

Karen drops Bill off at the Day Centre and drives back home with an idea taking shape in her mind. Over the past few weeks Bill has been much happier about going to the Centre, so whatever the problem was beforehand it seems to have resolved itself. Sally's theory, and she may be right, is that he's happier generally because of the GenClub, and now that he's spending time with other people outside the house he's better able to take things in his stride.

'It's a confidence thing,' she tells Karen. 'We're turning them into social animals. I mean, look at that night at Stella's – after that the Day Centre probably doesn't seem like much of a challenge.'

So Bill has stopped making a fuss about going there, and Karen now has a day a week to herself. It's a good chance to get on with some work, but the idea that's come to her has nothing to do with that.

She goes straight to the phone without taking her jacket off, because her courage is only waiting for an excuse to go into hiding, and a delay might be all it needs. And then she rings Graham's office number.

'It's about the Chapman contract,' she says when asked to identify herself, and just hopes that particular project – one that Graham had been working on for some time – is still on-going. It obviously is, because the girl on reception accepts this at face value.

'But I'm afraid he's not in the office today,' she says.

This is a setback, but now she's done it once and knows the way through there's always a chance tomorrow, or the next day...

'You might catch him at our Crawley office later this morning, though.'

Karen can't believe her luck.

'I can give you the number...'

Karen writes it on a pad, puts the phone down and then redials.

Once she's got the address out of the girl in the Crawley office she sits back with some satisfaction, and considers her options. She could try her luck at phoning using the Chapman contract again, but there's another possibility – she could get to Crawley and back with plenty of time to spare before Bill needs collecting. If she can just see Graham, face to face... She's not really sure what she'll say, but he'll be the one on the back-foot, and Karen needs to know now. She needs to be able to deal with this and move on if necessary. So she dismisses the phone idea, grabs her bag and car keys, and sets off again.

* * *

Bill's sitting round a table with several other elderly people, and a young girl who's getting them to cut pictures out of magazines and talk about the ones they choose. He's in a chatty mood today, happily chopping up a *Radio Times* and adding to his pile of pictures with an advert for a three-for-two plant offer.

'These need protecting from frost,' he says. 'Can't leave them out all winter without a bit of fleece over them.'

Next to him a frail old lady called Joan is very carefully cutting up a *Hello!* magazine. She puts her scissors down and places a picture of a scantily-clad B list celebrity on the table.

'That's my granddaughter,' she says, smoothing out the creases.

They all turn to look.

'You want to tell her to put more clothes on then,' says one of the other women. 'She'll catch her death going out like that.'

The young girl gathers up the discarded magazines from the floor.

'Could you put these out in the re-cycling bin, please?' she asks Bill, one of the more mobile of her charges, and points to the door to the courtyard. Eager to please, Bill does as she asks.

'It's started raining,' he says cheerily as he comes back in.

'That's OK, she's got her boots on,' says Joan, carefully moving her picture to one side and starting on one of Brad Pitt, who she claims as her grandson.

* * *

Karen drives into the car park, switches off the engine and sits, uncertain of her next move. She could just waltz in and ask to see him, but she'll have to give her name and that might not work. In any case if he's come over to Crawley it's probably because he's got meetings to attend, so she's unlikely to get past the reception area or get him to come down to her.

Her confidence is starting to drain away, and now she's wondering whether this was such a good idea. There are a number of firms within this office block, and as it's lunchtime plenty of people are coming out of the main entrance. She scans them all. The ones without umbrellas make a dash for it through the rain, juggling bags and keys, and the car park starts to empty out as people drive the short distance into the town centre or out to the supermarket. The rain starts to come down more heavily, and Karen turns the key and puts her windscreen wipers on intermittent sweep. She hasn't got an umbrella in the car, so the best thing seems to be to sit it out and wait. She can see Graham's car in the row in front of hers so he's not likely to get past her.

An hour passes, and the car park starts to fill up again as people return to work. And there's still no sign of Graham. Karen glances at her watch. Before much longer she'll have to make a decision about what to do next. Bill will need picking up from the Day Centre on her way back home.

When she looks up from her watch, it's to see Graham coming out of the main door. He's with a young woman and they're both sheltering under a purple umbrella, their heads close together and his shoulders hunched as he bends down to her height. Karen watches them run to his car, watches Graham unlock the passenger side, and sees that he's got his hand on her bottom as she struggles with the umbrella and then flings herself in the open door.

As the car edges forward and then turns a little it comes almost nose-to-nose with Karen's. Graham hits the brake as he recognises the number plate. His mouth falls open, then he says something to his passenger, which makes her laugh. His eyes meet Karen's for a second as he turns the car away from her and heads towards the exit. And his face tells her everything she needs to know.

She switches off the windscreen wipers and closes her eyes. Rain bounces off the car and tears start to build up and hurt the back of her eyes, but she swallows and fights them back. That's it, then, she thinks, my last romance. There won't be any more, not at my age, not now. No fool like an old fool.

She suddenly feels very tired and very sad. The sound of rain beating on the roof lessens after a time, and still she sits there. Immediately next to her a door opens, then slams shut, causing her car to rock a little. Karen opens her eyes and watches the car drive away in a rush. Then she sighs deeply and rouses herself, switching on the ignition and checking her mirrors before heading slowly for the exit, and home.

There's a short-cut she knows of that will get her back to Horsfield a bit quicker and where she can put on a bit of speed, so she turns off the main road and up the hill through the woods, leaving the traffic behind. Karen reaches across and puts the radio on, and immediately a slow sad song comes on, just at the wrong moment, and everything compounds itself in her head. A gulp rushes into her throat and catches, then the road ahead suddenly becomes blurry. She blinks furiously and wipes a hand across her eyes.

And then she sees a shape, a fox, dart out in front of her. She hits the brake, a reflex action, and the car skids across the wet road. Somewhere at the back of her mind she can remember being told that you should drive into a skid, but her actions now are all instinctive. Karen struggles with the steering wheel as the car spins round and heads sideways towards the edge of the road, and the trees.

Now she knows there's nothing more she can do. She takes her hands off the steering wheel and covers her head. The car tilts as it reaches the incline at the side of the road and the back end smacks into a tree, sideways on, before it bounces back into the carriageway.

And then it starts turning over.

Karen's suddenly aware that she's not going to get out of this in one piece, if at all. There's a crash as the car tips onto its roof, and scrapes along the surface of the road, where it meets the trees on the opposite side with a thump.

Her last thought, before the rush of blackness overwhelms her, is for Bill.

* * *

At the day centre, Bill is the last one there. The carers have phoned his home number, and nobody's answering.

'Bet she's got stuck in traffic,' they say to him. 'Nothing to worry about, Bill. We'll wait a bit longer then try again.'

But Bill is worried. Karen has never let him down before, and his worst fears are waiting in the shadows, ready to pounce out and terrify him again. He can't settle in one place, just keeps wandering up to the window and back. Every time he hopes to see her car outside, but it's never there.

'Have we got her mobile number?' one of the girls asks softly to another. They look in the office. Someone finds it. They call, but the number isn't connecting.

They wait a little longer, and Bill comes to rest in front of the main window. He stands there, staring out with his arms crossed tightly over his chest, rocking gently from side to side.

* * *

It's Tony who gets the call from Crawley hospital. At the bottom of Karen's handbag they've found a flattened piece of paper with his address and phone number on it. He can only think that it's been there since the first time the GenClub girls made their way over to his house. It seems suddenly like a lifetime ago.

'And her father?' he asks. But they don't know what he means. The driver, they say, was alone in the car. Tony rings Cathy, who is shocked and can't get her brain to work for a moment.

'What's today? Wednesday, yes, I think it's the Day Centre today. It must be, she wouldn't have left him alone and neither Jo nor Sally have got him. I'll have to go and pick him up, and break the news. Oh, God, poor Bill.'

'And poor Karen. Look, this isn't going to be easy – I can come with you Cathy, if you like.'

'Well if you could that would be great.'

'And where are we going to take him?' asks Tony. They're both struggling to get through the shock and onto a level where they can start dealing sensibly with practical issues.

'Their house, I think, he'll be better at home. If I put a few things in a bag, I can stay with him tonight. We'll think about what happens next after we've got tomorrow out of the way. I'll come by your place in about ten minutes and pick you up.'

'Maybe I should ring the Centre first?'

'Well, if you can find the number – I don't know what it'll be listed under. Don't waste time searching for it, let's just get there. You could give Jo and Sally a quick ring though.'

Jo is in the middle of cooking dinner when the phone goes. She wipes her hands on a tea towel, and takes it with her to the living room.

'Jo, it's Tony. There's been an accident...'

Her blood freezes. Don's safe, in his computer den, and her mind flashes through the others, one by one. She hasn't reached Karen by the time he tells her.

'... and she's in intensive care, but it doesn't sound good.'

Jo struggles to take it all in.

'What was she doing there? And where's Bill?' she asks.

'He's still at the Day Centre. I'm going with Cathy to get him now and she's staying with him tonight. Then we'll have to work out something more permanent, I suppose.'

Don shuffles into the living room, alerted by the tone of Jo's voice. She's got the tea-towel pressed to her face, and she's shaking.

'Whatever's happened?' he asks.

'Karen,' she says, 'an accident.' Then she starts crying and Don takes the phone from her hand.

* * *

When Cathy rings his doorbell, Tony hasn't had time to ring Sally.

'Jo was very upset,' he says, as they hurry down the front path towards Cathy's car. 'I'll have to call Sally later. And get back to Jo, see if she's OK. There might be some more news by then as well.'

It's a miserable evening. The rain has started up again and although it's only 5 o'clock it's so dull that it seems much later.

They pull up in front of the Day Centre, and there's Bill, standing up close to the window glass and gazing out through the drizzle. One of the staff meets them at the door, and she can see at once that it's bad news. They stand in the hallway, talking in low tones, discussing the options and making decisions for Bill that he'll never be able to make for himself. Then they go through to the main room.

Bill remembers Cathy and Tony, though he can't think of their names, but he knows they're Karen's friends and this rings more alarm bells in his head.

'Bill, let's sit down here for a moment,' Cathy starts, and takes him by the hand. 'We're going to take you home today because Karen's had a bit of an accident...'

A great cry of anguish bursts out of Bill.

'No...not again', he wails. 'Not my Karen... never find him... like Maureen...no...no...'

Tony supports Bill as he collapses into a heap. Great sobs convulse his body and strings of saliva join the tears that are running off his chin. Cathy finds some tissues in her handbag and puts her free arm around his shoulders. One of the girls at the Centre comes through with a glass of water and a whispered offer to call Bill's GP.

'We might need him later,' Cathy says to her. 'If you could let me have the phone number that would be a great help.'

'Bill, Karen's in hospital,' says Tony,' and we can't go to see her yet. But when we get home we'll phone again and find out from the doctors how she's doing.'

'... why has he... he done this again... Maureen didn't... she didn't come back... from the hospital...'

'Karen's going to come back, Bill. They're taking very good care of her, and she's doing fine,' says Tony, not sure if he's saying the right thing or not in the circumstances, maybe raising false hopes. How much truth do you tell? he wonders, and looks across Bill's head to Cathy, who shrugs one shoulder and shakes her head as if to say, I don't know either.

They let Bill cry the worst of it out. He's shaking from head to foot.

'I think we should try to move on,' Tony says quietly to Cathy once he seems a little calmer.

'Let's get you home, Bill. See if you can stand up and we'll get your coat on.' Cathy nods her thanks to the girl who's standing in front of them with Bill's anorak. He's very wobbly on his feet, and Cathy's glad of Tony there to support him. I couldn't have done this on my own, she thinks.

Together, with Bill supported between them, they make their way out to the car. As Cathy looks back in her mirror she can see Tony strapping him in and then putting his arm round Bill's shoulders. What a nice man Tony is, she thinks, and how lucky we are to have met him.

Once they get him into the house, he seems to rally a little.

'I want to see Karen,' he says.

'Yes I know, and you will,' says Cathy. 'But not right away, because the doctors have to do some work on her first. Tony's going to phone the hospital again in a little while, to see how she is.'

In the kitchen there's a baffling array of Bill's tablets, and Cathy tries to concentrate on making sense of the labels, with limited success.

'I think I'll ring the GP surgery,' she says. 'There must be an emergency number I can go through to and someone should be able to help. In any case, I think his doctor ought to know what's happened.'

She makes the call from her mobile, outside the front door, and she's in luck. Bill's GP is taking the emergency calls and says he'll be round within the hour. Tony has put the television on, more to establish normality in the house than with any hopes of Bill watching it, but eventually he does settle down with a cup of tea although every so often a small sob escapes from him and he whispers Karen's name. They can tell he's not really seeing anything on the screen.

Tony draws Cathy to one side.

'What's all that about Maureen?' he asks.

'I don't know. Karen's mother? I don't know the circumstances of her death, only that Karen was a teenager when she died.'

'Sounds like it could have been another accident. Poor old Bill.' Tony pulls his mobile out of his pocket. 'I'm going to ring the hospital,' he says, and disappears out to the front porch. Behind him Cathy calls, 'Don't forget Sally'.

He seems to be gone for ages.

'She's in surgery,' he says. 'There's been a lot of internal bleeding, a ruptured spleen, possible damage to other internal organs and some broken bones. I managed to speak to a doctor but he wasn't saying much more at this stage. I explained about Bill, so under the circumstances and because I was the first contact they're willing to talk to me. We can't go in to see her yet, they'll review it tomorrow after she's come back from theatre.'

Cathy lets out a sigh, and swallows hard. Keep going, she tells herself. Don't crack up because you've got to get Bill through this.

'Did you phone Sally?' she asks.

'I'm going to do that now,' says Tony, and disappears again.

It's Eleanor who answers the phone, sounding exactly like her mother.

'I'll just get her,' she says, then yells up the stairs to Sally, 'Mum! It's your friend Tony.'

This brings Sally to the phone quickly, and rather breathlessly. Eleanor looks up abruptly from the television when she hears her mother's initial response.

'Oh my God, that's dreadful. Oh Tony, I can't believe it, how awful.'

Alerted by Eleanor's reaction, Queenie pushes her hearing aids in more securely, and cocks an ear towards the doorway.

But by then it seems Tony is talking a lot and Sally is very quiet. Queenie and her granddaughter look at each other, and Eleanor turns the television down. Sally's end of the conversation doesn't give much away, but then she seems to find her voice again.

'Tell Cathy I'm on my way. And Tony – there's someone else we'll have to contact, though I've no idea how we're going to be able to do this. Mavis would want to know.'

* * *

It's about fifteen minutes later when Sally arrives, and they linger in the hallway, talking in low tones. Bill has refused to eat anything but managed a cup of tea, and is now sitting at the kitchen table staring into space and occasionally wiping his eyes with a hankie.

'I should be getting back to Mum,' says Tony. 'She won't have eaten anything yet.'

'Yes, of course, Tony. I'll drive you,' says Cathy. But he insists there's no need, and flips open his mobile phone to call for a taxi.

'I expect I'll be getting a phone call from the police tomorrow,' he says, while they wait. 'Not that I can tell them anything, but they'll have their paperwork to do, and I'm the only contact number. We don't even know where she'd been.'

'There isn't much between where she had the accident, and Crawley town centre. But I've no idea why she would go there,' says Sally.

'Maybe she has a client in Crawley?' Cathy wonders.

'I don't think Karen makes a practice of visiting her clients – isn't it all done by email?' asks Sally, realising suddenly that she hasn't actually got a very clear idea of what Karen's work entails.

'Presumably there are times when they need to get together, though.'

'Well, I can only tell the police what we know, which is very little,' says Tony. 'We don't even know yet if there were other cars involved.'

The taxi arrives.

'Are you sure you'll be OK now, with Bill?' Tony asks Cathy.

'I'll be fine. The doctor should be here soon, and Sally's staying for a bit, so you go ahead,' she says, her hand on his arm. 'Thanks for everything, Tony, you've been marvellous. I couldn't have done this without you.' Cathy would like to give him a hug, but she's afraid that will be enough to tip her over the edge and another emotional scene is the one thing they don't need right now.

No sooner has Tony gone, than the doctor arrives, sorts out the tablets and gives Bill something to help him sleep.

'Though I doubt,' he says privately to the girls, 'that any of you will get much sleep tonight. Just try to keep reassuring him that she's going to be all right.'

'And if she isn't?' asks Sally.

'We'll worry about that if it happens.'

He's right about the disturbed night. Sally stays till past midnight, and up to then Bill is very restless, getting out of bed and wandering around his room several times, coming out to them and going through the same questions again and again. Cathy finally makes Sally go home, and then she gets herself ready for bed.

Lying in Karen's bed, on pillows that smell of Karen's perfume, Cathy is wide awake and on constant alert. She hears Bill go into the bathroom, and listens for him to go back to bed. Twice he calls out for Karen, and she drags on her dressing gown, goes out into the hallway and puts an ear to his door, but can't hear anything more from him. Finally, in the early hours of the morning, he seems to settle down and sleep, and the house falls silent.

Cathy thinks of Karen in the hospital, and the tears she's been saving up all day start to roll down her cheeks and into her hairline.

'Come on Karen,' she whispers into the darkness. 'Keep going sweetheart.'

CHAPTER 17

PULLING TOGETHER

Bill sleeps late the next morning, and he's still in bed when Sally arrives.

'Did you get much sleep?' she asks Cathy in a low voice, as they sit together at the kitchen table with a pot of tea.

'Not much,' Cathy admits. 'He was very restless and to be honest I was on alert the whole time. I think we both nodded off in the early hours. How about you?'

Sally shakes her head. 'Couldn't get Karen out of my mind. Mum was upset too, and she couldn't settle. She was still in bed when I left, but Eleanor will see to her breakfast. Funny how things work out, isn't it?'

'How is Eleanor?'

'Fine, physically, everything's going to plan. She's still very shaken by the whole experience though. She hasn't contacted any of her friends, for fear of losing face I suppose, so she's got no company except for us and I know she's bored stiff. There's only so much reading and TV watching a girl of her age wants to do.'

'It's a pity that the rest of us haven't got kids around who might have been company for her. She needs to meet some new people.'

'Can't see that happening until she has the baby,' says Sally. 'Then at least she'll get to know other girls in the same boat.'

'What about Ian?'

'Yes, he's supportive, he rings her every couple of days. He'll take care of the money side of things, at any rate, if she wants to find a flat somewhere.'

There's a light tap at the front door, and Sally looks along the hallway. Through the circular stained glass panel of the front door she can see a tall, shadowy figure.

'That'll be Tony,' she says, and goes to let him in.

Too short for the glass panel and therefore a surprise visitor, is Beryl, who is standing in front of Tony.

'We're on our way to the supermarket,' says Tony. 'And Ma wanted to see how Bill's doing.'

'He's not up yet,' Cathy explains. 'It wasn't a good night for him.'

'Maybe best if we come in on our way back, then,' says Tony. 'Jo said she's coming over later, too. I've had the police round, by the way.'

'What do they think happened?' Sally asks.

'They don't really know. There were no other cars involved but it's a twisty road and the surface was wet, of course. They think she may have braked to avoid hitting an animal or something and got into a skid. The car ended up on the other side of the road, on its roof, wrapped round a tree.'

Sally winces.

'Speeding?'

'Possibly, but they didn't comment on that. She knew she had to get back in time for Bill, though. I told them we didn't know why she was there, so at the moment there isn't actually any more they can do.'

Cathy glances anxiously upstairs, not wanting to see Bill on the landing hearing any of this, but his bedroom door is still firmly shut.

'We'll have to tell Bill some of this sooner or later. We can't just let it all come out in a rush, he'll never be able to handle it,' she says.

'Well, I think we need to be careful. He's got enough to cope with already,' says Sally.

'Let's just hope it'll be better news from the hospital later. I'll ring them before I come back,' says Tony, and he ushers Beryl down the path and into the car.

Not long after they've gone, they hear Bill stumble out of his bedroom. He comes downstairs, where Cathy meets him, and into the kitchen. He looks dishevelled and confused.

'Karen's not here,' he says.

'No,' says Cathy. 'Remember we talked about Karen yesterday? And as soon as they will let us we're going to see her in the hospital. Do you remember that, Bill?'

Bill nods.

'Maybe you should get washed and dressed now, then have some breakfast. Sally's come round to help us get organised, you remember Sally, don't you?'

He nods again and lets Cathy guide him back upstairs to the bathroom, but closes the door on her.

'Don't lock it Bill, just in case you need us.'

Maybe he just didn't hear, but the lock goes across anyway, and then Cathy hovers on the landing, where Sally joins her.

'I don't know how much of this he usually does for himself,' Cathy whispers.

'I think assume most things, and then jump in when he gets stuck,' says Sally, who has recently learned the dangers of taking over too much when it's not necessary.

In spite of their best efforts, Bill won't eat anything when he reappears. They make fresh tea and pour him a cup.

'You must try to have something,' Sally says. 'We don't want you getting ill for when Karen comes home.'

'She'll think we didn't feed you, won't she?' says Cathy, taking his hand. A tear runs down Bill's face.

'She'll be all right?' he asks.

'Yes, of course she will,' they say together, and Sally hugs him.

'But it might take some time before she's back to her old self. So that's where we come in, Bill. While Karen's away we're all going to help look after you and the house.'

Bill thinks about this for a bit, but doesn't comment. 'I'll have a piece of toast,' he says finally, 'with marmalade.'

By the time they've washed up and got Bill settled in the front room, where he spends most of his time standing in front of the window, Jo has arrived.

'He's looking for Karen, I suppose,' she says. 'It must have been a dreadful shock for him.'

Tony and Beryl turn up again soon after, with the news from the hospital that Karen has come through surgery but there is no change in her condition. They don't pass this on to Bill.

'I couldn't talk to a doctor,' says Tony. 'They suggested I phone again later when they're on their rounds. Maybe we'll have more news then, and something positive we can tell him.'

'We should let Mavis know,' says Sally. 'Does anyone have Robert's phone number?'

But nobody has. They weren't expecting to have to contact Mavis. When she went away there was no crisis on the horizon that they knew of, no accident waiting to happen. Sooner or later she'll probably get in touch with one of them, and apart from waiting for that there seems to be little they can do. But then Tony has an idea.

'The estate agents must know where to contact her – what if someone makes an offer on the house? There's bound to be a board up outside.'

He says he'll drive back past her house and then go in to see the agents with a request that they ask Mavis to contact one of them, urgently.

They sit around in Karen's house, all on edge in case Bill needs them, all wondering what happens next, all thinking mostly about Karen. But the time needs filling, so Jo tells the story of her mother's visit, which takes a while and helps to keep their minds off the current situation.

'And has she gone?' Cathy asks.

'I suppose so. We haven't heard any more from her, and there's no other reason for her to stick around. I don't go past the Traveller's Lodge though, just in case.'

'Poor Don. How upsetting for both of you,' says Sally.

'I think we're OK about it now,' says Jo. 'Dad's feeling a lot better and back at his computer, and I'm just pleased to be able to draw a line under the whole episode.' She looks up at Tony as she says this, and they smile at each other in a conspiratorial way, which goes unnoticed by everyone.

Clearly, Cathy can't be the one to stay with Bill all the time. She still has a job, and there's Stella to consider too, so the next thing they need to do is work out a rota. Sally agrees to take tonight's shift.

'I'll have to go home to pick up some things,' she says, 'but Eleanor and Mum can cope without me.'

For Tony and Jo, the night shift is tricky since they can't bring Beryl or Don with them, so they take on the days. It's unlikely Bill will want to go back to the day centre on Wednesday, and by then they're hoping Karen will be able to have visitors and someone can take him up to Crawley. In the long term they might have to get a professional night sitter organised, but for the time being they can manage. By lunchtime they have a draft plan in place. Jo opts to stay with Bill for the rest of the day, and the others drift off home – Cathy to have a sleep, Tony and Beryl to unpack their shopping, and Sally to let Queenie and Eleanor know what's happening, and to pack a bag.

Bill keeps his vigil in front of the window.

* * *

Sally arrives home to find her mother and her daughter together in the kitchen. They have some recipe books and the kitchen scales out on the table, and they look up at her as she comes into the room.

'How's Bill?' asks Queenie.

'Well, not good as you might imagine. I'm going over there to stay with him tonight, so you two will be looking after each other,' she says, taking her jacket off and slipping it over the back of a chair. 'We've been sorting out a rota, and Cathy and I are sharing the nights.'

'We've also got a rota,' says Queenie.

'You and Eleanor? Sharing the cooking?'

'No, me and the other Old Gens,' says Queenie. 'We've been talking amongst ourselves – except for Beryl and nobody could get her on the phone.'

'That's because she was with Tony. I've seen her this morning.'

'Oh well, she'll fall in with it anyway,' says Queenie, as if Beryl's got no choice in anything.

'And what is this rota?' asks Sally.

'Well,' says Queenie, 'we decided *everyone's* got to pull together while Karen's in hospital. We're as much a part of this club as you lot, and we're not incapable you know.'

'And I'm in as well,' says Eleanor, much to Sally's surprise. 'I'll have to be the Third Gen.'

'We thought we would start by cooking something for tonight's dinner, enough for us, and for Bill and whoever – well, it's you now.' Queenie turns to Eleanor. 'Flour please, sweetheart,' and Eleanor goes to the top cupboard, which Queenie wouldn't be able to reach, and lifts down the bag of flour. They look back furtively at Sally, waiting for her to raise some protest, but none comes.

'Stella and Don will go round to Bill during the day to give you girls a break and a chance to do other things...' Queenie continues.

'How will they get there?'

'Taxi, or Eleanor if she can use your car.'

'And I'll get any shopping that's needed,' says Eleanor, and Sally has a ghastly moment imagining Eleanor lifting heavy bags of shopping, but bites back her immediate response in favour of a softly-softly approach later on. It seems we're all learning something, she thinks. She pulls a chair out from the table and sits down.

'And Stella and Don are OK with this?'

'Oh yes. Doing nothing isn't an option,' says Queenie, glancing at Eleanor, from whom she has obviously got this, and Eleanor winks back at her to confirm that she got it right. Then Queenie overdoes it by bringing out her other newly acquired phrase. 'There is no Plan B.'

Eleanor giggles.

'Right,' says Sally. 'Well, what's on tonight's menu?'

* * *

It's 9pm, and Cathy has cooked and made an attempt at eating a meal, checked her emails and phoned a work colleague to say she'll be back in tomorrow. It's been a peculiar day, her anxiety for Karen plus the stress of dealing with Bill and a sleepless night are all taking their toll on her. Although she had every intention of taking a nap when she got back home, it somehow didn't happen. She rang Stella, and found out about the Old Gens rota, then Tony phoned with more news from the hospital.

Karen's injuries are extensive, and the doctor he spoke to didn't want to commit himself to any kind of prognosis. Cathy's feeling even flatter after that. All the time she didn't know the extent of the damage it was easier to deal with, but now the vacuum of ignorance has gone and there's no getting away from the full horror of the truth. So far, they've agreed it's best to keep the details from Bill, though how much longer that can go on is debatable. If (God forbid, she thinks) Karen is going to die, Bill should be prepared for it. It's no good them all saying she's going to be fine and then springing the worst shock imaginable on him.

Since Tony's call, Cathy hasn't been able to rouse herself to do anything much. The television's on, but she's not watching it. The idea of sleep is delicious, but she doubts that she'll actually have a restful night. When the phone rings again her heart takes a huge leap as it tries to burst out of her ribcage. She can hardly bring herself to answer it, so for the first few rings she just stares at the phone, dreading that it'll be Tony and daring it to be bad news.

But it's Mavis.

'What's going on there? This strange email has come through and I've tried Sally but she's not in and her daughter answered – don't know what she's doing there and not in university – and she wouldn't tell me a thing.'

It's so clear that she could be in the next room instead of Chicago, and Cathy wishes she was.

'Mavis, it's bad news, and we thought you should know. Karen had a car accident yesterday.'

Mavis is quiet.

'Go on, tell me how bad.'

'It's serious. She's in intensive care, and she's had an operation to remove her spleen and a kidney. She's broken several ribs and fractured her arm.'

'Oh my God, poor darling girl. Was Bill with her?'

'No, he was at the Day Centre. She was on her way home from Crawley to pick him up when it happened. That's all we know. Sally's with Bill tonight, that's why you couldn't get her. We're taking it in turns to stay with him. You can imagine what a state he's in.'

'Is she going to be all right?'

'We don't know. It doesn't look good, but they're doing...'

'...everything possible, yes I know. Oh Cathy, this is dreadful.'

'I'm so sorry to spoil your trip Mavis...'

'No, no, you did the right thing. I just wish I could be there to see her, and Bill, and all of you.'

'We're managing. Everyone's doing their bit.'

They talk for a while, Mavis needing to get the picture straight in her mind regardless of the cost of a transatlantic call. When Cathy reminds her of this she shrugs it off.

'Robert knows I'm phoning you. He's not one to worry about a little thing like a phone bill,' she says.

It won't be a little thing, thinks Cathy, glancing at her watch.

'When are you off to Australia?' she asks Mavis.

'Next week, but I'll be talking to you before then, and I'll give you Martin's phone number and email address so you can keep in touch with me while I'm there and let me know how she's doing.'

* * *

When the shock has worn off a little, Mavis makes herself a strong coffee and takes it into the family room. The children's books and toys are still scattered around one end of the vast open-plan area, because Lori didn't have time to clear them away this morning before she went off to work, and Mavis said she'd do it. But then a neighbour came round and offered to take her off to the mall, and by the time she got back for lunch Robert had already been home and left again. He'd left her a print-out of the email attached to the fridge, where he knew she'd see it, with a message scrawled across it.

Call them soon, he'd written. *Remember 7 hour difference!*

Mavis starts picking up toys and putting them into large, plastic boxes – red for Amy, yellow for Kim and blue for Aaron – but she's not concentrating and they're all ending up in the wrong place. She stands up, with one of Amy's dolls in her hands, and straightens up its clothes absent-mindedly. Still carrying the doll, she goes back to the kitchen and calls Robert's work number.

'Can you get home?' she asks when he picks up. 'I really need to talk to you, soon. Before this evening.'

* * *

Cathy is just dropping off to sleep when the phone rings again, sending a jolt through her body.

'I'm coming home,' says Mavis.

Propping herself up on one elbow, Cathy reaches for her lamp and blinks against the light.

'Mavis you can't. It's so expensive and it'll ruin your whole timetable. You're off to Australia next week – you can't waste that ticket. And you've waited so long for this opportunity.'

'It's an open ticket, so I can go any time. Anyway, Robert's working on that, he's going to try to change it so I can go from England instead of Chicago.'

'But Dorothy's windfall won't cover the cost of an extra transatlantic flight you hadn't budgeted for – it's not a bottomless pit. Listen, we've got it all covered here Mavis, really we have.'

'Robert's paying for the flight home, and don't worry, they can afford it. Get a pencil and paper Cathy, I need you to write down my flight times so someone can meet me.'

It's obviously no use protesting any more so Cathy gets out of bed and rummages around in her handbag.

'OK, go.'

'The first flight I could get is next Monday, with British Airways. I get into Heathrow on Tuesday morning at twenty past nine.'

Cathy writes down the times and the flight number that Mavis reads out to her, also Robert's phone number.

'One of us will be there to meet you.'

'You'll let me know in the meantime if anything changes?'

If Karen dies, thinks Cathy, that's what she means. None of us can say it, but we all know she might not pull through.

'Yes, of course. Mavis – we'll be so glad to have you home.'

'Tell Karen I'm coming, if you can. And Bill, bless him.'

And then there's a click and she's gone. Cathy switches her light off and stares into the darkness. Between them they've got everything under control as regards Bill, she thinks, and if we have left any gaps then Mavis will be here soon.

But more importantly, Karen's made it through another day.

CHAPTER 18

SPREADING THE NEWS

The following day Tony gets a call from the hospital, and it's better news. Karen's still in Intensive Care, and still unconscious, but her condition has stabilised and they're allowing visitors. They decide to drive Bill up to Crawley the next day, Cathy volunteering as it's a Saturday, and Sally saying she'll go with her for moral support.

Bill is pleased and scared all in one.

'How will she look?' he asks. 'Is her face all right?'

'We don't know, probably a bit bruised,' says Sally. The hospital hasn't mentioned facial injuries, so she feels safe in telling him that much. 'But she isn't conscious yet, Bill. And she'll be attached to machines.'

'I miss her, you know' he says.

They reach the hospital, and then it's a long walk up to the Intensive Care unit and Sally takes Bill's arm because he's already stumbled twice in his eagerness to get to Karen, and they don't want another emergency on their hands. He seems to have aged years in the last few days, thinks Cathy, and it's clear that even when Karen gets back home they're going to need a lot of support for a long time.

The unit has a quiet serenity about it. Nobody bustles about in there, and there are no televisions or loud visitors to break the calm. Once they've said that they are there to see Karen, one of the senior nurses takes them to one side for a preliminary chat. She doesn't go in to the details of Karen's injuries, but prepares them for the shock of seeing her wired up to a number of machines.

'She's not awake yet,' she says, 'but do talk to her, won't you, so she knows you're there. She can probably hear you and it might help her to recover quicker. She's got pads on her eyes, but that's perfectly normal in cases like this, it doesn't mean there's any damage to her eyes.'

Then in they go, just Bill and Sally at first, and one of the nurses takes them to Karen's bed.

She's desperately pale and there's a dressing on her forehead, but apart from that there are no visible signs of injury to her head. She's wearing a hospital gown, and, as they were warned, there are pads on her eyes. She's on a drip, and around the bedside a number of machines are bleeping and winking, attached to Karen by multiple wires. Sally sits Bill down on a chair next to Karen and he leans forward. His lip starts wobbling, and when he reaches out to take her hand, he's shaking. Sally puts her arm round his shoulders.

'She's going to be OK, Bill,' she whispers. 'And you've got to be strong to help her, you know.'

Bill presses Karen's hand to his mouth and kisses it. A tear runs down onto her fingers. Sally looks away, blinks furiously and bites her lip. A nurse comes over with another chair, and Sally sits down next to him.

'Hello Karen,' she says, softly. 'Dad's here to see you. Cathy and I brought him here today, and she'll be in to sit with you a bit later. Everyone sends their love and we're all helping to look after your dad, so you mustn't worry about that.'

Bill stares at Karen, and strokes her hand, but he doesn't say anything.

'I expect she'll be glad to hear your voice, Bill,' says Sally, by way of encouragement. He sighs deeply, and his voice trembles.

'You get better,' he says to Karen. 'Get better, and then you can come back home and I'll look after you.' He touches the dressing on her forehead gently. 'You've hurt your head,' he adds.

Then he seems to cotton on to what's expected of him, takes a deep breath, and starts talking to her.

'I wanted to bring you some flowers, but they don't like them in here, that's what they said. There are still some dahlias in the garden, and some of those bright pink nerines that you like, but I wanted to buy you some roses in the flower shop. I think my Maureen would like to have some roses by her bed, I said, but it was no good getting any because I can't bring them in here. When you're a bit better I'll bring you some. I'll get some red roses for you.'

Bill turns her hand over and fingers the plastic bracelet on her wrist. 'Just get better,' he says.

In the waiting area, Cathy is explaining to one of the nurses about Bill.

'He can come in any time he wants to,' she says.

'That's good to know but it's not so easy having to bring him here from Horsfield,' says Cathy. 'Is there any chance they might transfer her to the local hospital?'

'Not yet, but once she's made a bit of progress, yes I should think they'll do that. Are you cousins or something like that?'

'No, we're just friends. She doesn't have anyone apart from her dad.'

'Thank goodness she's got you two, then.'

'There are another two of us as well – no three actually,' adds Cathy, as she remembers that Mavis will be there in a few days time. 'So you'll see us all at some time.'

'She's a lucky girl, to have such good friends,' says the nurse, who's seen it all in her time, 'and so's her dad.'

They stay for over an hour. Cathy tells Karen that Mavis is arriving on Tuesday, and that someone will be back with Bill each day. There's not a flicker from Karen, but they each kiss her goodbye, and Bill gently places her hand back on the bedclothes.

He doesn't say a word on the way home, but the following day, when it's Jo and Tony's turn to do the Crawley trip, he seems a little perkier on the journey there.

'I'm going to tell her about all of you. She'll like to know that someone's getting the dinner for me because I can't cook, you know.'

'My turn tonight, Bill,' says Tony. 'Beryl often likes a roast chicken on Sundays, so that's what we've got for tonight – OK with you?'

But then Bill seems to lose interest.

'Anything will do me,' he says. 'I'm not eating much.'

It's Jo and Tony's first time to see Karen, so they experience the same shock Cathy and Sally had the day before.

'It's all those machines,' says Jo, when they're sitting outside the main ward again, leaving Bill at Karen's side. 'Just makes you realise she's not doing anything much for herself. I can't bear to see her like that.'

Tony takes Jo's hand.

'Early days,' he says. 'Give her time.'

Sitting next to Karen, Bill gamely keeps up his monologue.

'I'm having roast chicken tonight, Maureen,' he tells her. 'Or did he say roast lamb? Well, it's roast something. And there'll be carrots and Brussels sprouts from the garden. You know, I was thinking this morning that those beetroots should be about ready to lift now. I must have a look at them when we get back home...'

It's later that evening that it strikes Tony they should start to let other people know what's happened. They've had dinner and washed up, and Bill's in front of the television with Beryl by the time Cathy arrives for the night shift.

'I was wondering about her work projects. In all fairness, if she's halfway through something then we ought to let the companies know she won't be able to meet her deadlines,' he says.

'We don't know who they are, though.'

'Well, no, but if we email to everyone on her contact list we'd be sure to hit them, plus others who maybe ought to or would like to know.'

'Perhaps we'd be able to find what she's working on,' Cathy wonders, but this idea has the words *needle* and *haystack* written all over it.

And so they go to Karen's computer and find her email addresses. Tony scrolls down through the list of names, but apart from themselves as they come up on the list, they don't know who any of them are. He goes past the address Graham and she used exclusively, which he's no longer checking, and past his work address. He goes past the companies she's worked for in the past and those she's working for now. None of these mean anything to either of them.

'You're right,' says Cathy. 'Send one to everyone then we can't go wrong.'

So they draft something out, with Tony's contact address for replies, and off it goes. Later, just to prove to himself that it's worked, Tony collects the message from his own inbox.

* * *

On Monday morning a parcel arrives at Jo and Don's flat, addressed to him.

'Ah, that'll be our phones,' he says as he takes it from Jo and starts picking the brown tape off.

'Why do we need more phones?' asks Jo.

'Not *our* phones, as in you and me,' he explains. 'They're for me, Stella, Queenie and Beryl. I'd have got Bill one too, but we didn't think he'd cope with anything more at the moment.'

Don manages after several goes to get into the package, and pulls out four mobile phones.

'Lovely,' he says, smiling broadly at Jo and holding one up for inspection.

'Dad, you don't need a mobile phone, you never go out alone,' she says. 'And nor do the others.'

'Ah,' he says, 'but you lot do. This way we're always in touch.'

'We all have landlines in our homes, Dad.'

'This is more flexible and more private – our phone is in the living room, Queenie's is in the kitchen...'

'I don't listen to your phone calls.'

'And it's cheaper to text.'

'You don't know how to text.'

'We're going to learn. Eleanor's going to teach us.'

Jo gives up. The Old Gens have obviously been talked into this by Don, who's then bought the phones over the internet.

'I'll just check with the girls and if you could get us all over to Queenie's tomorrow afternoon we can get started. They need charging up overnight,' says Don. 'The phones, that is,' he adds, with a wheezy laugh. 'But maybe the girls too, come to think of it.'

Don's excited about this venture, and quite his old self again. In spite of the fact that she's rushing about to get out, Jo smiles. It's good to see him like this. She hands him his anorak and checks her bag for house and car keys.

'We're due at Bill's any time now, so Cathy can get off to work. We can't hang about while you sort this, Dad. Can't you do it later?'

'No, it'll work out fine, I'll ring them from Bill's and fix it up. Come on Jo, no time to discuss it now or we'll be late,' he says, zipping up his coat and waving her towards the front door.

It's Jo's turn to cook for Bill tonight, and once they've relieved Cathy and she's explained everything to Bill again she needs to go out and pick a few things up from the supermarket.

'Now, I've got my mobile switched on – ring me if you need anything,' she says from the door.

'Handy things, mobiles,' says Don, grinning at her.

'Don't buy any veg,' says Bill. 'I've got some early leeks ready for pulling and there's plenty of cabbage... I'll just nip out and get us a good one...'

And while he's pottering about in the garden Don makes a few phone calls and gets the mobile session fixed up for the following afternoon.

* * *

Tony is the designated driver, co-opted to pick Mavis up from Heathrow. He gets there in plenty of time but as it happens the flight is delayed by half an hour. By the time Mavis finally comes through the arrivals gate, after everyone else from her flight, she looks harassed and completely exhausted.

'How's Karen?' are her first words after she's said hello to Tony. 'I've hardly slept since I spoke to Cathy,' she says, 'and all those hours crunched up in a plane didn't help much.'

Tony takes charge of her trolley and pushes it out towards the car park, updating her on the latest news as they go.

'Not much change yet,' he says. 'She's still unconscious, but they seem to think she'll be coming out of it soon. I don't know how they can tell, maybe from one of the many machines she's linked up to at the moment.' He loads her luggage in the car. 'It's going to take a long time to recover from this,' he adds, meaning Karen.

'I wonder if Bill will ever recover,' Mavis says.

'Are we going back to your house first?' he asks, because they don't know yet how Mavis sees this working out.

'I'll need to go there first, to drop off these cases and get some other clothes and things organised. A shower would be nice, too. I can't go into hospital today, Tony, I'm too tired at the moment and I'd just be over-emotional. I don't think Bill needs that at the moment.'

'Well there's no rush, tomorrow will be soon enough. You should try to stay awake till tonight, to get your body clock back in tune. And put your heating on when you get in, it's been chilly the last couple of weeks and your house has been empty all that time.'

'No, there's no need, I'm not staying there. I'm going to move into Karen's house with Bill, it's the most sensible solution. That way Cathy and Sally won't have to keep taking turns on the night shift.'

It's obvious Mavis has given this plenty of thought, and Tony doesn't try to talk her out of it. She's right, it is the best solution all round.

'We've been in touch with everyone on her email list,' he says, 'so her clients will know what's happened. Quite why she was in Crawley is a mystery, unless she went there to see somebody about work,' Tony adds, as they edge out of Heathrow and into the traffic.

'She'll have to be the one to tell us that,' Mavis replies, though she's got a pretty good idea in her own mind of the reason why. She's never forgotten how Karen looked after the afternoon when she was supposedly having a girl's day out with a friend, and how evasive she was about it. Now, it seems like light years ago and ever since Mavis heard the news she's been wishing she'd pushed Karen to talk to her about it at the time. Too late now, she thinks.

They get back to Horsfield in good time and Mavis is relieved when they turn into her road and her house appears.

'It's all very well being away,' she says, 'but no matter how nice the place you're staying in, it's still good to get home.'

***

'Right,' says Eleanor, 'so we've got your numbers programmed in, now we're going to try to make a call. So in turn you can each call the person on your right, and that'll give you all a chance to practice answering as well.'

They're sitting in Queenie's lounge, mobiles in hand, concentration etched on every face. Don starts, and he calls Eleanor.

'Hello Don,' she says chirpily.

'Hello Eleanor. I can hear you as clear as a bell!' and they all laugh, because he's only six inches away from her, after all.

'OK, ring off now, so I can call Grandma.'

Eleanor is having a better time than she'd have thought possible. For a start, the Old Gens spoil her in a way the Young Gens don't. Don arrived with chocolates for her, and the old ladies keep fussing her and asking if her back's aching sitting in that chair and does she want to swap with them. There's been no hint of disapproval from anyone, in fact they all seem quite excited by the prospect of a baby, wanting to know if she's thought of any names and would she like a boy or a girl. Beryl has offered to knit her some baby clothes, and although Eleanor knows they'll be old-fashioned little matinee jackets she's touched by this, and determines that her baby will wear them.

But also, the Old Gens are fun to be with. Stella has a wicked sense of humour, and although it's taken them a long time just to get to this stage with their mobiles, they've had plenty of laughs along the way. And because she's got them all together it means Cathy and Sally have been able to go off shopping together, and Jo and Tony can do the hospital run without worrying about getting back. For the first time since she came home, Eleanor has started to feel she's able to make a contribution.

They go right round the circle, with a few hiccups, and then she moves the lesson along.

'OK, now we'll start texting.'

A cheer goes up and Stella waves her magnifying glass in the air.

'Then I'm going to get you all to send a text to your Young Gen,' she says.

'Ooh, this is such fun,' says Beryl, clapping her hands.

* * *

Tony doesn't hang about at Mavis's house. He's got things to do in town, including his weekly visit to the office, where his partner Roger updates him on current projects they're involved in. Tony doesn't really have much input into the business any more, but just likes to feel he's still on the loop. His partner certainly has no need of these visits, since he has everything ticking over perfectly well, but he goes along with it largely because the firm is financed mainly through Tony. They've suffered a bit in the downturn, but not as badly as others because many years ago Tony had the foresight and good fortune to start taking on contracts for the local Council. This has proved to be steady work over the years, but new opportunities come along all the time, and Tony's never been one to turn anything sensible down without a good reason.

The morning's post has brought a proposal in that's worth considering.

'They're an IT firm based in South London,' says Roger, unfolding architects drawings on his desk, 'with a couple of offices in Sussex. We've been asked to tender for a complete refurb of premises in Crawley. Bursting out of their current office there, apparently.'

'So they're doing well?'

'It seems that way.'

Tony leans over the plans, and Roger flicks through the tender document.

'They're tendering separately for the plumbing and heating, so we won't be involved in that. Bit of outside work, but mainly inside,' he tells Tony. 'Could be a nice little job,' he comments.

'Do we know anything about them?'

Roger shakes his head.

'No, they came to us through the structural engineers, this is the third tender Gregson's have put our way – I think there's a Council connection there. I could have a word on the quiet with someone at Gregson's, sound them out first.'

Tony straightens up, considering. He's always cautious at first. You have to know they're good for the money before getting in too far – that's always been his way, and it's never let him down.

'Good idea. Let's not waste too much time on the tender if we don't want to work for them. When's the deadline?'

'Fifteenth of November.'

Tony looks at the plans again, his eyes coming to rest on the client name in the bottom corner.

'Rawson IT Solutions,' he reads. 'Why do I know that name?'

Roger shrugs. 'No idea. I don't.'

Tony taps his fingers on the plans, thinking about the project, but mostly wondering why the clients seem to be familiar to him.

'I'll be in Crawley tomorrow,' he says. 'Maybe I'll take a look at the building while I'm there.'

'You want me to fix something up?'

'No, I won't do a site visit, just walk round the outside. Whereabouts are they based now?'

Roger refers to his notes, but he's only got the head office address in Streatham.

'Give me that anyway, and a phone number, just in case there's something I want to check out.'

Roger folds the drawings up again and they move on to talk about a couple of other issues involving some of the men. Before Tony knows it an hour has passed. Although he wouldn't want to be doing this every day now, he still gets a buzz out of the business sometimes, and it's good to feel the pulse every so often.

He's on his way out of the office when his phone beeps at him. A text, from a number he doesn't recognise.

hello tony, it says. **this is nun lol www**

He frowns. For a second or two it doesn't register, then he realises what it's all about, and bursts out laughing.

hello mum, he texts back to Beryl. **well done xxx**

* * *

Tony drives Mavis and Bill up to the hospital, then goes off in search of the building Rawson's are moving into. It's just off the town centre, and judging from the condition has obviously been empty for a long time. Three floors high, it's a block that was probably built in the 1970s, with no architectural merit whatsoever. Vandals have necessitated the boarding up of the ground and first floor windows, but there's no gate at the side so it's possible for Tony to get round to the back.

He puts his hand up against the lowering sun and squints up at the roof. He makes a mental note that there are patched areas of tiling and places where the guttering is hanging loose, and notices the general condition of the brickwork and rendering. He takes a penknife from his pocket, stabs the blade into a wooden windowsill in a few places and chips out some rot. Then he stands back and looks at the building from a different angle.

And all the while he can't understand why the name of the company is ringing bells with him.

* * *

Mavis and Bill sit on either side of Karen, each holding a hand. Mavis tells Karen about Chicago, and Bill tells her about the lamb chops Jo cooked for him the night before.

'She used our mint from the garden to make the sauce, just like you do Maureen, but it wasn't as good as yours. The pudding was champion though. Can't quite remember what it was…'

'They don't eat proper puddings in the States, you know, not like ours. Anyway those kids eat far too many sweet things the rest of the day in my view.' says Mavis. 'That little Amy is such a naughty thing – learned it from her big brother and sister I suppose – but…'

Mavis stops abruptly in mid-sentence, her mouth open.

'Her hand…' she says. 'She moved her hand, I'd swear it, Bill.'

They look at Karen's hand, as if it were suddenly going to take on a life of its own and start waving and pointing and clicking fingers. Nothing happens, and the relentless rhythmic bleep of the machines continues unbroken.

'I'm sure I didn't imagine it…' says Mavis. 'No! She did it again – Bill, she moved her fingers…'

Now Mavis is on her feet and they're both leaning over Karen.

A nurse comes past. 'Everything OK?' she asks.

'She moved her fingers,' says Mavis looking up at her.

The nurse homes in and checks Karen's pulse, looks up at her screens and speaks to her.

'Hello, Karen,' she says. 'Are you coming back to us, dear?'

She takes her hand and holds it, waiting for the movement that Mavis noticed.

'I'll call the doctor over,' says the nurse, and pads off to the desk where the doctor is discussing something with one of the other nurses.

Mavis and Bill look at each other, not really knowing if this is a good sign or not and hardly daring to speak to each other. The nurse comes back.

'I'm afraid you'll have to wait outside for a bit,' she says.

'I want to stay with her,' says Bill.

'Yes, I know you do,' she replies, 'but the doctor will want to examine Karen and he'll need room round the bed to do that.'

Reluctantly, Bill lets Mavis lead him out to the waiting area when the doctor arrives. They sit for what seems like hours. Someone gives them tea, which neither of them wants. Tony joins them, thinking they'd be ready for the return journey but prepared to stay for as long as it takes. Eventually, the doctor re-appears.

'Mr Kennedy,' he says to Bill, 'your daughter is coming out of her coma. You can go back in for a few minutes, but then she needs to rest as much as possible.'

And Bill's only response is something that's halfway between laughing and crying.

CHAPTER 19

PLAYING POIROT

Tony's inbox has thrown up a lot of replies to the email he sent to Karen's contact list. There are a few from old school friends, one from a man in Canada she once worked with, and two from firms she was working for at the time of the accident. There's also a response from her hairdresser, which makes him smile, and several from people who just describe themselves vaguely as old friends. He replies to all of them, with a promise to keep in touch with news of her recovery.

It's while he's doing this that it suddenly strikes him. Rawson IT Solutions was on Karen's contact list. This is when Tony starts to add two and two incorrectly, though his skill at maths improves later on in the day.

That's the answer, he thinks, Karen had been to see them at their Crawley office. Odd then, that they haven't responded to the email. Maybe they didn't get it, or it found its way through to the wrong department.

It seems sensible to send another one, though he can't do it from home, it'll have to wait till later this evening.

The good news about Karen has spread quicker than a bush fire, thanks to Don sending a group text out, and plans are already afoot for a mini celebration this evening round at Bill's house. Mavis has started to get organised there, found out about the washing machine's little foibles and how to override the central heating timer, but she's got no idea about computers, so it's no good Tony ringing her and expecting her to extract Rawson's email address for him. So when he and Beryl arrive at Bill's, ahead of all the others, he goes onto Karen's computer again himself.

It's not as simple as scrolling down to R, he tries that first and is surprised to find nothing there. It's only when he runs through the contact names again that he finds it. GrahamSJ@ RawsonITSolutions. What strikes him as strange though, is that immediately above that is another address, for the same name. GrahamSJ@ hotmail. So one way or another, this person has had Tony's email, possibly twice, and yet he hasn't replied.

Tony sits back, crosses his arms and thinks about it. Why would she have two email addresses, unless one was personal? And why would she have a personal email address for someone in a firm she was simply doing some work for? And why was there no reply?

On a whim, he Googles Rawson IT Solutions. Their website tells him a bit about the company, but more importantly it lists the four directors, and one of them is Graham Seaton-Jones.

There's a ring at the doorbell, and from their voices he knows that Sally, Queenie and Stella have all come bustling into the house, followed immediately afterwards by Cathy. Jo and Don will be there, too, any time now, and he doesn't want to have to explain what he thinks he's just found. So he shuts the computer down and joins the assembled GenClub members in the lounge.

And they're in party mood. In spite of the fact that Karen's still in hospital, with a long way to go, their relief that she's back in the real world is making them behave as if all their birthdays and Christmas have come at once.

'You haven't got another bottle of that sherry, have you?' Tony asks Don, and Bill laughs for the first time in a week.

'I frisked him before we came out,' says Jo, 'but we do have this.' She delves into her bag and produces a camera. 'We were going to get a card for Karen, but then we decided there was something she'd like more than that.'

'A picture of all of us together,' says Don. 'A sort of wish you were here.'

It takes them ages to get the camera set up on timer, to get everyone in place and in shot, and to get everyone's eyes open at the same time, but eventually and after several goes, they manage it.

The incomplete GenClub are captured for all time, smiling and happy, every one of them looking through and past the lens and straight into Karen's eyes.

* * *

'I doubt now if I'll go till spring. It would probably be too hot for me through the winter, anyway.'

Mavis has had a call from Robert, and when Sally drops by the following morning she fills her in on her revised travel plans.

'He changed that ticket, I don't know how. The money's going back into my account, but to be honest I think he might be standing the loss himself,' she says from behind the ironing board.

'That's very generous of him,' says Sally, watching Mavis ironing a shirt for Bill. 'Are they wealthy?'

'Loads of money, my dear. You should see the house! And two enormous cars – well Lori works as well, of course, she's a divorce lawyer and there's plenty of money in that. Those kids don't want for much, I can tell you.' There's a hint of disapproval in her voice as she says this.

'Spoilt?'

'Not by me. Probably glad to see the back of nasty Granny from England,' she adds, but smiles as she says it. 'You wait – it's not always easy being a granny.'

'It's not always easy being a mother,' says Sally, ruefully, although she's getting on much better with Eleanor these days, and is the first to admit it. Their relationship seems to be getting back on to a normal footing and, true to her word, Eleanor has been on hand to take Mavis shopping, and do other little errands for any of the others during the days of the hospital visiting regime. Not only that, she seems to be positively enjoying it

'You'll have to learn to bite your tongue at times,' Mavis goes on.

'I've already got that off to a T,' says Sally. 'You couldn't pass that tip on to my mother, could you?'

Mavis laughs. 'I wouldn't dare!'

'So will you stay here now until Karen's home?'

Mavis puts Bill's shirt on a hanger and switches the iron off. 'Probably. It suits all of us quite well, as things have turned out. The agent phoned today and it looks as if I've got a buyer for the house, so that can go ahead as quickly as they want and staying here means I can look around at my leisure for something else.'

'Karen will need a lot of help at first, I expect.'

'Yes, I'm sure she will. And physical scars often heal faster than emotional ones. That's going to take longer.'

Sally isn't sure what Mavis is referring to here, but assumes she means the trauma of the accident.

Bill wanders in through the back door rubbing his hands together.

'Chilly out there today Mavis,' he says, finally getting her name right, and adds 'Hello Susan.'

'Must be time for your coffee, then,' Mavis replies, getting mugs and kettle organised. Sally smiles at the speed with which Mavis has slotted into the Kennedy routine, and the patience she shows towards Bill. But he looks older, and more hunched than he did less than two weeks ago. There's trauma here, too, she thinks.

'Now then,' says Mavis, sitting down at the kitchen table while she waits for the water to boil. 'Let's have a look at this catalogue of yours, Sally. I could do with a winter coat now, seeing as I'm going to be here and not in Australia after all.'

* * *

'Let me know what's arranged. I'd like to come with you.'

Tony is talking on the phone to Roger, about the plans for a site visit to Crawley. At least two of the directors plan to be there, Roger has told him. Tony's banking on one of them being Graham Seaton-Jones, so he wants to be included too.

'Your friend still in the hospital there?'

'Yes, but they may be able to transfer her to Horsfield soon. They've done a brilliant job on her.'

'Well if she's still there next week you'll be able to kill two birds with one stone,' says Roger.

If Tony's right, and he thinks he is, he would certainly like to kill one of the birds.

* * *

Friday evening, and Moira is holding auditions for her play. She's fooled them all this time, not gone with any of the dire choices they read recently and instead come up with a comedy called *After Hercule*.

'Not something she's written, surely?' asks Stella when Cathy tells her about it. 'She doesn't sound like a woman who'd be able to write anything you'd laugh at.'

'No, I don't know where she found it, but actually it is very funny,' says Cathy. 'It's a 1930s piece, so lovely costumes and set. And it's quite a clever idea, set at an Agatha Christie-type country house party, the day after Hercule Poirot has been there and sorted out a murder. Except that the little grey cells have let him down this time and he's got it all wrong, hence the title and the comic opportunities.'

'Well that's something different for the Players to tackle. It sounds more like a farce.'

'Well, not really, but there are elements of farce in it. Everyone's at each other's throats because of Poirot's solution being way off the mark. He's added two and two and made fifteen.'

'What part are you auditioning for?' asks Stella. 'Not one of the servants I hope. You want to get something where you can wear at least a couple of gorgeous evening dresses.'

Cathy laughs. 'Oh, yes. I made sure of that!'

'And no doubt Andrew will get the male lead. It sounds right up his street.'

'Mmm. It does rather, doesn't it? Well he won't have to do much acting to play the lord of the manor, he's like that all the time.'

'Let me know how you get on – you could pop in on your way back home if it's not too late,' says Stella, who loves to hear Cathy's theatrical tales.

'I don't know how long it will take, there are loads of people auditioning – it's a cast of seven, and Moira's expecting at least twenty to turn up,' says Cathy, adding, 'so I might not even get a part.'

Stella doesn't say so, but she's thinking that Moira would be barking mad if she didn't cast Cathy in one of the major roles.

'We've had to hire the community hall for the auditions, we'd never all squeeze into Moira's bungalow. And I bet they'll all turn up for this one.'

And sure enough, when Cathy arrives at the hall later that evening there are already fifteen or so Players there and HiDog is in a state of complete excitement, dashing about on the stage. There's no sign of Andrew so far, but Cathy knows he won't try pulling the late arrival trick that works so well with Barry. Moira would simply tell him he's too late and show him the door.

Cathy has chosen to audition for the part of Martha, Lady Hawley. She gets some wonderful lines, and although Cathy hasn't played comedy for a long time, she's fairly sure she can handle it. Andrew is, naturally, auditioning for Lord Hawley, and the rumour is that he's the only one up for it.

A sudden bout of frantic barking from HiDog heralds Andrew's arrival in the hall. He strolls in, ignoring the racket the dog is making, takes his jacket off, puts it over the back of the nearest chair and sits down.

'Hi dog!' Moira shouts, then picks him up in case he has another go at chewing a lump off Andrew's leg.

Andrew runs his hand through his hair and acknowledges Moira first, then Cathy, then the rest of the room. Two or three other people wander in, Moira calls everyone to order, and the auditions start. The smaller parts are cast first, then Cathy reads one of Martha's speeches, opposite Andrew.

There are two other Players auditioning for the part of Martha, so they go next. Andrew is unopposed, so the part of Lord Hawley is automatically his, and rightly so in everyone's opinion since he's the only one who could carry it off.

'Now we come to Robina,' says Moira. 'Jackie and Sarah are up for this one, but I'd like Cathy to read for it too, if you don't mind.'

Cathy is surprised by this. Robina is a large part but not the one she chose, thinking herself too old for it. So she hasn't prepared for it at all.

'No matter,' says Moira, dismissing her excuses. 'Just read it.'

So she does, as the other girls do, in a scene opposite the butler.

At the end of the evening, Moira makes her final decisions.

'Lord Freddie Hawley, naturally, goes to Andrew.' One or two people clap, and HiDog growls a couple of times in Moira's arms. 'Anne, I'd like you for the part of Martha.'

Cathy is disappointed but carries it well.

'Now we come to Robina. Very difficult choice here girls, but in the end I think Cathy just has the edge.'

'Well done,' says Andrew, leaning across to Cathy. 'Nobody I'd like better for my mistress.'

Everyone disperses pretty quickly once Moira's gone through the rehearsal timetable, and in the end there are just three of them left. Cathy's got her coat on and is heading for the door when Andrew calls her back.

'Erm, I was just wondering,' he says, hesitantly, 'if you were free one evening next week? Maybe we could go for dinner somewhere – La Boheme perhaps?'

Cathy's taken aback by this. In all the time she's known Andrew they've never actually spent an evening together, alone. Well, that's if you don't count the hour or so at her house a week ago, she reflects.

'Well,' she says, 'I don't really know…'

'Oh, come along you two, for goodness sake get on with it,' says Moira, coming up behind them. 'Sort out an evening, or I'll have to get HiDog onto you.'

They turn and look at her in amazement.

'Is that really his name?' asks Cathy.

'Of course not!' says Moira. 'But I know that's what you all call him.'

'So, what *is* his name?' asks Andrew, keeping his hands in his pockets and standing well back from the dog, who's staring malevolently at him.

'Ralph,' says Moira, 'after my late husband. He irritated everyone, too. Now, can you please get your diaries together and make this date at long last, so I can turn the lights off and lock up.'

So they do. And on the way back, Cathy stops off at Stella's flat, even though it's a bit late, to tell her. Stella's in her dressing gown and ready for bed, but is still delighted to hear how Cathy's evening went.

'La Boheme!' says Stella. 'Only the best restaurant in town!'

'Yes, worrying, isn't it?' Cathy laughs. 'Hope he's not expecting me to foot the bill.'

'Well, you've had a good evening all round,' says Stella. 'You also got one of the main parts in the play.'

'But I don't know why she cast me as Robina, who I hadn't considered, instead of Martha, who I'd really worked on.'

'Well I do,' says Stella. 'If you're the mistress she needs the spark of electricity that runs between you and Andrew for it to work. And she definitely doesn't need 240 volts running between a married couple.'

Cathy laughs.

'You're such an old cynic, Stella.'

'Yes, and I'm usually right, my dear.'

CHAPTER 20

TOMORROW, THE WORLD

La Boheme is right in the centre of Horsfield, and Cathy has never been there before. It has a reputation for fine food and wine, excellent service and large bills, so it's something of a treat to be taken there by anyone, let alone Andrew.

After much agonising, and consultations with Sally, Eleanor and Jo, she's opted to wear a black dress, with some glitzy jewellery hastily bought in town.

'*Cosmo* always says you can't go wrong with the LBD and a bit of bling,' says Eleanor.

'Shoes?' asks Sally. 'What does *Cosmo* have to say about them?'

'As high as you can walk in, I think.'

Cathy sticks her head in the bottom of her wardrobe and starts opening boxes. 'I won't have to walk anywhere other than from the car to the restaurant, so I think I can manage in these,' she says, emerging with a pair of stiletto heeled sandals she's had for years.

'They won't make you taller than him, will they?' asks Jo, because Cathy is already tall and surely Andrew isn't Tony's height, she reckons, mentally sizing them up.

'That's a point.' Cathy rummages around again and comes up with a lower pair of heels. 'These?'

So Cathy is now ready to go. And ridiculous though she feels about this, she's actually quite nervous. Don't be so stupid, she tells herself. You've known him for years, slapped his face on several occasions, kissed him passionately umpteen times and laid in bed with him for the entire duration of an Alan Ayckbourn play. It doesn't leave much to be nervous about.

The restaurant is small, and fully booked most nights, so they were lucky to get a table at fairly short notice. And it's a good one, away from the window in a secluded corner. Cathy wouldn't normally have been seeking seclusion, but the other girls jokingly threatened a walk past, and she wouldn't want to be in full view in case Andrew's being outrageous and kissing her hand or something theatrical like that at the time.

Bur Andrew's not in thespian mood this evening, he's just being himself for once, which is something most people don't usually see. Cathy's not seen it often herself.

The menu is fabulous, and she's got the one without the prices on it, so that's comforting. She's trying to memorise all the dishes, as she knows Stella will want to know what she's missed, but it's difficult because they're quite complicated. Difficult enough to choose for herself, but in the end she does at least manage to do that and resigns herself to the fact that by the end of the evening she'll have forgotten everything else on offer.

'I wondered if you'd come,' says Andrew, lifting his glass to hers.

'Why? I said I would.'

'No, I mean when I first asked you. Only because when you've known a person for as long as we have, it's sometimes difficult to relate to each other in a different situation.'

'We've been together in loads of different situations,' she says, replacing her glass. She reminds him of the Ayckbourn play.

'It was a bit like like lying in state, wasn't it?' she says.

'Well I rather enjoyed it, and if you remember we had a good laugh under the duvet. But that wasn't the real you and me, only our stage people. So this could have been awkward,' says Andrew.

'No, it's a lovely idea. And coming here is perfect,' Cathy says, looking round at the restrained décor and subtle, contemporary lighting, which is only just bold enough to whisper the word *lavish*.

'Well, yes I hoped it would be.'

'Anyway, I didn't dare refuse, not with Moira on the warpath.'

'*Surely* they haven't been talking about us,' Andrew says, in mock astonishment. 'And did you see that bloody dog giving me the evil eye? He's like the crocodile with Captain Hook, one bite and you're his for life.'

'He's all right, little Ralphy. I'm sure he just wanted to make sure your intentions are honourable,' says Cathy, primly.

'Oh, was that it? Then he's even more stupid than I thought.'

Cathy catches his eye across the flickering light of the candle, opens her mouth to say something, and then the waiter arrives with their starters.

* * *

Meanwhile, it's a perfectly ordinary, quiet evening in the Taylor household. There's nothing on the television, so Don is at his computer and Jo is sewing a zip into a black Prom dress. It's difficult working on black, even under the special lighting she's got, and it makes her eyes ache after a while. So she takes a break from sewing and wanders in to see what her dad's up to.

'What d'you think of this, love,' he asks, and turns the screen so she can read an email he's just picked up, in reply to a recent one from him.

'I played with Sonny back in the late sixties,' he says. 'Brilliant pianist. Didn't know he had a daughter though.'

Jo reads both messages through.

'I've heard that programme once or twice,' she says. 'They wouldn't really be interested in us though, would they?'

'Well, she seems to think so. I might give Stella a ring,' he says, reaching for his now indispensable mobile.

He relates the story to Stella.

'I don't know her name,' Jo hears Don say, 'but it sounds as if she just works on the show. Maybe she's a presenter.'

There's a short silence, then he calls to Jo. 'Stella says if you look in the *Radio Times* where the programme's listed it should give the name of the producer underneath,' he says. 'Radio 4,' he adds, 'she thinks it's on a Wednesday afternoon.'

Jo gets the *Radio Times* and flicks through the pages till she finds what she's looking for.

'Alan Pettigrew,' she reads.

'Alan Pettigrew,' Don repeats into the phone, then there's another silence, and Don turns round to face Jo and gives her the thumbs up.

'Stella knows him,' he mouths to her, and after a few more minutes he says goodbye and puts his phone down.

'He was her office junior in research, if it's the same Alan Pettigrew, shortly before she left to join television. She's going to ring him on Monday.'

But Jo still isn't convinced this is going anywhere.

'Why would anyone want to know about the GenClub?' she wonders aloud.

'Because there are thousands, probably hundreds of thousands, of other people out there just like us,' says Don. 'It's a human interest story.'

'Oh, right. Are you going to reply to Sonny's email?'

'I think so. I only mentioned the GenClub in passing, but maybe now I'll give him some more information for his daughter.'

'Stick to the facts, Dad,' says Jo, knowing how Don so often gets carried away with enthusiasm, 'and don't overdo it.'

'Did I hear the kettle go on?' he asks, ignoring her.

* * *

'I wonder how Cathy's getting on,' says Eleanor, painting her nails at the kitchen table. 'He might have proposed by now!'

'I hope not, she needs to get a few more candlelit meals under her belt before they get to that stage, because she won't get any afterwards.'

'*Mum*! That is so cynical!'

'Yes – but true,' says Sally, clearing up dishes around Eleanor.

'What do you think she'd say to him?'

Sally stops for a moment and considers.

'She was pretty excited about this date. I don't know, I suppose she'd say yes. But I shouldn't think he will, Eleanor.'

'Why not? They're both on their own and they've known each other for a long time.'

'Yes, but why marry her? They could just carry on as they are, moving between his house and hers, people do that these days. Sounds like a very good idea to me.'

'Keep his clutter out of her place, you mean. And keep control of the remote.'

'Now you're getting the idea,' Sally laughs. She pulls a chair out and sits down with her daughter.

'I don't want to push you, Eleanor, because you know you're welcome here for as long as you and the baby want to stay,' she says gently, 'but have you had any thoughts about a place of your own? I don't suppose you'll want to live with us forever.'

Eleanor screws the top back on the nail polish and starts waving her hand about.

'Well, I don't want to go before the baby's born,' she says, 'but it would be nice if the two of us had our own place later.'

Sally's touched by the way she puts it – *the two of us*. In spite of her initial shock, she's getting excited now about the baby and her catalogue has already delivered several parcels of clothes and equipment.

'Would you consider council housing?' she asks, her fingers crossed under the table. 'Because if that's want you want you'll need to get your name on the list.'

'Don't think I'd fit in down at the Westbourne estate,' says Eleanor, to Sally's relief, 'and that's probably where I'd end up. Dad's said he'll help with rent, though.'

'Yes, I know he has. Well then, maybe we ought to start looking around, just to see what's available.'

'Yes maybe. There's plenty of time though, I've got another seven weeks to go, and that's if it's on time.'

Sally gets up from the table and crosses to the sink.

'Mum...'

'Mmm?'

'Thanks for being so good about everything. You and Grandma have been great.' Eleanor hauls herself up from her chair, goes over to Sally and puts her arms round her.

'You will stay with me, won't you, during the birth?' she says into Sally's neck, in a small anxious voice.

Sally feels like she's just got six numbers up on a Lottery rollover week.

'Even if they send in a dozen big men to drag me away,' she says.

* * *

'We don't have to stay here for coffee,' says Cathy. 'I expect I can run to a couple of cups of Nescafe at a push.'

'OK. We'll do that then.'

They're the last ones to leave the restaurant, and although nobody starts putting chairs up on tables or getting the Hoover out, Cathy senses that maybe the staff would all like to go home.

Andrew gets the bill, doesn't turn a hair as he hands over his credit card, and leaves what seems to Cathy a huge tip. At the usual rate of 10%, she thinks, this evening hasn't come cheap to him. She's never thought about his financial standing, never considered the quality of the clothes he wears and never even seen his house, though she does realise it's in an expensive part of town.

'Fantastic meal,' she says on the pavement outside La Boheme. 'Thank you so much, it was a really lovely evening,' and on an impulse she kisses him.

'Am I forgiven now,' asks Andrew, taking her hand, 'for the Carol episode?'

'Nothing to forgive,' she says, 'I don't have any claims on you.'

'Mmm. Well, maybe we can talk about that,' says Andrew, opening the car door for Cathy. She pauses, stops in the act of getting in the car, not sure how to respond.

'But not right in the middle of the High Street,' he adds as Cathy still doesn't move. 'Don't look so worried. Come on, it'll keep till we get to your place.'

She's not worried. She's intrigued, and quite excited by the possibilities Andrew has laid enticingly before her. But he doesn't say any more, not till they're established in Cathy's lounge with their coffee, by which time her anticipation levels have shot off the top of the scale.

'So, what did you mean by that remark?' she asks, unable to contain it any longer.

Andrew takes his time before replying. He puts his coffee down and strokes the cat as it wanders up to him.

'*After Hercule* will be my last play in Horsfield,' he begins. 'I'm leaving town come the summer. In fact I'm leaving the country.'

'Oh no,' says Cathy, as all the scenarios she's built up in the last half hour come crashing down around her. 'Why? Work transfer?'

'Quite the opposite,' he says. 'I'm taking early retirement, and going to live in Cape Town. I worked there for five years back in the eighties, and I've never sold my house, just kept it rented out. So I have somewhere to go that I'm familiar with. They won't give me a resident's visa at first, I'll have to come back every six months till the paperwork gets sorted out, but because I own the house it makes a difference and I hope I'll move up the list pretty fast.'

'So you want somewhere to stay when you come back, is that it?' asks Cathy, struggling to keep the disappointment out of her voice.

'Well,' says Andrew, 'I will have to get that organised of course, but that's not want I wanted to ask you.'

Then he drops his bombshell.

'Come with me, Cathy.'

'Oh, don't start all that again...'

'No, I mean it this time. Come to Cape Town. We'd be great together, we *are* great together...'

'But I can't. I mean, this is a bit sudden...'

'You don't have to decide tonight.'

'Andrew, I have my aunt here, all my friends, my job...'

'The cat?' He takes her hand. 'OK. Then tell me there hasn't always been a frisson between us or that we've never had good times together. Tell me that you and I could never be anything other than friends.'

Cathy's mind whirls around. She's stuck for something to say.

'Well?'

'No, I can't... you're right about all of that...but going to South Africa is a hell of a way to prove it.'

'It's not tomorrow we're talking about, it's seven or eight months away. And a lot can happen in that time.'

Cathy swallows hard. 'Well...'

'But only if you let it. At the very least, will you keep an open mind about this? Give it some serious consideration?'

'Yes...yes OK.'

'And first of all, decide if you want to be with me, because if you do then everything else will fall into place somehow or other. If you're already certain you don't then I won't mention it again, I'll go off home now and see you at the first *Hercule* rehearsal, no hard feelings.'

It's a risky strategy, and Andrew knows it. He doesn't say anything. Cathy doesn't say anything. The cat wanders away from the silence in a huff.

'Then... does that mean to say that you want to be with me?'

'If I didn't I wouldn't even have suggested it, would I?'

'I don't know, Andrew, I'm totally confused by all this. It's come as a bit of a shock.'

'Listen, Cathy. I'm going to go, and I'll go on my own if I have to. But...let me put it like this, I'd rather go with you than without you.'

'Oh. Oh. Right...'

'We've got plenty of time to see if it's likely to work or not,' Andrew says, 'but we've got to start sometime or we'll never know.'

Cathy gulps. This isn't quite how she saw the evening developing. She thinks about Stella, and she thinks about the GenClub. But they're not there right at that moment, and Andrew is.

'No commitment?' she asks, finally.

'None at all,' he says.

'Well, in that case...' says Cathy, 'I guess I've got nothing to lose.'

Except you, she thinks, or everyone else.

* * *

Next morning, Cathy arrives at work with only a couple of minutes to spare before they throw the doors open to the public. Her early morning routine was all out of gear due to Andrew being there, and then after she saw him off she just couldn't get back into her usual rhythm. There was no time to wash her hair, and she's got baggy eyes because she's not used to having anyone else in her bed so she couldn't sleep. Now, she feels as if there's a sign on her forehead that says *I had sex last night*, and she's having trouble making eye contact with people. But strangely, nobody else in the office seems to think there's anything different about her.

When Cathy leaves work at lunchtime, she's ambushed outside the agency by Sally and Jo, who whisk her off for lunch with the intention of prising the whole story out of her. Once they've ordered and set her up with a large glass of wine they proceed to grill her.

'Eleanor was convinced he'd propose to you,' says Sally.

'Well, she was half right,' says Cathy, picking at a salad while her stomach keeps up its constant whirling, round and round like a tumble dryer. It's been like that all morning, since Andrew left and the real world started to claim her attention again.

'How can he half propose?' asks Jo, slicing up garlic bread for them to share.

'It wasn't marriage he was proposing.'

'NO!' they cry together. 'Then what?'

'He wants me to go to Cape Town with him.'

'Fabulous! A holiday together,' Sally enthuses. 'That'll do the trick.'

'Not a holiday. For good.'

Jo stops in the middle of licking garlic butter off her fingers and Sally nearly chokes on her wine.

'Beware of men wanting to take you off to another continent,' says Sally, half-jokingly. 'Remember Eleanor.'

'Maybe not quite the same situation,' says Cathy, 'And it wouldn't be till next summer, so I've got time to decide. But he's thrown me into a real quandary.'

Jo gets her voice back. 'Go,' she says. 'Just do it.'

'But Stella?' asks Cathy.

'She'd say the same,' says Jo.

'I know, and that's the problem. I can't just leave her.'

'Well,' says Sally, 'what do you think we're here for? You were the one who came up with the GenClub, so we'd all be there for each other.'

'I didn't envisage a situation quite like this,' says Cathy, completely off balance now.

'Nor did we,' Sally replies, 'like we didn't envisage a serious accident happening to Karen. But if you want to go, you should have the chance to go. Right?' Sally looks across to Jo for confirmation, who nods in agreement.

Cathy puts down her fork, tired of playing with frisee lettuce that keeps springing off it.

'This wouldn't be a temporary situation, though, like Karen's accident. If I go it'll be for good, well... that's assuming residents' permits would be granted.'

Cathy tells them about the six-month clause, and Andrew's house, which may give him a lever in the permits office.

'But what I'm saying is, I wouldn't be coming back and taking over the reins again,' she goes on. 'And Stella is my responsibility, not yours. Helping out is one thing, but this is different.'

'Well,' says Sally, 'in all fairness we didn't know that Karen would be coming back.'

'But it wasn't planned.'

'Maybe,' says Jo, 'you could go for the first six months, and then see how things are working out. Or for less time to start with – you might not like it there after all.'

It's an option. They mull this over a bit, but there are still lots of questions hanging in the air.

'She wouldn't go with you?' ventures Sally.

Cathy shakes her head. 'She won't fly,' she says.

They fall silent, trying to figure this one out.

'I don't want Stella to know,' Cathy says. 'Not yet, anyway. Not till I've got my head round this and made the decision on my own.'

* * *

Stella's conversation with Alan Pettigrew has done the trick. The piece about the GenClub, previously no more than a possibility, is now definitely happening. The plan is for an interview to take place at the local BBC studio, for inclusion in the programme the following week. The timing is opportune, since a previously scheduled piece has had to be dropped for sensitive reasons relating to a current news story.

There is a problem, though. They only want to interview two of the GenClub and opinions differ about who this should be. Initially, Cathy and Sally are the ones everyone thinks should go, since the club was their baby in the first place and they were the ones who got it started. But there is also a feeling in some quarters that Tony should be one of the interviewees – as the only man in the YoungGen group it would demonstrate inclusivity. Then Queenie pipes up.

'Well I think one of the OldGens should be included,' she asks. 'That would make it more interesting, and it's fairer.'

So, now they're into a whole new ball game and it seems they could make out a case for every one of them to be chosen, except for Jo who has already ruled herself out of the running.

'Definitely Cathy,' says Sally. 'It was her idea.'

'In that case, Stella should be the other one to go,' says Tony and in the end this is the pairing that wins everyone's vote.

The whole thing is being put together in a bit of a rush, due to their last minute inclusion in the programme, so the interview has been fixed for two days time. For now, all they can do is speculate on what the interviewer will ask them.

As Cathy drives Stella back to her flat, the subject of Andrew and Cathy's dinner date inevitably comes up.

'It was lovely,' says Cathy. 'I had a great time.'

'And?' asks Stella, who's nobody's fool and has noticed a look in her niece's eyes that she doesn't remember seeing there for a long time.

'And… em…well, he stayed the night, actually.'

'Good,' says Stella. 'About time, too.'

Then she gets to the heart of it, and Cathy has to stop herself from spilling all the beans.

'So is this going to be a lasting relationship, do you think?'

'I don't know,' Cathy replies, honestly. 'I can't think like that at the moment. Who knows what's around the next corner?'

Stella turns in her seat to look at Cathy. 'What does it matter what's coming round the corner?' she asks. 'Either you want to be together or you don't. And let's be honest, Cathy, this has already been brewing for years and neither of you wants to wait too much longer at your age. Grab your chance of happiness while you can and let the future take care of itself.'

Cathy doesn't respond. If she mentions Cape Town, if she lets on about her misgivings or if there's a hint of indecision on her part she knows Stella will urge her to go, putting Cathy's needs before her own. And then it will simply be down to her, and that's scary.

'I don't believe for a moment that this is just a passing fancy,' says Stella as she opens her front door, 'and I'm going to be very cross with you if you let this man get away,' she adds.

'What makes you think I'll do that?' asks Cathy, laughing and trying to make light of it.

'You seem less than thrilled. In your place I'd be walking on air.'

'I am! It's just that I need time to get used to the idea. It's all a bit sudden,' replies Cathy, and they both choose to leave it at that.

* * *

The traffic on the way to Tunbridge Wells is very heavy and Cathy starts to wonder if they'll make it in time for their interview. Stella is thrilled to be going back into her old working environment and looking forward to seeing how things have changed, so she's quite bubbly on the way and doesn't notice Cathy's frustration at the hold-ups as they get into town. Finally they make it with a few minutes to spare.

The interviewer chats to them for a bit, mostly about Stella's career in the BBC, then they go into a studio and record far more material than will be needed. It all seems to go well, and they're made to feel very welcome. Stella is full of questions, and takes it all in. Not once does she say *in my day*, which makes Cathy feel proud of her. Then a great surge of guilt envelopes her when she thinks of what she's considering doing, and at that moment the idea of leaving Stella and going halfway round the world seems quite preposterous to her.

Trouble is, when she's with Andrew, the idea of staying seems preposterous, too. They've seen each other a couple of times since the dinner date. He's deliberately not been pushy, not mentioned South Africa once since, and neither has Cathy. They've just concentrated on spending time together.

Sensing that Cathy needs time to adjust to this new regime, Stella has avoided the subject altogether, but now, on the way home, she allows his name to drift into the conversation in what she hopes is a casual way.

'Will Andrew be joining us for the bonfire?' she asks.

The GenClub are planning a Bonfire Night party, in Mavis's garden since there's nothing there to spoil. The idea is twofold: partly to burn a lot of old rubbish from Mavis's loft plus some bits of furniture from the house that Tony has broken up in preparation, and partly as a celebration. Firstly, Karen is being transferred to the local hospital in a couple of days, and secondly Jo's birthday is on the fifth. The OldGens are keen on the idea, and Queenie has been making Parkin, telling them this is traditional for the event.

'No,' says Cathy firmly. 'This is a GenClub party, so he's not included.'

'That's a bit harsh, isn't it?' says Stella. 'Don't you want him to meet your friends?'

'It's not that, it's just that he isn't involved in this part of my life.'

Stella has the feeling there's something more to it than that, so she doesn't press the point. But her mind is working ahead, and taking her on excursions that all seem to lead back to one place.

Karen has been making a good recovery and is now in an ordinary ward and starting on physio. The doctors think she's been very lucky and her injuries, serious though they were, could have been a lot worse. She's obviously strong, and starting to mend. Bill, seeing an improvement in her, has settled down better, although he won't entertain the idea of going back to the day centre, which he seems to blame in some way for Karen having the accident in the first place. Mavis, at the hub of the Kennedy household, has everything under control and seems to have gained Bill's trust completely. So, the immediate crisis seems to have passed, although there will be difficult times ahead, once Karen comes home. Tony has kept all her friends informed of progress by email and checks daily for a response from Graham that never comes.

It drizzles with rain on Bonfire Night, but Mavis's old conservatory is a good, warm viewpoint from which to watch Tony and Jo struggling to light fireworks and keep the fire going long enough to burn everything. The sound of their laughter floats in from the garden every so often. When they come back in, pulling off wet, woolly hats and gloves and trailing mud in on their boots, they bring with them the smell of the bonfire and a whoosh of cold air.

Once they've had soup and buttered rolls, and squares of gingery Parkin, Queenie reveals her *piéce de resistance*, an iced birthday cake with candles, which Jo blows out then gets embarrassed when they all sing to her. Someone puts a glass of mulled wine in her hand, and the toast is to both her and Karen.

Later, in bed, with her hair smelling of bonfire like it used to on birthdays when she was a kid, Jo smiles to herself. She can't remember the last time she enjoyed the occasion so much, or that she felt so happy.

CHAPTER 21

FAIRLY HIGH NOON

'Gregson's weren't giving much away about these guys, but they wouldn't be dealing with them if they weren't good for the money,' says Roger, as he and Tony drive to their site meeting in Crawley.

'No, I suppose not. Just wondered if they'd worked for them before.'

'Not as far as I could make out.'

'Then we're all in the same boat,' Tony says. 'They don't know any more than we do.'

It's the day after Karen's transfer to Horsfield General, and Tony is glad it's the last time he'll be making this particular journey. He's never liked Crawley, and from now on it will always have unpleasant memories for him.

When they arrive on site, the structural engineer and architect are already there and the main doors are open. They wander in, Roger with a folder and clipboard under his arm and carrying a camera, and introductions are made. It's as cold in the building as it is outside, cold, bleak and echoing, a depressing interior in any weather. At this stage it's hard to believe that this will actually become a working environment for a whole lot of people who will never be able to imagine how their office looked today. Tony walks around some of the ground floor rooms, coming back to the reception area when the sound of more voices reaches him.

Two men in suits and overcoats have joined the party.

'David Jennings, from Rawson's,' says one, stepping forward, hand outstretched.

'Graham Seaton-Jones,' says Graham.

Bingo! thinks Tony as he shakes each of them by the hand and carefully avoids giving his name.

'I'm from the builders,' he says cagily. 'But it's my partner Roger you need to deal with. I'm only here for the ride.'

The party moves off, taking a room at a time. Roger is busy with his clipboard and his questions as he casts a practised eye around. Tony hangs back, behind the others, keeping an eye on Graham, sizing him up. In literal terms, Tony is a good head taller than Graham, and although he wouldn't dream of attempting anything physical that extra bit of height does give him a psychological advantage.

He can appreciate that Graham is, even seen through the eyes of another man, very good looking. He's dressed well – both directors are – and looks somewhat incongruous in the midst of all the rubble and dust of an abandoned building. This is usual though, and Tony has made hundreds of site visits that are no different to this one. The one difference for him today is the outcome he's looking for.

Graham's input is minimal. He seems to defer in most things to David Jennings, only expressing an opinion or asking for clarification occasionally. From his vantage point at the back of the group, Tony is forming an opinion of Graham that is only partly based on what he sees. He's a chancer, he thinks. Grabs a good thing when he sees it, moves on when something better turns up.

Tony's own chance comes as the party goes up to the top floor and Graham pauses on the landing to look out onto the car park below.

'Not much parking available there for the staff,' he comments to Tony. 'That was one of our concerns. Maybe if it were marked out differently we could squeeze a few more in.'

Behind him, leaning on the handrail, Tony doesn't reply.

Graham turns to face him.

'What do you think?' he asks.

'It's possible,' says Tony, not taking his eyes off Graham, then adds, 'I believe we have a mutual friend.'

'Oh? Who's that?' asks Graham, all smiles.

'Karen Kennedy.'

The smile fades slowly from Graham's face, and his eyes shift away from Tony. A silence develops.

'Karen... ah, yes, Karen,' he says, and coughs nervously. 'How is she these days? Still busy?'

'Not exactly. Still in hospital, as you might expect after a serious car smash.' Ignoring Graham's attempt at a shock-horror look, Tony ploughs on. 'Actually I'm the guy who emailed you with the news of her accident. Twice,' he adds for effect. 'Strange you haven't replied.'

Graham says nothing, but his eyes slide to the staircase and his route out of the building.

'Yes... yes, I've been meaning to get back to you,' he lies. 'I thought I'd send her a card or something, you know.'

'Oh, I wouldn't be doing that if I were you,' says Tony.

Graham coughs again. 'Might upset her, you mean, a bit too late now?' he asks.

'Might upset me,' says Tony, 'that's what I mean.'

Graham's eyes narrow a bit as the penny drops.

'And that's something I wouldn't recommend,' says Tony, putting paid to any remaining doubts.

'Ah. So maybe not.'

'Definitely not. Is that clear enough for you? I've got a pretty good idea now of why she was on that road when she had the accident...'

Graham cuts in.

'Now hold on a minute...it was over between us a long time ago. In the end I felt like I was being stalked, I couldn't shake her off.'

'At the moment,' says Tony, ignoring Graham's outburst, 'nobody else knows what I know. Shall we both see if we can keep it that way?'

'Yes. Right.'

There's a sound from upstairs and Graham glances up the staircase.

'I think maybe I'll get back to the office,' he says. 'I'll just have a word with David...'

'No need,' says Tony, still neatly positioned in his way at the turn of the staircase. 'I'll pass on your apologies.' He takes a step to one side, allowing Graham the option he's been looking for.

Graham nods, and clatters past him down to the ground floor, and Tony watches from the window as he crosses the car park, gets in his car and drives away. He can't resist a small smile of satisfaction.

'Spineless little shit,' he mutters.

The rest of the party appears on the staircase at that point.

'Your friend had to go,' Tony says to David Jennings. 'There was a call on his mobile that sent him back to the office.'

They spend another twenty minutes on site, but Tony's got no interest at all in the job now. In the car on the way home, Roger expresses some reservations about the logistics of the project.

'I shouldn't worry about it,' says Tony. 'We won't get it anyway.'

'What makes you think that?' Roger asks.

'Intuition,' Tony replies. Roger glances across at him, but Tony's face is giving nothing away.

* * *

It's a beautiful, crisp November day, and when he gets back home at around midday Tony needs a diversion to make him wind down and forget about his showdown with Graham. He has a good idea and rings Jo.

'Gnasher could do with a long walk,' he says. 'Let's take Don and Beryl off to the seaside for the afternoon. We can park them somewhere with a cup of coffee while we have a walk along the seafront.'

They decide to drive down to Eastbourne, where they know it will be fairly easy walking from the car to a café overlooking the sea. Gnasher is excited and spends a bit of time chasing his tail, but once in the car he sits obediently on Jo's lap and watches with interest as the world whizzes by outside the window.

When they get to Eastbourne the breeze is only light, and it's coming from the south-west so it doesn't have much bite to it. It's a sunglasses and gloves day, with a brilliantly blue sky and high puffy clouds, and there are a surprising number of other people who've had exactly the same idea as Tony. They park the car and help the OldGens up the slight slope, slowly and with plenty of stops en route, and into the café. It only needs a couple of coffees and buns to keep them happy, although Don has already got his mobile out and is absorbed in texting as they leave them and rejoin Gnasher, tethered outside.

Jo and Tony set off along the promenade towards Beachy Head and from inside the café Don and Beryl can watch the start of their walk, as the path passes just below and away from where they're sitting.

As they look out, it's clear that Tony has just said something to Jo to make her laugh. Don and Beryl watch her double up in laughter, and Tony stops and turns towards her, hands spread out, saying something else which starts her off again. On his lead, Gnasher sits patiently in front of Jo and gazes up at her.

'That funny little dog seems to love your Jo,' says Beryl.

Tony steps forward to Jo's side, and puts his arm around her as they walk on again.

'I don't think he's the only one,' says Don, and as they watch, Jo's arm comes up and circles Tony's waist.

'Well I never!' says Beryl, gleefully clapping her hands.

* * *

On the day of the radio broadcast, Eleanor borrows Sally's car and volunteers to take Mavis and Bill in to the hospital, while the rest of the GenClub gather together in Tony's house. By three o'clock they're all settled in Beryl's lounge. Their piece is the third one up.

'Now,' says the presenter, 'how many of you listening are finding that life with an elderly dependent relative can be both difficult and isolating? Well, we hear now from a group of people in Sussex who found their own way of dealing with what is, in today's society, a growing problem. Stacey Potter caught up with them recently in our Tunbridge Wells studio.'

Clustered around Karen's bed, Mavis, Bill and Eleanor are also listening to the radio, and one of the nurses, who's already been told the story, stops for a few minutes to join them.

The interview has been cut to about eight minutes in all, from the twenty or so that was recorded. Cathy is disappointed by this.

'No, that's perfectly usual,' says Stella. 'They caught the essence, nothing important was left out. You've got to remember, people don't want too much detail – they can't concentrate for any longer than about ten minutes on any one thing.'

The final piece of the programme follows, and Tony gets up to switch the radio off.

'No, leave it on till the end,' says Stella. 'They take phone calls on this programme – we might get some reaction to the GenClub piece.'

So they have half an ear on the radio until the final round-up.

'We've had lots of calls and emails in today,' says the presenter, 'on all the issues in the programme, but overwhelmingly from people interested in the Generation Club concept. Mary from Bristol is typical of those phoning in. She says; *Something like this would be a life-saver for me. Is there a group in my area?* We don't know of one, Mary, but if anyone else does, please call in and let us know. We'll try to get more to you about this in a later programme, but that's all for today...'

In Beryl's lounge the cheers ring out.

And in Horsfield General's *Ardingly* ward, the reception is only slightly more subdued, with much self-congratulation going on around the bed. It's been a huge success.

'Come on, Bill,' Eleanor says. 'Let's you and I go off and find something nice to celebrate with – some of those marzipan chocolates you told me you like so much?'

She mouths to Mavis; *Give you a bit of a break,* and Bill lets her lead him off in the direction of the shop.

'Well,' says Mavis, 'that girl's done a lot of growing up in a short time. She's an angel.'

'You're all angels,' says Karen, and takes Mavis's hand. 'I'll never be able to thank you enough...', and then her voice cracks.

'Now, let's have less of that, my girl. We've always said, if it works for one, it works for all. Seeing you recover is all the thanks we need.'

Mavis passes Karen a tissue and she blots her eyes.

'If only you knew what a complete idiot I've been, and all over a man. At my age I really should have known better.'

'You don't surprise me, and these days nothing shocks me. I had a rough idea what was going on, but there was nothing I could say to you because when you're only adding two and two it can so often come to five.'

'I so wanted to tell someone.' Karen reaches for another tissue with her un-plastered arm, and winces as she does so. 'Shouldn't be bending over sideways like that,' she explains. Mavis puts the tissues on the bed, on Karen's lap.

'Don't go through the whole box,' she says. 'He's not worth it.'

'I realise that now. Do any of the others...?'

'No, not a thing. They think you were in Crawley seeing a client there. Probably best they carry on thinking that.'

'I'll never drive again, Mavis, the thought absolutely terrifies me. There was a point when I thought I'd die in that car, and even though the whole thing must have only taken seconds, I still had time to think *What will happen to Dad after I'm dead*? I never want to get behind the wheel again.'

'Then you don't have to, nobody's going to make you do it. Karen, you do know Tony emailed everyone on your computer?'

'Yes, he said. I've had lots of cards from old friends – even one from a chap in Canada I used to work with. And my hairdresser sent a card, too, he wants to come in and see me! Perhaps I can get him to do something with this while he's here...' She runs her fingers through her hair and ruffles it up. 'I was in the middle of doing work for two companies and they've both been in touch to say they'll be using me again once I'm back.'

'Well, that's good.'

'I know what you're thinking, Mavis. Everyone got an email, so he would have known.'

'And... nothing?'

'No.'

'Well then, there you are. Karen, there are good men out there, and you're an attractive woman...'

'It's going to take me a long time to want to commit to anyone again. So difficult to know who you can trust and who you can't. There aren't all that many like Tony around.'

'No, you're right there. Nobody's saying anything, but we all think he and Jo will get together.'

'Fabulous! She needs someone like him to bring her out of herself.'

'He's certainly done that and it's good to see the difference in her. And I've got a feeling there's something going on with Cathy and that Andrew from the play...'

Eleanor and Bill arrive back at that moment.

'No marzipan chocs, we got these instead.' Eleanor gives Karen a box of Belgian truffles.

'I'll be huge by the time I get out of here,' says Karen, laughing. But that doesn't stop her peeling the cellophane off, awkwardly with one arm in plaster, and taking the first truffle.

* * *

After all the excitement of the afternoon, Cathy drops Stella off first at her flat, then continues on with Sally and Queenie to their house.

'They're not back yet,' Sally says, noticing that her car isn't amongst those parked along the road.

'Eleanor's very good to take a turn on the hospital run,' says Cathy, as they get out and Sally escorts Queenie to the gate.

'She's glad of something to do,' says Sally. 'I think she's getting a bit nervous now, and this takes her mind off it. It must be a strain when you haven't got a partner to go through childbirth with you.'

'She's got you, and Queenie.'

'Yes, but it's not the same.'

Queenie disappears into the house, and Sally lingers on the pavement with Cathy.

'I was wondering,' she says. 'All those people calling in after the programme – there's obviously a need out there. Do you think we ought to set up a website or something like that?'

'Well, it's a thought. I don't know anybody who could do that for us, do you?'

'No I don't, but they can't be that difficult to find. Eleanor might know someone from university. Shall I ask her?'

'Why not? And I'll ask around, too.'

'Well that's something we didn't imagine right back at the start,' says Sally, smiling.

Cathy agrees, and she's thinking, like so many other things we didn't imagine happening when we all met for the first time. Then her mind takes another leap in a similar direction and she remembers she's going round to Andrew's house later on and she hasn't even thought about what she'll wear yet.

'I've got to dash,' she says to Sally. 'I'm due in wardrobe and make-up soon!'

CHAPTER 22

BABY GEN

Feedback from the radio programme is astonishing. Their original contact, the daughter of Don's friend, phones Cathy a few days later.

'Record numbers of calls and enquiries,' she says. 'We've been inundated, and we may want to do a follow-up in a few weeks so I'll be keeping in touch with you. I've also been approached by a national magazine for your contact details – is it OK if I release that information to them?'

The magazine in question turns out to be a glossy monthly for women, definitely from the top end of the market.

Cathy can't quite believe the response they've had. In their own small way they seem, unwittingly, to have opened up the floodgates. People from across the country, in similar situations, want to join groups or get advice on how to start up groups. Sally's idea of a website starts to look less like an option and more like a necessity.

Eleanor hasn't kept in touch with her university friends, and seems unwilling to step back into that circle, but Cathy has better luck with her enquiries.

'I know just the man,' says Andrew. 'I've played golf with him, and he did a very good job on the golf club website. I'll set up a meeting.'

After so many years on her own, it's come as something of a revelation to Cathy that she hasn't felt protective of her own space. She likes having Andrew around her house, and doesn't mind that he puts the kitchen utensils back in the wrong places, or that he bunches up the towels in the bathroom. It's taken one or two visits, but she's starting to feel comfortable in his house too, which is twice the size of hers and positively opulent in parts. Andrew, clearly, likes the good things in life and has no trouble financing them.

She's seen pictures of his stunningly beautiful house near Cape Town, with fabulous views of the bay, and she's taken travel guides out of the library so she can get a feel for the area. The prospect of going there is one that she finds intensely exciting, but the subject of Stella is still unresolved. All the YoungGens are in on it now, but nobody has mentioned anything to the Oldies, in case one of them forgets Stella's still in the dark and lets the cat out of the bag.

Andrew is philosophical about the whole thing.

'If it's meant to be, we'll find a way,' is all he'll say on the topic, and there's still plenty of time to make the final decision. Cathy has decided she'll definitely go with him for a holiday, but staying on after that or going back there for longer is still a big step away.

On rehearsal evenings for *After Hercule,* they've always arrived separately at the appointed house. It's going quite well, considering nobody has bothered to learn any of their lines yet, except Cathy, who has at least made a start. The latest rehearsal is in her house, and when the Players arrive she's already cleared the furniture back to the sides of the room to give them a reasonable rehearsal space.

Moira arrives, with HiDog tucked under her arm of course, and Cathy's cat takes one look and shoots off, scrambling through the cat flap in a panic.

'I'm tempted to join him,' says Andrew, as HiDog licks its lips and snarls in his direction.

The rehearsal staggers along, it seems nobody is in the mood. By now, the end of November, the shops are all full of festive decorations and that pre-Christmas shopping panic has set in. The Horsfield Players are not immune to this feeling, it appears.

'Oh, come along,' says Moira. 'Concentrate, Anne. This is your husband, who you adore. Try to forget it's only Andrew and give it a bit of warmth.'

'Well thank you so much,' says Andrew, not in the least slighted but determined to make capital out of it.

The scene they rehearse between Andrew's character and his lover Robina, played of course by Cathy, goes much better.

'Well,' Moira comments. 'I certainly felt the heat there! Anybody would think you two really were about to jump into bed together – well done!'

Andrew and Cathy look at each other and smile.

'That's because we are,' he says.

And so the news reaches more people.

* * *

The magazine is quick off the mark, phoning Cathy only days after their radio broadcast.

'We're planning an article for the March edition, so we'd like you all to come up to our offices for an interview as soon as possible, and we'll get you into the studio for photos on the same day. Now, let's find some dates...'

Cathy explains about Karen still being in hospital, and far from this being a problem the woman she's speaking to seems to think this part of the story will give a very positive slant on the way they write the article.

'We'll get a photographer in to the hospital,' she says, 'and we can talk to her on the phone while we interview the rest of you. Fabulous,' she adds, enthusiastically.

When Cathy relates this to Karen her immediate response is to phone her hairdresser, who arranges to come in so she can have her cut, colour and highlights all done beforehand.

'And I'll make sure I'm there on the day darling, so don't worry about a thing,' he says, contemplating the advantages of a bit of free advertising in an up-market monthly magazine.

There's a bit of a flurry amongst the girls as the interview day approaches. They all book in for hair and facial appointments, and Jo actually takes the plunge and has some blonde highlights put in.

'What are you all wearing?' asks Sally.

But nobody has the definitive answer, except for Tony, who's planning on his standard kit of jeans and a sweatshirt.

'Maybe we should all wear jeans,' Cathy speculates.

'Not me!' says Mavis. 'I don't want the whole nation to see this crammed into a pair of jeans,' and she slaps her bottom. 'Besides, I haven't got any.'

In the end, a call comes through from the stylist working on their article. All the women are to be kitted out in black trousers and white tops, courtesy of the magazine, and there'll be a hairstylist and make-up artist in attendance. Tony's asked to wear exactly what he had in mind anyway, and Don & Bill have a free hand in their choice of clothes. This is going to be a big, multi-page feature for the magazine, and they're pulling all the stops out.

It's getting very exciting, and Don has emailed everyone he knows to tell them about it. The other OldGens are a bit bemused by this turn of events, but they go along with it. Except for Queenie.

'I can't see why we can't just stay the way we are. Just because they've got a lot of hoity-toity readers, they want us to look like something we're not,' she moans.

'Grandma, don't be silly,' says Eleanor. 'You get to keep the clothes, and you know how much better you feel after you've had your hair done. What's not to like?'

'I don't want them plastering make-up on me.'

'They have to put a certain amount on, because of the lighting for the photos,' Eleanor explains. 'Otherwise you'll look dreadful. It's a free makeover, I wish I was getting one.'

Queenie's objections crumble at the mention of the word *free* and as always, Eleanor's opinion carries far more weight than if Sally had said exactly the same thing.

'Well I'm keeping my own shoes on.'

'OK, make sure you wear a black pair and I should think that'll be fine,' says Sally, rolling her eyes at Eleanor.

It's another mini-bus trip, and Tony volunteers to be the driver again. Finding the offices of the magazine in the City isn't easy. None of them are familiar with this part of London, and there's no SatNav on the vehicle so Jo acts as map-reader, a job she doesn't really feel confident about. They make a few inevitable mistakes, find themselves in the wrong lane more than once and when they do get there parking isn't easy, but in the end they're able to announce themselves in reception with nearly ten minutes in hand.

They get whisked off to a hospitality suite, and the stylist comes along and sorts out the clothes for each one at a time, before they get their make-up and hair done. Then it's off to the studio.

The interviews and the photo shoot are done at the same time. This way, in addition to the posed group photos, there are a lot of informal shots of them in conversation, laughing, leaning across each other and gesticulating as they make a point. A very small percentage of the pictures taken will actually make the final cut, the photographer explains, but they will get the chance to see them all.

Once they get going, everyone relaxes, and even Queenie starts enjoying herself. The interviewer, Barbara, is friendly and helpful and asks pertinent, intelligent questions. She's happy to let them talk amongst themselves when answering, and she coaxes something out of everyone until most of the story has been told. After a while, Karen comes on the phone and tells Barbara about her accident, the most dramatic bit of all. She edits it lightly, for reasons which only two of the people in the studio will ever appreciate.

'Without the GenClub,' says Karen, 'my Dad would have ended up, eventually, being taken into care – and who would have taken the trouble then to bring him in to see me every single day?'

'And how do you think this has helped with your recovery?' asks Barbara.

'Knowing he was with people I trust who genuinely care, someone being with him every day and every night – it gave me the chance to concentrate on getting better. I didn't have to worry about a thing.'

They have this on speaker-phone, and hearing Karen back in Horsfield General, removed from the rest of the GenClub, is strangely affecting. The room becomes still and very quiet, except for an occasional question from the interviewer. The photographer declines the opportunity to capture the tears in Bill's eyes, but the interviewer makes a note of it.

'Plans for the future?' Barbara poses as her final question.

'We're looking at starting up a website,' says Sally, 'because it seems there are a lot of people out there who want to know more about us...'

'...and how they can start their own group,' adds Cathy.

'Well, keep me on the loop with that one,' says Barbara. 'If you can get your web address to me before we go to print I'll put it in.'

Then it's all over. They're taken back to the hospitality suite, and given tea and biscuits. Publishing is a facet of the media Stella has never had any involvement with before, and she's fascinated by everything she sees, asking questions of everyone they come into contact with. In the end, they have to prise her away and make their way back to the minibus.

They're in high spirits on the way back to Horsfield, going over and over different things that happened.

'I don't know why my hairdresser can't get it to look as good as this,' says Queenie, patting the back of her hair.

'I was just thinking the same thing about mine,' says Tony, completely deadpan, looking back at her in the rear mirror. 'I'll have to have words with him.'

'Wasn't that photographer good?' asks Mavis. 'He took such a lot of trouble to get us arranged just right. I can't wait to see the photos.'

'A very interesting morning,' comments Stella, 'and I'll think of it every time I wear that outfit,' she adds.

'Now we really *must* get that website moving,' says Cathy. 'I'll get onto it straight away.'

They're getting close to home before the general excitement dies down. At the back of the bus, Beryl and Don both start to nod, before the distant sound of a mobile ringtone jerks their heads up again.

'It's mine,' says Sally, fishing her phone out of her handbag.

'Hi Eleanor, we've had...oh my God...OK sweetheart...ring the hospital, they'll tell you what to do...I should be home in ten minutes.' She flips her phone closed and looks up at Queenie.

'Her waters have just broken,' she says, 'four weeks early.'

Ignoring the speed restriction and the cameras that may or may not have any film in them, Tony puts his foot down.

* * *

It's 11pm, and the maternity unit at Horsfield General is having a busy night. Queenie, sitting in a waiting room with Cathy, is starting to look jaded.

'Why don't you let me drop you off home?' Cathy asks. 'I'll be going past your door, so it's no trouble. It could be hours yet.'

'I'm not leaving till this baby's born,' says Queenie, then remembering her manners, adds 'but thank you for offering, Cathy.'

Cathy has been at the hospital for the past couple of hours. She hasn't seen Sally or Eleanor because by the time she got there they were already in the delivery suite. This baby is obviously in a hurry to arrive, and things have so far progressed quite quickly. Now it's just a waiting game, and there's no telling how much longer it'll be. Cathy has to work the next morning, but she's reluctant to leave Queenie on her own, although there are other people sitting around in a similar situation.

'Let me get you some tea before I go,' says Cathy. 'And maybe something to eat? There must be a canteen open somewhere.'

'Tea would be nice, but I don't think I'll eat anything,' says Queenie.

Cathy goes out in search of a drinks machine, and someone else from the waiting room follows her.

'We'll keep an eye on her,' she says to Cathy. 'She's not going to give in, is she? We could all be here till morning.'

So once she's got Queenie set up with some tea, and a KitKat that she might be glad of later, Cathy decides she'll go.

'Ian should be here sometime soon,' says Queenie.

They've left messages for him but he's obviously out somewhere and hasn't responded so far. When he does find out Eleanor's in labour he'll have an hour's journey to get to Horsfield.

'Let me know as soon as there's any news. You can text a message,' she says to Queenie, thinking what foresight Don had in setting them all up with mobiles.

Out in the car park it's a raw December night, with the first signs of a frost on the top of the cars and a biting wind blowing. The sky is clear and a big pale yellow moon is hanging overhead.

Poor little thing, thinks Cathy, pulling her coat collar up, being born only three weeks before Christmas. There'll be no birthday parties in the garden for this little one, or outdoor birthday treats. Her own birthday is in August, nicely spaced out with Christmas for presents, and ideal as a child for a special picnic. Eleanor's baby will miss out on those treats, but she can't imagine Sally allowing birthday and Christmas to merge into one for her only grandchild. It's a shock suddenly to think of Sally as a grandmother, and Queenie as a great-grandmother.

By the time Cathy gets back to her house the heating has gone off, and she potters about with her coat on till she warms up a bit. There's a message on her answerphone from Andrew.

'Come over if it's not too late,' he says.

She checks her watch. 11.45pm. It *is* a bit late now to turn up on his doorstep, much as she'd like to. She sorts the cat's food bowls out, switches off the lights, and goes up to bed.

In the hospital, Eleanor is reaching the point of exhaustion. The baby that started off in such a rush to see the world, is now refusing to budge. Sally feels helpless, and just wants it to be over for her daughter. Meanwhile the nursing staff are discussing the lack of progress, and the possibility of a Caesarian, although that's still some way down the line. Time ticks on.

* * *

At 3.20am, all the GenClub mobiles bleep at the same time. Some hear it, but most don't.

Jo is having a restless night, with too much adrenalin running round her body and making her wake up at regular intervals. She hears the bleep at 3.20 and gets out of bed for her mobile, scurrying across her bedroom in the cold and pulling the duvet up round her ears as she gets back into bed. There are two messages for her, one left at 12.30, which she must have slept through. It's from Tony.

I meant it is all he says. Jo hugs herself, smiling broadly, and there's a delicious feeling in her stomach like going too fast over a hump-back bridge. She considers her response, then texts back to him;

Me too, and tries to picture his face when he reads it.

Thinking the other message might also be from him, she retrieves it in a fever of excitement.

It's a boy, is all it says. More good news, Jo thinks. If it wasn't so cold she might just fling the window open and shout out into the street. She laughs quietly at the idea and wonders what her neighbours would think if she did. She's wide awake now, accepting the fact that sleep is out of the question for the rest of the night.

Leaning back on her pillows and watching an occasional car headlight streak across the ceiling, Jo feels a surge of the purest happiness she's ever known.

* * *

When Sally emerges from the delivery suite, she looks as exhausted as if she's given birth herself. Ian has arrived, and the three of them sit together until they're able to go back in to see Eleanor and the baby.

He's a tiny thing, just under six pounds, and he looks very cross, as if the world's already a huge disappointment to him. But he's healthy and Eleanor's gazing at him as if she can't quite believe she's managed to produce anything so wonderful. She hands him to Queenie first.

'Meet Oscar,' she says.

'Come on now, little boy,' Queenie says to Oscar. 'Stop that grizzling for your great-granny.'

Amazingly, and maybe because he already knows what's good for him, he does as he's told.

CHAPTER 23

GENCLUB DOT COM

There's a patch of sunlight on the floor in front of Cathy's French windows, and it's right on this spot that three-month old Oscar is snoozing in his baby rocking chair. Also in Cathy's lounge, although he's oblivious to this, are his mother, Grandma and great-Granny, plus another nine adults that he doesn't know well yet although some of their voices are becoming familiar to him.

The occasion is the launch of www.genclub.com. uk. It's almost a year since the Generation Club was born, in this very room, so it was considered fitting that they should gather here for their launch party.

A photographer from the local paper has been round, making them gather in a tight group, heads together, coffee cups (empty) raised and smiling at the camera. The minute he goes Cathy collects up the cups and deposits them in the kitchen, where Tony is in the process of opening a couple of bottles of champagne.

'Get the real stuff,' Don instructed him, 'none of that fizzy wine.'

The magazine featuring their story has just hit the shops and newsstands, with details of the website address, and they're ready for the first enquiries to come in. Eleanor's in charge of administering the website and dealing initially with all emails. Sally and Queenie have encouraged this from the start, mainly because it will give them the chance to take Oscar off her hands for an hour or so at a time and have him all to themselves.

Tony brings in a tray loaded with glasses.

'You'd better have this little one, Ma,' he says to Beryl. 'We don't want you getting up and dancing, you know what you're like.'

'I've no objection to her dancing,' says Don. 'In fact it's something I'd rather like to see, especially those high kicks.'

Bill produces a wolf-whistle, though he hasn't really been following the conversation up to now. Beryl laughs, Stella looks at Don with raised eyebrows, and he winks back at her and gives a wheezy chuckle. Jo leans forward to create a space on the coffee table for the tray of glasses, moving to one side Cathy's copy of the script for *After Hercule* and a glossy hardback book entitled *Seven Days in Cape Town*, which Stella bought for Cathy on a recent trip to Horsfield.

'You'll have to go to each place three times,' Stella had said as they queued at the till. 'They don't have a twenty-one day version.'

'Come with me,' said Cathy suddenly, more out of guilt than anything else.

'And play gooseberry for three weeks? Thank you, dear, but I don't think so. Of course,' she added,' if you were there for longer...'

Cathy held her breath. But Stella was in the process of getting her purse out, and didn't comment further.

Now, as the book is moved along the coffee table, Karen remarks on the cover picture.

'Do you think the sea's really that turquoise colour?' she asks.

'They probably touch it up a bit, like they did with us after the magazine shoot,' says Mavis, who had one of the group pictures framed and hung on the living room wall in her new flat. 'There are pictures like that of the seas around Australia. I'll let you know next month if it's real or not.'

'Who'd have thought,' says Sally, looking round the room, 'that we'd have come this far in such a short time. Less than a year.'

Tony, now sitting on the arm of Jo's chair, lifts his glass.

'Well, here's to us,' he says, 'and GenClub dot com.'

Eleanor nips off to the kitchen and comes back with a plate of cheese straws. 'Grandma made them this morning,' she says. 'They're gorgeous.'

Over in the sunshine, Oscar opens his eyes and gazes about till he finds his mum. He yawns, and his little fists punch the air a couple of times before he looks round again and his eyes lock on Bill's, sitting right next to him. He smiles a gummy smile at Bill, who responds by reaching down to pick up his hand. Oscar holds on tightly to Bill's finger and then dribbles onto it.

In the middle of the celebration nobody else in the room notices that an old man and a baby are doing their small bit to bridge the generations between them in the only way they know how. It's the GenClub philosophy at its best.

Annette Keen lives on the south coast, where she runs a jazz club and spends most mornings walking along the seafront with a dictaphone, recording plot ideas and scraps of dialogue.

The Generation Club won the Yeovil Literary Prize in 2008, and is her first full-length novel. A second novel is in preparation, with publication expected in 2013.